Praise for

A COLD AND LONELY PLACE

"Henry follows up her award-winning debut novel, *Learning to Swim*, with a strong second effort also featuring freelance reporter Troy Chance. . . . Featuring a strong cast of female characters and a measured pace, this sophomore novel also perfectly conjures the lure of living in a small and beautiful mountain town during a bitterly cold winter. Featuring an independent and immensely likable lead, riffing on the complicated nature of friendship, and boasting a solidly plotted mystery, this may well appeal to fans of Gillian Flynn."

—*Booklist*

"[A] haunting follow-up to her Agatha Award–winning debut, *Learning to Swim* . . . Adding considerably to the compulsively readable mystery that unfolds . . . is Henry's bone-deep sense of this terribly beautiful place."

—*Publishers Weekly*

"There is a mystery at the cold and lonely heart of this book, but first and foremost, it's a poignant and haunting story about Troy's search for the truth behind a young man's life. . . . This is a powerful, emotional journey for Troy, but ultimately a hopeful one, as she uncovers the stories behind one young man's traumatic childhood, stories that will finally redeem him."

—*BookPage*

"[The] sense of severing all previous ties and never truly getting close to people permeates Sara J. Henry's insightful second novel. As she did in her 2012 Agatha Award–winning debut, *Learning to Swim*, Henry explores the complicated nature of relationships while delivering a suspenseful novel full of unpredictable twists."

—*South Florida Sun Sentinel*

"A chilling mystery about families and friendships . . . the cold atmosphere of a wintery Lake Placid fits in perfectly for a winter read."

—*Parkersburg News and Sentinel*

A COLD LONELY

A NOVEL

Sara J. Henry

AND
PLACE

B\D\W\Y

BROADWAY BOOKS / NEW YORK

Copyright © 2013 by Sara J. Henry

Reading Group Guide copyright © 2013 by Random House LLC

All rights reserved.
Published in the United States by Broadway Books, an imprint of the Crown Publishing Group, a division of Random House LLC, a Penguin Random House Company, New York.
www.crownpublishing.com

BROADWAY BOOKS and its logo, B\D\W\Y, are trademarks of Random House LLC.

Originally published in hardcover in the United States by Crown Publishers, an imprint of the Crown Publishing Group, a division of Random House LLC, New York, in 2013.

Library of Congress Cataloging-in-Publication Data
Henry, Sara J.
    A cold and lonely place : a novel / Sara J. Henry
        p.   cm.
    1. Women journalists—Fiction.   2. Family secrets—Fiction.
3. Adirondack Mountains (N.Y.)—Fiction.   4. Saranac Lake (N.Y.)—
Fiction.   I. Title.
PS3608.E5796C65   2013
813'.6—dc23   2012032575

ISBN 978-0-307-71842-6
eISBN 978-0-307-71843-3

Printed in the United States of America

BOOK DESIGN BY ELINA D. NUDELMAN
COVER DESIGN BY ALEX MERTO
COVER PHOTOGRAPHS: (WOMAN) DAVE O. TUTTLE/FLICKR/GETTY IMAGES;
(CABIN) RYAN MCVAY/GETTY IMAGES

10 9 8 7 6 5 4 3 2 1

First Paperback Edition

TO REED FARREL COLEMAN

PART ONE

ICE CAN ASSUME A LARGE NUMBER OF DIFFERENT CRYSTALLINE
STRUCTURES, MORE THAN ANY OTHER KNOWN MATERIAL.

CHAPTER 1

We could feel the reverberation of the ice-cutting machine through the frozen lake beneath our feet. Matt Boudoin was telling me this would be the best ice palace ever, and I was nodding, because of course every year the palace seems better than the one the year before. At the same moment, he stopped talking and I stopped nodding, because the machine had halted and the crew of men was staring down at the ice. Then, in unison, like marionettes with their strings being pulled, they turned their heads to look at Matt. Their faces were blank, but we knew something was wrong, very wrong.

We started moving forward. Because this is an Adirondack mountain town and Matt has an ingrained sense of chivalry, he held his arm out in that protective gesture you make toward a passenger in your car when you have to slam on the brakes. But it didn't stop me.

Later, I would wish it had.

For the first few months of winter, this lake is an expanse of frozen nothingness. Then, seemingly overnight, an enormous palace of ice appears, blocks melded together with a mortar of frozen slush, infused by colored lights that turn it into a fairy-tale castle. You can wander through it, footsteps crunching, breath forming icy clouds, and feel a sense of wonder you haven't felt since you were a child.

It's part of the fabric of this town, and the flow of winter is based around it. Never mind the huge expenditure of time and energy. This is Saranac Lake; this is Winter Carnival. Up goes the ice palace, every year with a different design, a different form of magic. This year I was going to track its progress for the local paper, with a photo and vignette every day—I thought I'd write about the homemade ice-cutting contraption, interview one of the ice cutters, talk to the designer. There was a lot you could write about palaces built of ice cut from the lake.

As we reached the circle of men, they stepped back, and Matt and I looked down. What I saw looked at first like a shadow under the ice—a dark mass, debris somehow caught up in cast-off clothing and trapped underneath as the ice had formed. I was wondering why the crew didn't simply move on to clean ice when I realized the mass had a shape, a human shape. You could see something that looked like eyes and a mouth that seemed open. Right about then Matt grabbed my arm and walked me away from the thing under the ice. We stopped about ten feet away and I sank to my heels, trying to process what I thought I'd seen. Matt whipped out a walkie-talkie and began barking orders as he gestured the men farther back.

For once my journalistic instincts had shut down, and I had no urge to record any of this. I could still envision that face under the ice, as if it were looking at me through a rain-distorted window.

And it was a face I knew.

I live in Lake Placid, ten miles away, in a house so big I rent out rooms, usually to athletes in town to train for bobsledding or kayaking or skiing. But sometimes a local turns up, and one day late last summer a girl named Jessamyn knocked at the door. She was thin with long black hair and green eyes that shifted as she looked at you. I wasn't sure I trusted her. But she didn't smoke—I've had people stare me in the eye and swear they didn't smoke when they reeked of it—and something about her made me like her. She was happy to take the smallest upstairs room, the one with just a twin mattress on the floor, a child-sized dresser, and a rod to hang clothes on.

She moved from job to job, but that's not rare here. Lake Placid is a touristy sports town with plenty of low-paying jobs, and people come and go, moving on to Boulder or Salt Lake City or giving up on their particular dream and heading back home to the unexciting job they never thought they'd have to take. Jessamyn had a quick wit and a sardonic manner, and men flocked to her. She'd date them for a few weeks, then discard them as if they were an article of clothing that didn't quite fit—apparently with no hard feelings on either side. She partied hard in the local bars but didn't bring it home with her. I never encountered a drunken paramour stumbling down the stairs; her employer never called because she missed a shift. And, like me, she never got involved with any of our roommates. You don't fish in your own pond; you don't hunt in your own backyard.

Then she met Tobin Winslow.

I would have pegged him for trouble from the start, with his frat-boy good looks, floppy hair, sleepy brown eyes, and diffident manner. It was written all over him that he was the sort of person who assumes life should go his way, no matter what. He didn't have a job to speak of, nothing steady, and drove a rattletrap pickup that seemed as much a prop as his Carhartt pants and flannel shirts. I suspected he'd grown up in a world of crisp khakis and button-downs and gone to an elite prep school, then partied himself right out of Harvard or Princeton before drifting up here, where no one ever asked where or if you'd gone to university.

It surprised me that Jessamyn fell for him—actually it surprised me she fell for anyone, because I hadn't seen her let anyone get too close. But Tobin seemed to appeal to something in her in a way the local guys hadn't. Maybe she was looking for someone who might take her away from here. Maybe she was yearning for conversation about more than ice fishing or carburetors or whatever game had been on television the night before. She'd been steadily working her way through the shelves of the Lake Placid library, and most of the guys she dated probably hadn't cracked a book since high school. And while Tobin may have been playing the role of good old boy, I suspected there was a lot going on behind that sleepy-lidded look.

But it didn't take a rocket scientist to see that Tobin Winslow likely wouldn't be leading Jessamyn down a path to anything new and improved. Falling for him meant giving up a big chunk of herself—although maybe that would have happened no matter who she fell for. Maybe she didn't know how to love without giving up herself. I'd figured that Jessamyn's flippant manner, hard drinking, and serial dating had been the veneer she'd adopted to cope with things life had thrown at her, things I could only guess at. But it had worked, in its way. Sure, she dated guys who were completely unaware of her intellect and she hadn't been able to settle down, but that happens to a lot of us. She had a life she could handle and at least pretend to be happy.

But Tobin had changed all that. Around him she dropped her sardonic edge and became close to meek. It didn't seem a change for the better. I didn't expect it was going to end well—I couldn't see Tobin settling down here, or whisking Jessamyn off to the bosom of his family, wherever they might be.

Tobin would periodically disappear for a week or two—no one knew where—and while he was gone Jessamyn would show glimmers of her old self. But once he came back she'd take right back up with him again as if he'd never left, an Adirondack version of a Stepford wife.

And the face beneath the ice was his.

CHAPTER 3

The ice harvesters had begun to talk in low tones. I heard Tobin's name, so they'd recognized him too. Tobin had spent a lot of time in the Saranac Lake bars, which were in general grittier than the ones in Lake Placid, and without the cluster of shiny-faced tourists trying a little too hard to have a good time.

Someone appeared from the Lakeview Deli across the street, carrying a cardboard carton of steaming drinks. One of the men handed me a cup. It was cocoa, hot and sweet, not the black coffee the guys almost certainly were drinking. This was their concession to my being a woman, one who had just seen a dead man under the ice, someone she knew. Fine by me, because in all the ways that mattered, the guys treated me as an equal. I'd covered their softball games and dart tournaments and ice-fishing contests, taken their photos and spelled their names right, so to them I was okay. And maybe cocoa was just what I needed now.

I took another sip and walked over to the guys. I nodded at them. They nodded back.

"It's Tobin, right? Tobin Winslow?" I said.

They nodded again.

"How . . ." I began.

They shrugged in unison. "Takes a while for that much ice to form," said one.

I'm from the South, where a dusting of snow means that schools close, life comes to a standstill, and everyone stays home until the white stuff disappears. It had been a rude adjustment to live somewhere so cold that lakes freeze into solid masses that people walk on, cut holes in for ice fishing, and drive sled-dog teams across. It took my first long winter here to learn to gauge the weather and dress in layers so I wasn't cold to the bone most of the time.

We stood there, no one saying anything. It wasn't all that rare in the Adirondacks for vacationers to get stranded in a sudden snowstorm on what they had thought would be a pleasant afternoon hike and freeze to death before anyone could find them. Far too often a local would drink too much on a Saturday night and drive off the road and die in a deep ravine. And sometimes, in the middle of a jobless, loveless winter, someone would write a note, put his mouth around a shotgun barrel, and thumb down the trigger. Or go out for a long walk and never be found. Someone cried for them, or no one did. Someone cleaned up the mess, and life went on.

And with all the lakes here, people find plenty of ways to drown. In winter they'll take a Ski-Doo out when the ice isn't thick enough and go under. Maybe they have the time and presence of mind to toss a child or grandchild to firmer ice before they sink, maybe not. Or in spring someone will go boating without a life jacket and drown under a bright shining sun, in water so cold it saps your will to keep moving until you give up and slide under, maybe on the way down thinking of the rest of your life you'll never have.

Last summer I'd nearly drowned in Lake Champlain, and sometimes in my dreams I'm back in that water, cold and alone, wondering if I'll ever take a breath of air again.

Matt came over and nodded at us, shaking his gloved fingers hard to warm them. A police car drove up and a policeman got out, walked over, and peered down at the ice for what seemed like a long time. Then he looked up and beckoned to Matt. Another policeman arrived, then a rescue squad. They all walked over, looked down at the ice, retreated to talk it over. Finally Matt came and asked me if I would take photos of the body before they started trying to remove it.

When I'd been the sports editor here, I'd covered everything from kayaking to boxing to luge to snowshoe races. But I'd never photographed anything under ice, and it was tricky with the sun reflecting off the surface. I concentrated on exposure and tried not to think about this being the body of a man I'd known.

After I'd taken multiples of every shot I could think of, I nodded at Matt. The men moved in with saws and began to cut the ice around the body. I kept shooting. It was something to do, and I needed to do something. Someone brought me another steaming cup from the deli, and I gulped it down. This time it was coffee. I kept clicking.

It seemed to take a very long time to free the block of ice, lever it out, and wrestle thick flat canvas bands under it to slide it toward shore. By now a crowd had gathered at the edge of the lake. I kept pressing the shutter button as the body slid along in its ice coffin. I saw it but didn't see it. I let the camera see it for me.

If I had simply heard that Tobin had died in a car crash downstate somewhere, I don't think I would have mourned him. But that dark shape in the chunk of ice sliding past hit me in a way I wouldn't have expected. Jessamyn had cared for Tobin, and somewhere were friends he'd grown up with, gone to school with, shared his rich-boy escapades with. Somewhere there was a family who would mourn his death and the extensions of him that would never exist: wife, children, grandchildren. And no mother is ever ready for a phone call telling her that her child has been found frozen into a lake.

The good thing about weather this cold is that tears freeze before they fall, so you can brush them away without anyone noticing.

On the shore, paramedics were having a discussion with the police, apparently adamant that this giant chunk of ice was not going into their ambulance. Finally someone drove an oversized pickup out onto the lake, which always makes me nervous. It seems to break one of the immutable laws of nature—water isn't meant to be driven on, and there's water on the other side of that ice, cold and dark.

Every man on the crew went to help hoist the slab of ice and slide it into the pickup bed. Probably they weren't all needed, but wanted to feel they were doing something. Off drove the truck, to a heated municipal garage, I imagined, where they'd wait for the ice to melt from around Tobin's body. Or maybe someone would chip away at it. There were people around here skilled in ice sculpting, and I supposed this would use the same basic skills, sort of in reverse.

Matt appeared at my side, and I was cold enough that I could almost sense the heat coming from his body. "We're going to go to the tavern, Troy," he said. "Do you want to come?"

I shook my head. I knew the guys needed to unwind before they went home, where their wives and children would want to hear the story. This would be told and retold in years to come, an almost apocryphal tale to keep kids from venturing too far on thin ice. It would be an easier story to tell, I thought, if you hadn't been there, if you hadn't seen Tobin's body being sawn out of the lake. If you hadn't known him when he was alive.

There would be a lot of beers downed this afternoon. The guys would talk about Tobin, how much he liked to drink, the crazy things he'd done, how he had ended up under the ice. Maybe it would be good to hear all this, but I couldn't handle it. I needed to get home.

Most of all, I needed to tell Jessamyn before she heard it on the street.

CHAPTER 4

It's about twenty minutes to Lake Placid, if you don't get stuck behind tourists. With my car heater blasting on high I had just about stopped shivering by the time I got home. But I was still cold, too cold to go looking for Jessamyn. I ran water in my tub, as hot as I could stand it, and crawled in and lay there, all of me submerged but my face, steam coming off the water, and thought about Tobin, under the ice. My dog, Tiger, lay in the doorway watching. She's half German shepherd and half golden retriever, and just about the best dog on the planet.

It seemed to take forever to warm up.

I toweled off and dressed as fast as I could, but I was moving slowly, like in one of those dreams where you just can't get anywhere. The walk up to town took longer than usual.

Jessamyn was working at a restaurant up on Main Street, where she regularly had the weekend shift. Tourists come into town determined to spend money, and they're happy to drop it on tips for a smiling waitress. And Jessamyn could play charm-the-tourists as well as anyone.

This was your standard steak and seafood restaurant, with the requisite Olympic kitsch: hanging ice skates and hockey sticks, photos of ski jumpers and bobsledders. I kicked snow off my boots at the door and stamped more off in the foyer. It was the after-noon lull before the dinner rush, and I saw Jessamyn refilling coffee cups for a table of tourists and laughing as if they'd said something incredibly witty. I waited until she headed back my direction.

"Hey, Troy," she said, surprised. "Did you want to eat?" She knows I don't often eat out, and if I do, it's Desperados, where the food is cheap and the service fast, or The Cowboy if someone's visiting from out of town.

I shook my head. "Can you take five minutes?" I asked.

She narrowed her eyes. She knew I wouldn't be here if it wasn't important. She set down the coffeepot, told the cashier she'd be right back, and grabbed her jacket.

Outside she crammed her gloveless hands into her pockets and looked at me. There was no easy way to say this. I would rather have told her at home, but word travels fast. Somewhere in town somebody probably was already telling the story.

I took a deep breath, and spoke. "I was over in Saranac Lake today—they started building the ice palace. They found a body in the ice."

Now her eyes shifted. I'd learned with her this didn't always mean she wasn't telling the truth; sometimes it just meant she was uncomfortable.

I made myself say the next words. "It was Tobin, Jessamyn."

She seemed to stop breathing. She stared at me, eyes wide, and swayed on her feet. I took a step toward her, but she righted herself. Her face was chalk.

"You're sure?" she whispered.

I nodded. She didn't ask any questions. She just stood there and breathed: in, out, in, out.

When Tobin had disappeared this last time, she had held out hope for a long time that he would return as usual. But as weeks turned into months, even she had given up. I think both of us had assumed he'd gotten tired of playing Adirondacker. I'd pictured him back at whatever posh home he had come from, living off

family money or making the motions of going into Daddy's business, and frequenting bars more expensive and sophisticated than
here. I'd imagined he'd dropped the Carhartts and flannel shirts
into a Goodwill bin, or given them to the hired help.

Our breath formed little clouds.

"I didn't want you to hear it from someone else," I said. The
words were thin in the cold air.

"I need a drink," she said.

She told her boss she was taking the evening off, and after one
look at our faces he knew not to protest. If Jessamyn was passing
up a prime winter Saturday evening slot, there was good reason.
He'd call in someone who'd be happy to take her shift and the fat
tips that came with it.

We walked down the street wordlessly, our feet crunching on
the packed snow. When we reached ZigZags, she opened the door,
and I followed her in. She nodded at the bartender; I'd seen him
around town but didn't know his name. He served us efficiently,
refilling her glass when she gestured to it, and topped up my Diet
Coke without asking.

She didn't cry; she just drank. She asked the bartender if he
had any cigarettes, and he handed her an open pack and didn't say
anything about smoking not being allowed. There were no other
customers. She smoked four in fast succession, lighting one from
the butt of the other. I didn't complain about the smoke. I didn't
remind her how hard she'd told me it had been to quit. I just sat
there.

She spoke only once, and I had to lean in to hear her. "Damn
him," she whispered. I didn't know if she meant damn him for
dying, or damn him for things he'd done when he was alive. I
didn't ask.

Eventually I went off to the bathroom, and on the way back
asked the bartender if he had any food—I figured that liquor and
shock weren't a good combination on an empty stomach. I thought

he might find some pretzels or nuts, but he came back with two thick sandwiches on sturdy plates and sat them on the bar in front of us. Maybe he'd heard about Tobin, or maybe he could just tell when someone needed to have food set in front of them. Jessamyn picked her sandwich up almost unseeingly and ate most of it, then put it down and emptied her glass.

"Let's go," she said, and stood. She pulled some bills from her pocket and dropped them on the bar. I caught the bartender's eye with a look that said *If it's not enough, let us know,* and he nodded. I grabbed my jacket and followed her outside.

It was snowing softly, the flakes falling on our faces and sticking in our hair. Dusk was settling. We walked to the house in silence. As Jessamyn turned to climb the stairs to her room, I saw a tear trail down her cheek. Maybe she'd cry up there, or maybe she'd just go to sleep. But I knew she needed to be alone.

CHAPTER 5

It was past Tiger's dinnertime, so I filled her bowl and left her in the kitchen while I climbed the steep stairs that led to my rooms. I have an outer room I use as an office, a tiny bathroom, and a small bedroom, all nicely separate from the rest of the house. I turned on my computer and clicked on my portable radiator. This is the only heat up here, plus whatever makes its way up through the stairwell and vents in the floor. But at night I have a down comforter and the warm weight of Tiger in the crook of my knees, so I do all right.

I sat at my desk. I could feel the heat from the radiator, but I didn't want to. I wanted to feel numb. I wanted to forget the grinding sound the block of ice with Tobin's body had made as it had slid past me, the grunts of the men struggling to move it into the truck, the look on Jessamyn's face when I'd told her the news. And I wanted to forget that glimpse of Tobin Winslow's face, frozen into the ice.

But I couldn't.

I pushed my camera's memory card into my computer, let Photoshop start uploading the photos, and turned away as they began flashing past. I rummaged in my dresser for some thick wool socks, pulled them on, and went down to the kitchen to brew some tea. Then I climbed under my covers to warm up.

There, while I sipped my tea, I realized I needed to talk to someone. This still doesn't come naturally to me. But I do have people I can call: my brother, Simon, in Orlando, with his cool, logical policeman's brain. My friend Baker, in Saranac Lake, with her kids and more routine life, always calm and pragmatic. Alyssa, a reporter in Burlington who'd been there for the worse parts of last summer. And Philippe, in Ottawa, whom I'd come oh-so-close to falling for.

But it was Jameson I wanted to talk to.

He was a police detective in Ottawa I'd met after I'd dived from a Lake Champlain ferry to rescue a small boy who turned out to have been kidnapped, a small boy whose father was Philippe. Jameson had seemed to consider me a prime suspect in the child's abduction, or at least an accomplice. He could be insufferably rude; he was brusque and direct.

I trusted him absolutely.

Something was tickling the back of my mind, a memory of the week Tobin disappeared, of seeing Jessamyn coming in the kitchen with a fat lip and a stiff way of moving. *Walked into a door,* she'd said. I hadn't believed her. I'd once worked with a woman who would come in with heavy makeup that didn't quite cover the bruises on her face—*I fell off the porch,* she'd say, or something similar, and we would nod and pretend to believe her. But in the afternoon roses would arrive from her husband, and I knew that husbands don't routinely send flowers whenever you're careless enough to fall off a porch.

The phone rang three times before he answered.

"Jameson," he said, as he would at work.

"Hey, it's Troy."

Something changed on his end, as if he had shifted in his chair. "Troy. How are you?"

"Something happened today," I said. He knew I wouldn't be calling about something mundane, and I knew he'd want to hear it from the beginning. So I told him about my roommate and the guy she had dated, a guy who had disappeared regularly, who may have mistreated her, whose body had just been found frozen in Lake Flower.

He listened without a word. "Fully dressed?" he asked when I stopped.

I closed my eyes, and I could see the contorted figure in the block of ice. One arm, off to the side, fingers splayed. A shiver ran through me. "Yes. Coat. No hat. No gloves, at least on the hand I saw."

"He was a drinker?"

"Oh, yeah. And he smoked weed, I think. He never seemed entirely sober."

I've never seen the logic in drinking to excess—it makes people act stupid and feel bad later. But plenty of locals drink hard and regularly, and many vacationers seem to think it's a requirement for stepping foot in town. More than once I've hollered out my bedroom window at two a.m. at firemen here for a convention and so drunk they couldn't find their way back to their motel. Maybe visiting horse-show people got plastered as well, but didn't wander the streets being loud about it. Maybe they sat around in their trim riding jodhpurs and neat buttoned shirts and got quietly, desperately, privately drunk.

Even I knew if someone had imbibed enough they might think it a great idea to amble across a half-frozen lake. Alcohol seems to go a long way toward convincing people they're immortal.

"They'll do an autopsy," Jameson said. "Even the basics will take a few days; tox screens take longer. Then they'll likely know if it's anything besides him just falling through the ice. But tell your roommate not to talk about this. To anyone. Not even casually."

"What about the police?"

Silence for a moment as he negotiated between his sense of duty and what was best for Jessamyn. "She doesn't want to impede the investigation," he said finally. "She should tell them what's relevant: when she saw him last, who his friends were, but nothing that's not facts—nothing they can misinterpret. Not without a lawyer."

"Okay," I said, and suddenly it was. Without me having to spell it out he knew I was worried, and he knew why. If I had noticed Jessamyn's fat lip and pained way of walking, other people would have too. It wouldn't be a giant leap for someone to assume that Tobin had been the one to hurt her, and that she might have decided to do something about it. Because the Jessamyn before Tobin came along wouldn't have put up with anyone raising a hand to her.

"Let me know what they find out," he said.

"I will," I said, and hung up.

I did realize that on some level there was a thread of something deeper between Jameson and me, but neither of us seemed to want or need to acknowledge it. Jameson was single, and that was the extent of what I knew about his personal life. And of course he knew how intertwined my life had been with Philippe's last summer after I'd rescued his son.

It was getting late, and had gotten colder. But I needed a walk, and Tiger could use one. It's one of the great things about dogs— they're always ready for an outing. I pulled on my wool-lined Sorel boots, zipped up my parka, and wedged my neck warmer under my hat so only my eyes and nose were exposed. This is my secret to beating the cold: blocking the little crevices that let the cold creep in. This, plus my puffy insulated gloves.

I didn't bother with a leash, because Tiger always walks or runs beside me. No credit to me; she was born that way, pre-trained. I let her know what I wanted, and she'd do it. We headed out past Town Hall and the police station and turned onto Mirror Lake Drive for the three-mile loop around the lake.

I love this walk at night, especially in the winter. Almost no one is out; the air is still; the snow and ice crunch underfoot. As you move along you can forget the bad stuff that happened during the day.

Or almost, anyway.

I don't often have female roommates, because usually it's guys who show up looking for rooms. And guys are easier to live with.

They don't care if you don't feel like talking and they don't get involved with your life, except around the edges. They never want to make the house rules or take over running things, and they don't complain about the décor or much of anything.

But Jessamyn hadn't been the typical female roommate. She didn't want to take over anything. She didn't want to always be doing things with me. She didn't want to tell me her problems or hear about mine, and she was tidier than most of the guys. Tobin I'd seen a lot of, because he was often at the house, and nothing had given me a reason to change my impression of him. Not that I'd told Jessamyn. She hadn't gotten where she was in life by listening to good advice. Few of us have.

As I walked I pictured Tobin, drunk or foolish or both, crunching across the early winter ice of Lake Flower until he fell through, or passing out or falling asleep and sliding under as the ice gave way. At least then, I thought, he would have been spared the shock of plunging into the frigid water and that final awful moment when he knew he wasn't going to be able to save himself, that today had been his last tomorrow.

Or he could have been ice diving. It's crazy, but people do it. I'd seen it during Winter Carnival—unofficial, of course. Someone dives through a circular hole cut into the ice, a rope tied to one leg, and comes up through a second hole nearby, presumably after drinking enough to decide it's a good idea. Maybe Tobin had missed the second hole and had no one to haul him out. Or tried it without a rope, or the rope came loose, or his friends lost hold of it. It would be a terrible secret to keep through the winter, waiting for the body to be found. But because of Winter Carnival and the vagaries of the lake, it had appeared sooner rather than later.

It didn't yet cross my mind that someone might actually have a reason for wanting Tobin gone.

My eyelashes were beginning to freeze. I broke into a jog, taking choppy, short steps, all you can do in clunky boots on icy ground. Tiger kept pace without missing a beat. I switched to a brisk walk when I reached town, passing restaurants and gift shops, the Olympic Center and then the speed-skating oval with its skaters in tights and long blades, bent low, gliding around the track.

In the kitchen, Brent glanced up and nodded. He was working his way through a plateful of spaghetti and a paperback copy of *Of Human Bondage*, a book I've never been able to make myself finish. Brent, like most of my athlete roommates, was quiet and dedicated—a biathlete who spent long hours skiing, lifting weights, and dry-firing his rifle at a tiny target taped on his bedroom wall. He'd lived in the Olympic training center a while, but I suspected there'd been too many boisterous bobsledders and snowboarders for him.

I wondered if I should tell him Jessamyn's boyfriend had been found frozen in the ice of Lake Flower. But it's a hard thing to work into conversation: *How's your book? Say, did you hear Tobin Winslow was found dead today?* I nodded back at him and climbed the stairs to my room.

I pulled on the sweatpants and old pullover I sleep in, and thought about e-mailing or calling Philippe. But I didn't feel like talking, and this wasn't something you could rattle off in an e-mail. I'd tell him about it, but not now. I grabbed my favorite Josephine Tey novel, and forced my eyes to follow the words until I could go to sleep. It took a while.

CHAPTER 6

I awoke abruptly, with that disquieting feeling you have when the world has shifted on its axis. I pulled on boots, parka, hat, scarf, gloves in quick and practiced succession. Some mornings I just let Tiger out the back door, but this morning I needed movement, brisk movement. I went up the hill behind the house and down Parkside Drive, then circled down Main Street. As we neared the house I saw a Saranac Lake police car pull up. And my brain, without pause, went straight to: *The police must think Tobin's death wasn't an accident.*

The policeman got out of his car as I approached. He was young, probably not long out of high school, and wore his uniform like a suit of armor.

"Does Jessamyn Field live here?" he asked. Something, his tone or how he stood, made me think he'd become a policeman for all the wrong reasons. I imagined he'd been a gawky kid, bullied, never taken seriously.

I nodded.

"She dated Tobin Winslow?" he asked.

I nodded again. "Off and on," I said, as if this made it less significant. Never mind that the "off" parts had been Tobin's choice.

"I need to talk to her," he said.

"I'll go see if she's here," I told him. I wished I'd been able to warn Jessamyn, to pass along what Jameson had said. The policeman followed me into the front hallway, as if I'd invited him in. At the base of the stairs I turned and said, "I'll be right back," so he wouldn't try to follow. Jessamyn didn't need to wake up to see a cop at her door. Policemen seldom arrive with good news—they don't come knocking to tell you you've won a sweepstakes or a home makeover.

I tapped on her bedroom door. No answer. I tapped again and called out her name. I pushed the door open a few inches and peered in. The room was empty, covers pulled up tidily. Normally Jessamyn wasn't an early riser, but the day after your boyfriend was found frozen to death wasn't a normal day. Not even here in the Adirondacks.

"She's not here," I told the policeman as I came down the stairs.

"Not here?" he echoed. "Doesn't she live here?"

I tried not to sound sarcastic, but I hadn't had breakfast and wasn't in the best of moods. "Yes, she lives here," I said. "But at the moment she—is—not—here."

"Do you know where she is?"

I suppressed the urge to tell him I didn't have my roommates sign in and out. I shook my head. "She works at a restaurant up on Main Street, but it's not open yet. Maybe she went for a walk." Not that I'd ever known Jessamyn to walk anywhere unless she had to.

At that moment the front doorknob clicked, and we turned. The door opened and Jessamyn entered, carrying two steaming cups and a paper bag giving off a rich, buttery smell. She smiled at us.

"I thought you might like some coffee," she said, handing me a cup. "Cream, right?"

I nodded. I was surprised she knew I ever drank coffee, let alone how I took it. She turned to the policeman. "Would you like a croissant?" she asked, holding the bag out. "I'm sorry, I didn't know you were here or I would have gotten you a coffee."

I tried not to laugh; she was acting as if this were an early-morning date. The policeman's ears turned red, and he shook his head. I had no idea why Jessamyn was suddenly playing Rebecca of Sunnybrook Farm, but I reached into the bag when she held it out to me. It was from the bakery next to the movie theater, too pricey for my budget, and usually for Jessamyn's. The croissant was warm, the crust flaky. I bit into it.

"Are you Jessamyn Field?" the policeman asked.

She nodded, setting down the bag and shrugging off her jacket.

"You knew Tobin Winslow?"

She nodded again.

"You know he's dead."

I thought, *You idiot; if she didn't, that would be a heck of a way to tell her.*

Jessamyn took a sip of coffee. "Yes," she said. "Troy told me."

The policeman looked at me, almost accusingly.

"I was there when he was found," I said.

He frowned, and turned to Jessamyn. "I need to ask you a few questions."

Jessamyn didn't respond, and something uneasy flickered through her eyes. Suddenly this didn't seem like a game.

"What sort of questions?" I asked, to buy her some time.

He glanced at me. "Where he's from, full name, date of birth, all that."

Jessamyn took a deep breath and her eyes shifted. I doubted she knew much of this, and for her and Tobin this was perfectly normal. Jessamyn didn't tell anyone about her past and she didn't ask any questions about anyone else's. But to this policeman it was going to sound odd that she didn't know these details about someone she'd dated for months. And Jessamyn being Jessamyn, she might make up stuff that would come back to bite her in the ass.

I spoke up. "His name was Tobin Walter Winslow." They both looked at me as if the kitchen table had spoken. "I saw it on his driver's license. He was showing us his photo." It had been one of those comparing-awful-driver's-license-picture things. And it wasn't as if Walter was a common name: I could think only of one of Anne of Green Gables' sons, after she'd grown up and married, which had seemed strange to my eleven-year-old self. Children in books aren't supposed to grow up and turn into married ladies with kids. They're supposed to stay children forever.

"Birth day or year?" the cop asked.

"Didn't see it."

He looked at Jessamyn, and she shook her head.

"How long did you know him?" he asked her.

"Since June," she said. "I met him at Mud Puddles. Across the street." That bar's called Wiseguys now, but it was Mud Puddles for a very long time.

"Do you know where he was from?"

She shook her head.

"It was a New York license," I said.

"Family?" he asked.

Jessamyn looked blank.

"I think he had a sister," I said. Now they both looked at me as if I were the annoying kid in class who kept supplying answers. I shrugged. "He once said someone was like his older sister nagging him."

"Friends?" said the policeman, frowning. This Jessamyn knew. She rattled off names, although she didn't know full names for some of them. Now she looked unsteady, and the policeman noticed it.

"I'm sure this was a shock to you," he said belatedly, and she nodded. I don't think she was acting.

"Why don't you call if you have more questions?" I said, moving toward the front door to urge him out. He seemed none too happy, but he must have realized he wasn't going to get much more out of Jessamyn at the moment.

As the door closed behind him I turned to Jessamyn. "My gosh, coffee and croissants. What's next, you start cleaning house?"

She gave a crooked smile, and the last of her façade of functionality disappeared. Whatever impulse or energy had sent her out that morning was gone, and she looked thin and tired. I followed her to the kitchen, where she sat and put her head on her arms. I sat down across from her.

When she lifted her head, she opened the pastry bag and took out the last croissant. "How did you know that stuff about Tobin?" she asked.

I shrugged again. I can't help noticing things, and I can't help remembering them. Which is probably why I started writing as a kid, journals and stories I never showed to anyone. You have to do something with all that stuff in your head.

She pulled off a bit of the croissant and put it in her mouth. "You didn't like Tobin, did you?"

No one wants to speak ill of the dead, as if dying gives them a grace they lacked in life. I chose my words carefully. "I wasn't sure he was good for you."

She gave a short bark of a laugh. "You know what's funny? What's funny is that when I met Tobin, I thought my whole world was going to change. He seemed like someone who could make anything happen, that anything was possible. That I could be anybody I wanted to be."

She looked up. Her eyes were shiny with unfallen tears, with grief and pain and confusion. I could have told her this was a knack Tobin had, a skill set he used to get what he wanted when he wanted it. I could have told her that had he put his mind to it, Tobin probably could have made anything happen and could have accomplished whatever he wanted. But what he had wanted was to live here, to mingle like a disreputable royal among commoners, where people thought he was great because he could crack jokes and drink hard and attract whatever woman he wanted, and get by with doing as little work as possible.

I wasn't going to say any of that.

Besides, she knew it all.

CHAPTER 7

My phone rang, and I ran up to answer it. It was my friend Baker in Saranac Lake—she'd just heard about Tobin. Then another call came in, from the editor of the paper, and I clicked over to him.

George cleared his throat. "You saw them find Winslow."

"Yep."

"You got pictures."

"Yep."

He got right to the point—one of the things I liked about George. "Can you do a first-person piece?"

I thought about it as I listened to Jessamyn moving about in the kitchen below, speaking to my dog. I could write a piece that would capture being there on the lake, the air so cold you couldn't stand still for long; the sound of the saw blades chewing through the ice, the men's breath rasping as they worked, the slide of the ice coffin across the lake. George didn't need to tell me this story would almost certainly hit the wires, that it would run nation-wide, that this would help me break into bigger magazines than I wrote for now.

I shook my head before realizing I was doing it. "I can't," I said.

Churning out a first-person piece about being there when

Tobin was found would seem a betrayal in a way I didn't begin to understand. Maybe I could write about it later, maybe in a magazine piece, but not now. Not when it had just happened and Jessamyn was still reeling from it. And maybe I was too.

"Have you got someone on it?" I asked.

"Yes," he said, and told me who, a kid named Dirk who had been at the paper a few months, whose writing hadn't impressed me. My silence told George what I thought of this. "He really wants to do it," he added. "And everyone else is tied up or on vacation."

Long pause.

"Can you work with his piece?" he asked. "Review it, add some stuff? Dual byline."

This I could do. "Sure. Send it over."

"Photos?"

"I'll let you have a couple. Nothing real specific. You don't want a body on your front page, George." Even if he did, I didn't. "Are you clear to run it? Have they notified next of kin?"

"Yep. I heard someone's on their way here."

I was surprised. "They didn't have trouble tracking down the family?"

"No, Barry at the police station said the wallet was still in his pocket. I'll send the story to you when it comes in. Won't be for a while yet."

I thought as I hung up. So the police knew perfectly well where Tobin was from and who his family was, and the officer at the house had asked Jessamyn questions the police already knew the answers to. Maybe that particular policeman had been uninformed—or was shrewder than he'd seemed. Maybe he had been the one playing games.

I went down and told Jessamyn the newspaper editor had called, that I was going to look over the article they were doing on Tobin. Then we heard the door open, and steps coming down the hall. We looked at each other, both of us maybe wondering if the policeman had returned and waltzed in the front door we never locked.

But it was Brent, carrying a plastic bag from Stewart's up the street. He raised one eyebrow but didn't say anything. He pulled a box of oatmeal from the bag, and we watched him dump some in a pot, mix in water, and turn on the stove.

Jessamyn looked at me. "Tell him," she said. So I did, succinctly, while Brent was stirring his breakfast.

He listened, then ladled his oatmeal into a huge bowl, topped it with raisins and cinnamon, and sat down with us. There was something comforting about the smell of that oatmeal.

"So what happened to Tobin's truck?" he asked.

We gaped at him. I hadn't thought of this; apparently Jessamyn hadn't either. Of course we'd assumed Tobin had driven his truck out of town—but he'd never left. *So where was his truck?*

Brent misunderstood our confusion. "Didn't Tobin have a pickup truck?" he asked.

"Yeah, he did," I said. "Maybe it's still out at his cabin." Tobin had stayed in a cabin outside of town, where he'd had some kind of deal with the owner who lived downstate and used it only rarely.

Jessamyn was shaking her head. "No, I went out there a couple of times, to see if he'd come back. No truck."

"Maybe it was impounded," Brent said. "Did he own it?"

"I guess so," said Jessamyn, frowning. "But if he'd left it anywhere around here, someone who knew him would have seen it and mentioned it."

I think the thought came to her the same time it did to me: *Maybe Tobin had tried to drive across the lake and crashed through—and maybe his truck was on the bottom of Lake Flower.*

We sat there a long moment.

I cleared my throat. "No," I said, shaking my head, sounding more confident than I felt. "No way he would have tried to drive across the lake, even drunk, not that early in winter. Walk maybe, never drive. And if he had, a truck going through the ice would have left a hole someone would have noticed."

Brent said nothing. He was probably calculating how thick the ice had been and how fast a hole would ice over, but was smart enough not to say any of this.

"Then where's his truck?" Jessamyn almost whispered.

"He must have parked it somewhere, or it broke down and got snowed in, and no one's noticed it," I said. "Then he hitched a ride."

Around here a vehicle could get completely buried by snow on a back road and not reappear until spring. But it seemed an odd and unlikely coincidence that a truck would disappear at the same time its owner drowned. From the look on Brent's face, I guessed his brain was going the same direction.

The fact was, there were plenty of reasons that could lead to someone ending up dead around here. Tobin could have smarted off to the wrong person, dabbled in the North Country drug trade, gotten involved with someone whose spouse didn't take kindly to being cuckolded. He could have been in a fistfight that went bad— you could break your skull on a rock in a bad fall; a blow to the wrong part of your chest can stop your heart. I'd once read in a John D. MacDonald novel that hitting someone's nose at a certain angle could send fatal shards of bone into the brain—one of those tidbits that sticks in your mind when you're thirteen, whether true or not.

Jessamyn nodded. She stood. "I'm going to go work a shift for the girl who filled in for me last night."

"Listen," I said, talking fast to get it out. "I talked to a friend who's a policeman. He said you shouldn't talk about this to people, and if anyone asks you questions, don't answer."

She gave me an odd look.

I'd rather have tried to explain this when Brent wasn't around, but it wouldn't have been easy even then. I didn't want to tell her that her lippy repartee wouldn't look good in print. I could hardly say *Someone could start a rumor that you had something to do with Tobin's death* or *Hey, the police may think you were involved.* I tried again: "This could be a story that other papers want to cover, Jessamyn. It's better if you just don't say anything— then no one can misquote you."

From the look on Brent's face, I saw he got it. I hoped she did too.

CHAPTER 8

It would take a while for the article to arrive, and I didn't want to sit around waiting, so I loaded up skis and dog and headed for the trails behind Howard Johnson's.

It was in the low twenties, pretty much perfect for cross-country skiing if you knew not to overdress. It was a bright clear day, and the glide of my skis and the motion of my muscles let my brain start to unwind. I only had to stop once to clear out snow from between Tiger's paws where it had melted and refrozen. You can buy dog booties, but dogs mostly don't like them—I think they consider them an insult.

In the snowy woods with the sun bright overhead, it seemed absurd to think that anyone had caused Tobin's death. This was an unlucky confluence of a late night, poor judgment, cold weather. Tobin had run out of gas or had a breakdown; his truck would be found, cemented in place by snow. He'd hitched a ride to town, decided to walk across the lake, and fallen in. He had died, grotesquely and accidentally. It happens all too often around here. You could fill a book with grim and sometimes mysterious Adirondack deaths—actually, someone had, a book called *At the Mercy of the Mountains*. Jessamyn would recover; she'd regain her old personality or form a new one. Everyone would talk about Tobin for a while, and then move on. Like they always did.

I slid my skis into the back of my car, and then decided to drive on to Price Chopper—this was a day that called out for a hot dinner. Back at the house I chopped vegetables and tossed them in a big pot with stew meat and diced tomatoes, left it simmering, and went upstairs. After a quick shower, I turned on my computer and saw that George had sent the article. I opened it and started reading.

> *When Matt Boudoin and his workers went to work on*
> *the Ice Palace Saturday, none of them had any idea what*
> *horrible discovery they would find under the ice.*

I winced. Maybe George had left it this bad to goad me into doing complete rewrite. He knows I loathe incompetence, and that competitiveness runs deep within me.

I read on. Near the end of the piece I found a sentence that made me cringe:

> *Before Tobin Winslow disappeared, he had been dating*
> *Jessamine Fields of Lake Placid.*

The kid had not only misspelled Jessamyn, but had gotten her last name wrong. I highlighted the sentence and hit Delete without a qualm. Who Tobin had been dating wasn't relevant—it wasn't as if they'd lived together or been engaged—and the last thing Jessamyn needed was to be forever linked to this guy.

I called Matt Boudoin, who told me they were continuing the ice harvest from a different area. I tracked down the number of the guy who owned Tobin's cabin, and left him a message. I called the Saranac Lake police and found out precisely nothing about Tobin's truck, Tobin's family, or much of anything. I didn't push it. I wasn't the primary reporter on this, and I'd already annoyed one local cop.

Then I Googled "Tobin Walter Winslow"—something the reporter apparently hadn't bothered to do—and within minutes turned up Tobin's hometown, the name of his prep school, and a photo of him at a lacrosse game at, yes, Princeton, during his freshman year. It was unsettling to see this younger, happier person with Tobin's face, hair shorter and face brighter.

A few more clicks, and I found his parents: Mary Martha and Bertram Martin Winslow II. I learned the name of the insurance company Tobin's father owned, his private club, the hefty donations he'd made; the groups his mother belonged to, events she'd attended. Then I saw a link for a Bertram Winslow III and clicked, and started reading. When the words penetrated, I pushed back from my desk.

Tobin had had one brother, four years his senior, who had died in a boating accident while Tobin was with him, the summer after graduating from Princeton. The Tobin I'd so disliked had seen his big brother drown; this set of parents had just lost their second son.

I got up and walked around. Then I sat down and read more. There was one sister, Jessica, neatly spaced between the brothers, a tidy two years apart. It did occur to me that it was odd that Tobin's sister had a name so similar to Jessamyn's—I think it was Freud who said there are no coincidences.

But I had an article to rewrite.

Before moving to the Adirondacks, I'd worked part time at a paper out West, writing features, which I'd liked, and engagement and wedding announcements, which I'd hated. I'd applied for the sports editor job here partly because I was desperate, and partly because it was a long way from home. It took a while to figure out how to cover so many sports I knew next to nothing about, but once I did, I'd loved it. Athletes had passion for what they did— whether Olympic kayaker or sled-dog racer or the five boys on a tiny high school basketball team that didn't win a game until the last one of the season. And I loved translating that passion onto the page.

A benefit of having written so many articles on deadline is

that you learn to work fast—very fast. In less than twenty minutes, I was done.

I proofed, printed it to read again, and made a few more tweaks. I chose a photo with the crowd on the shore and the ambulance, and one of the ice cutters with their saws, working on the ice but not quite showing what was under it. I sent it all off to George, along with links to the Princeton photo and one of last year's ice palace. I knew if he wanted to use them he'd get permission. That was another thing I liked about George—he wouldn't cut corners. To him journalism was journalism, no matter how small your circulation numbers.

Suddenly I was deeply fatigued. I went into my bedroom and plopped on my bed. When I opened my eyes it was dark, and I could hear voices downstairs. I could smell my stew, and something baking. Something chocolate.

I went down, still groggy. I saw Jessamyn at the stove, stirring my stew. I blinked. This was as unlikely as her bringing me coffee and croissants that morning, maybe more so. Brent turned from the sink. "Hey," he said. "Do you want to share? We made rice and a salad, and Patrick's baking a cake."

This seemed an odd dream, conjured from fatigue and shock. We'd never all eaten together—the extent of our togetherness had been running into one another in the kitchen or happening to watch a TV show in the living room.

"Sure," I said. "Why not?"

Brent grinned. He had an open face, straight blond hair he kept short, and an athlete's lithe body that was no mystery to any of us—cross-country ski suits don't leave much to the imagination. Jessamyn had never shown a glimmer of interest in him, partly because he hadn't been her type, I thought, and partly because he was a roommate. Home was where you relaxed, not where you picked up the next man in your life. But maybe it would be good for her to get to know a guy who didn't spend every spare minute and spare dollar in the local bars, someone with a brain and goals and a passion for something.

Maybe, I thought, she deserved more than she'd been settling for.

Maybe many of us do.

Patrick, our youngest roommate, wandered in. He had finished high school in California a year early, and at eighteen was planning to travel the world. First stop: Lake Placid, where he was scrounging free lift tickets and skiing his brains out. He pulled the cake from the oven and set it aside to cool while we ate bowls of stew and rice with salad and garlic bread. We talked about weather and skiing and made fun of tourists, which is what you do when you live in a resort town. The guys tossed bits of bread for Tiger, and Jessamyn ate more than I'd ever seen her eat. No one spoke of Tobin.

It was strange in a way, but in a way it felt right. When we finished, we spooned all the leftover ice cream in the freezer over the still-warm cake and devoured it. It was one of the best evenings I'd had in a long time.

Sometimes home is where you're at, and family is who you're with.

CHAPTER 9

The next morning my phone was ringing as I was coming in from taking Tiger out. It was Baker.

"Look at the online edition of the newspaper," she said without preamble.

"What?"

"Look at the newspaper online."

"What's wrong?"

"Just read it," she said, and hung up.

I moved to my computer and to the paper's website. I winced at the headline: BODY HAUNTS ICE PALACE. At a glance the story seemed as it was when I'd turned it in, except the bylines were reversed, with mine first.

But there was a sidebar, a box with just the kid's byline. And as I started reading it my throat went dry.

WAS THERE FOUL PLAY?

Did Tobin Winslow die a natural death in Lake Flower when he disappeared in December, or did someone hasten his demise?

Saranac Lake police will say only that an autopsy has been scheduled, but refuse to divulge any other information.

"No way could Tobin just have drowned," said one of Winslow's friends. "He was too smart for that. He wouldn't have gone way out on that ice. Someone must have dumped his body."

Friends say that Winslow had been buying drinks for them at the Waterhole the last time they saw him, and he had had a large wad of cash. Some suggested the money was for drugs.

I was reaching for the phone when I saw the last few lines: "A source says that Winslow and his girlfriend Jessamine Fields of Lake Placid had been fighting the week he disappeared and that she had been complaining about him. Fields was unavailable for comment."

My heart seemed to skip a beat. What *had* the kid been thinking? He might as well have headlined this LOCAL GIRL SUSPECT IN DRUGGIE BOYFRIEND'S DEATH. What had George been thinking? Tobin's family would pitch a fit, the local cops would be ticked off, and Jessamyn—well, the word "pilloried" sprang to mind. I speed-dialed the paper; George wasn't in. He liked to come in early and set the front section, then go home for a leisurely brunch. I called his home and told his wife it was urgent. George was on the phone in seconds. I imagined an omelet getting cold, toast growing soggy.

"Did you okay this sidebar?" I asked.

"What?"

My voice got louder. "Did you okay this sidebar? On Tobin?"

"Well, yeah," he said, puzzled.

For a moment I couldn't speak. "George, are you crazy? This is horrible—it's lurid, it's probably actionable."

Silence. "Let me get to my computer."

I listened to his footsteps, the creak of his desk chair, the clicking as he navigated to the story. I could hear his breath suck in when he saw the article. Then I knew what must have happened: this reporter, annoyed by having his story edited so extensively, had done something very stupid.

"This isn't what he turned in," George said. "The sidebar I

saw was a collection of quotes from Winslow's friends. Somehow he went behind me and switched them. And changed the headline."

"Could he have changed the print version too?"

George said a word I'd never heard from him. "I'm calling the press room now," he said. I could hear him punching buttons on his cell phone. "Call Sheena for me and tell her I said to kill this story on the website. Take the whole site down if she has to."

We hung up. As I dialed the paper I saved a copy of the web page, and hit Print. This would disappear soon, and I wanted a record of it.

Sheena answered, and I filled her in. "It's urgent," I told her.

"The site's down," she said a moment later. "I'll pull the story and we'll redo the page. For now, people will just see a message that says 'Down for Repairs.'"

"Great. Are the presses running?"

"I think so, the front section anyway," she said. "Is the same story in the paper?"

"I hope not, but probably. George is on the phone with them now."

"So they're going to have to reprint it."

"Sounds like it."

She said a word that was an interesting variation of the one George had used.

"Look, I'll come over to help," I said.

"Great." She hung up. I grabbed my parka, pulling it on as I headed for the door, and reached the paper in record time. The presses were ominously silent. George was at his desk, pounding away at his keyboard. The kid, Dirk, was nowhere in sight.

"Can you finish this, Troy?" George asked as he stood. "I changed the headline and pulled the sidebar, but I don't want his name on this, not anywhere. If there's anything left from his piece, change it. And when you're done, get Sheena to put the new story on the website."

George didn't often get his back up, but when he did, he meant business. I slid into his chair as he headed back to the press room, probably to calm the press room guys and the women waiting to slide in inserts and bundle the paper. If he was smart, he'd send out for doughnuts and pass out cash bonuses at the end of the day. It was going to take a lot of work to get the paper out anywhere close to on time.

I went through the piece. There wasn't much left from the kid's original copy, and it didn't take long to redo those parts and add some background on the ice palace. I enlarged the photos to fill the rest of the gap, proofread, and clicked Save. The press room foreman was watching through the door, and I gave a thumbs-up. Within minutes the presses were rolling.

I stayed a few hours, helping where I could—I can stuff inserts in papers as well as the next person, but it's hot, dirty work. I tried to call home to let Jessamyn know what was happening, but no one answered. After the papers were loaded for distribution, I helped pull the front pages from the discarded ones headed for recycling. George worked alongside me, grimly.

He set a few copies aside and let me take one. "Lock it away," he said. He didn't need to tell me.

"What are you going to do with them?" I asked.

"Burn them. I've got a barrel behind my house."

I helped him carry them out and put them in the trunk of his car.

As I left, I saw the kid arriving. Probably Sheena had tracked him down. George was easygoing for the most part. You could make mistakes in stories, especially when you were new. You could turn a story in late and you could get away with showing up hungover to work a few times. But this George wouldn't let slide.

I'd never known him to fire anyone, but I had a feeling it was about to happen.

CHAPTER 10

The parking lot was icy, so I stepped carefully. Once I'd fallen flat here and cracked an elbow that still ached whenever a storm was coming in.

I'm not particularly tuned in to the sound of cars and trucks, although of course dogs can tell when their owner's car is approaching. But something about the vehicle driving past caught my attention—the sound of the engine, a bounce of springs, or something more subtle. I turned in time to see a truck go past.

It was Tobin's truck, or its twin.

I stood there a moment, staring after it, my breath making billows of steam in the cold air. For one crazy, time-shifting moment, part of me thought the shadowy figure behind the wheel was Tobin.

But it wasn't. And it wasn't Tobin's truck. No one would be merrily driving it through town, where locals could identify it at a glance. It was just one that resembled his—not even, I thought, quite the same color.

I've done this with people, ones no longer living: my grandfather, a soldier friend killed in Afghanistan. You see someone in a store or out working in the yard and you do a double take, because for an instant it *is* that person, with their height, their appearance, their mannerisms. Then when you look again, you see the resemblance is only slight.

I started my car and flipped on the seat heater, one of the greatest inventions in the history of the automobile. I tried calling the house again, but the line was busy. I'd never spent the extra to get voice mail on the house phone—it's a pain with a group of ever-changing roommates, and most people had cell phones. Jessamyn didn't, and Tobin hadn't either. I'd figured he didn't want people to be able to find him.

I pulled out onto Broadway and made the turn on Route 86 toward home.

Something really ugly had just happened—for the newspaper and for anyone who had cared about Tobin. Something I'd played a role in. I suppose I could have e-mailed the reporter, letting him know how much I'd changed his piece, but one, it never occurred to me, and two, it would have seemed patronizing. This was how I'd learned to write on a newspaper, without any hand-holding or babysitting. You turned in your work; you paid attention to what was done to it. You did it better the next time.

But part of me had reveled in fixing that article, in slashing out the kid's bad writing, showing him how it was done. And I hadn't given a thought to how he would react when he saw what had been done to the article. This is one of my flaws, a blind tunnel vision, where I concentrate so much on getting a job done that I don't consider other people. There's a reason my list of friends is short.

And there are no true do-overs on the Internet. It takes only seconds to take a screen shot or for a web page to be cached. I just hoped that few people had seen this piece, and that fewer had taken note.

Sometimes when I drive home I take the shortcut by St. Agnes that bypasses most of town and goes past the Crowne Plaza— what used to be the Holiday Inn—and reconnects with Main Street at the Olympic Center. But that route has a lot of stop signs, with figure skaters traipsing up and down the hill to the rinks, so today I decided to skip it.

I was partway through town when something caught my eye: a woman, her stance fierce, her face contorted, facing two men, locals from the look of them. It took a moment to realize it was Jessamyn. I'd never interfered with her life, not even when maybe I should have, but she'd never just had a boyfriend found dead. And this looked ugly.

I pulled over, and closed my car door loudly to get their attention. "Hey," I said as I walked toward them, trying to sound casual. "What's up?"

One guy turned. He'd long passed the stage of needing a haircut and shave, and his clothes looked like he'd slept in them for a week. I knew before I got close what he would smell like—long-unwashed clothing mixed with that boozy aroma that seems to emanate from the pores. Every village had one of these: not quite the town drunk, not far from it.

"What's up is that this bitch had Toby killed," he sputtered, waving a clutched piece of paper. Even from where I was I could see that it was a printout of the article from the Internet. My heart sank.

People across the street glanced over, and the second of the two men looked as if he wished he were somewhere else. Jessamyn's mouth opened and closed. This was worse than I'd feared.

I said the first thing I could think of: "No, she didn't."

"Yeah, he got tired of her and dumped her and she had him taken out." His voice was louder, spittle spraying.

I glanced at Jessamyn. Her eyes had a look I never could have imagined in her, like a cornered fox I'd once come across. The guy took a step toward her and without thinking, I moved between them and grabbed the paper from his hand.

"You need to go home," I said, enunciating clearly, staring straight at him. "You need to go home and you need to do it *now*." I was calm, oddly calm. Something had kicked in, the opposite of adrenaline.

He bristled and for a moment I thought he was going to hit me. But the other guy, one who looked like he had slept in his clothes only one night rather than a week of nights, tugged at his friend's arm.

"Hey, Stevo, it's not worth it, let's go. C'mon. Let's go to Al's."

After a moment the guy let his friend pull him along up Main Street.

I turned. Jessamyn was staring at me.

"Troy, you're shaking," she said.

I crammed the piece of paper in my pocket and looked down at my hands. "Guess I am." Common sense should have told me to have eased Jessamyn away, to not have stepped into the fray. But my brain had disengaged and I'd moved without volition. Like when I was nine and saw a man beating a dog with a stick, and had run between him and the dog and ended up with the dog following me home and adopting me. Like when I'd dived into the lake last summer to rescue a small boy and had changed my life forever.

Jessamyn looked over my shoulder toward my car, and then back at me. She gestured toward the café across the street. "How about some coffee?"

"No, I'm fine, I just need to eat, and I'm tired. I've been at the paper for hours." I moved toward the car. She followed and got in, and we rode to the house in silence. I went straight to the kitchen, sliced a banana into a container of yogurt, and devoured it. Jessamyn waited until I had a steaming mug of tea in front of me.

"So what was that about?" she asked. "What was that piece of paper?"

How do you tell someone *Oh, just an article suggesting your boyfriend was killed and that you had something to do with it?* You can't—at least, I couldn't. I reached into my pocket for the page I'd pulled from the guy's hand and held it out to her.

"It was just in the online version, and not for long—the editor took it down," I said.

She straightened it out and read it, slowly, then read it again. It took her a moment to speak. "What the— Where did he get this stuff?"

I shook my head. "I don't know. Maybe he heard guys in the bar talking or just made it up. You don't know him?"

"No," she said. "I mean, I guess I could have run into him somewhere, but I'd remember the name Dirk. What else did the paper say?"

I pulled a newspaper from my bag and handed it to her, pointing at the main article. I hadn't wanted to be here while she read this, but maybe this was the honest way to do it. Maybe all journalists would be more careful if they imagined being in the room as the people involved read their articles. I watched her eyes move down the page.

"Did you know—about Tobin's brother?" I asked. She shook her head. I wasn't surprised, not really. People who ended up here often had something they wanted to leave behind, something they didn't talk about. Jessamyn never talked about her past either. And, well, neither do I.

She pointed at the photo of the ice cutters on the page. "Do you have more pictures?"

I wanted to say no. I didn't want Jessamyn to see those photos. I didn't want anyone to see them. That was one reason I hadn't copied them onto a flash drive and taken them over to the Saranac Lake Police Station. But if anyone had a right to see them, she did.

She followed me upstairs and I showed her how to scroll through the photos. She went through them, one by one, while I sat on my sofa, Tiger at my feet. This was harder than watching her read the article. Her gaze lingered on some of the long shots, then she pushed back from the desk.

"What was Tobin doing out on the ice?" Her voice was so low I barely heard her.

There were no easy answers here, and none, I thought, that would bring her any peace. I shook my head. "Drunk, maybe. Or maybe someone from the bar dared him to see how far out he would go."

"And no one noticed he didn't come back?" She sounded incredulous.

"They might not—you know how those guys are. They'd just assume he went home." I didn't want to tell her I'd wondered if someone had been with Tobin, if they'd seen him fall through thin ice and panicked; if an ice-diving attempt had gone very wrong. Or worse. Neither did I want to point out that we might never know what happened, that this might be one of the Adirondack deaths for which answers were never found.

I looked at her. Her face twisted.

"I loved him," she said, her voice thick and odd.

"I know you did." And the next moment she was crying, full-body crying, the retching, gasping kind when it seems part of you is dying. I reached out and she grasped my hand for a moment. Then she curled into herself and cried hard for what must have been five minutes straight, then got up and went into my bathroom for a long time. I heard water running.

When she came out, her eyes were red. "Tobin didn't kill himself," she said, as if I'd suggested it.

I shook my head. "I wouldn't think so." And I didn't, not really. Tobin's existence here had been on the marginal side, with the borrowed cabin, a battered truck, and odd jobs here and there. But this wasn't his real life. It wasn't like the people who lived here, who had families to support, who had nowhere else to go. Who weren't playing at this.

She spoke again. "Everyone's going to think I had something to do with this—that I had him killed or somehow made him kill himself."

"I don't think so, Jessamyn. It was a dumb article, and badly written—nobody sane or not perpetually drunk will believe it. And not many people will have seen it—it wasn't up long. Those guys today were being stupid. This will be nothing."

I may have been more wrong before, but I don't remember when.

We had about ten minutes of quiet before the phone started ring-ing. The first call was from someone Jessamyn knew who had heard about the deleted article but hadn't seen it. Then it rang again, and again. All these callers had seen the article that had been on the Internet less than half an hour. Some were friends; some weren't. Some were reporters, from television and radio and newspapers; some looking for Jessamyn, some looking for me. Before long, we learned that some enterprising soul had e-mailed a copy to a bunch of locals, plus pretty much every news outlet in the area. Then people forwarded it, because spreading bad news apparently is the great American pastime. You'd think points were awarded for disseminating this stuff.

I called Baker. Pulling the article likely would have worked, I told her, if someone hadn't grabbed a screen shot and decided to send it around—no one seemed to know who. She said she'd ask some people.

George called to tell me he had fired the reporter, the second time in his life he'd let someone go. The kid, he said, wouldn't admit he'd done anything wrong—he seemed to think he was a modern-day Woodward or Bernstein. More like Matt Drudge, I thought, but didn't say it.

"Did he actually talk to someone, or just make that stuff up?" I asked.

"He claims his sources were 'privileged.'" George made a sound like a snort. "Probably someone in the bar, probably drunk, and likely he didn't actually get a name."

The paper had been getting calls too. George had heard about the article being sent around, and he'd try to get a copy of the e-mail. He cleared his throat. "People are saying that you got the piece pulled, Troy, because you're friends with Jessamyn."

He went on to tell me the wire had picked up the news story on Tobin, along with my two photos, and they'd be running nationally. So I'd have the clip I hadn't really wanted, and some extra income because of it. It wasn't any comfort—it was the opposite of comfort.

That evening I called Philippe and told him about my roommate's boyfriend being found in the lake and all the rest of it.

He listened and made commiserative sounds. "Do you want to come up for a visit?" he asked. "Your friend could come up too."

I was tempted, but it would have felt like running away when we hadn't done anything to run away from. "It should die down soon," I told him. "If we just don't respond, people will stop calling."

But it was early winter and a slow news cycle. One reporter dubbed Tobin the Ice Man of Saranac Lake, which caught people's attention. The story made the TV news; it made every paper within a two-hundred-mile radius and some farther afield. My inbox was flooded with Google Alerts with Tobin's name.

Going viral is great if you're a cute sixth-grade boy with singing talent who ends up on *Ellen* and gets a record deal. It's not so great if what's going viral is an article suggesting you were involved in the death of your boyfriend found frozen in a lake. None of the articles mentioned Jessamyn and none approached the kid's bad writing and clumsy innuendo, but in the hands of skilled writers, it was worse—implying a giant cover-up raging in this tiny town, where rich boys could be bumped off and salted

away under the ice without anyone knowing about it. Sort of a
North Country *Deliverance*.

When Jessamyn went to work, her boss told her it was best if
she didn't come in for a while. Business was slow, he said. But this
was a snowy January—business wasn't slow. Slow is April, when
the snow turns into a trickle of melting sludge and places close for
the month. She knew it, and he knew she knew it.

George got an editor friend to forward a copy of the e-mail
with the screen shot, which was of course anonymous. But no
one does something as vindictive as this without a reason, real or
imagined, and I wanted to find out why.

We ended up unplugging the house phone. After the first reporter showed up, we stopped answering the door. For the first
time since I'd lived here we locked it, and everyone had to search
out their house key. I thumbtacked a towel over the front door
window as a makeshift curtain. By midmorning the next day I'd
retrieved a batch of reporters' business cards stuck in the door.

Enough was enough. I climbed the stairs to Jessamyn's room
and knocked.

"What?" said a faint voice.

"What do you think about getting out of town?" I noticed her
door could use a coat of paint. I heard the springs of her mattress
shift. The door opened a few inches.

"What do you mean?" she asked.

"A road trip."

She didn't hesitate. "When?"

"Now. As soon as we can pack. You have a passport or en-
hanced driver's license?" I remembered her having taken a day
trip to Montreal, so she must have something to get across the
border.

She nodded.

"Bring it," I said. She didn't ask any questions.

Back in my room I called Philippe. "Come on up," he said. "I'll
call Elise to let her know you're coming, and I'll try to get home
early."

I sent Baker a note that I was going out of town for a few days. Then I e-mailed Jameson: *Things went nuts here after an article about Tobin's death. Coming to Ottawa with my roommate—will be at Philippe's.* It would be good to see Jameson, good to tell him about this. In the back of my mind did I realize that leaving town with Jessamyn might not be the smartest move, that it might appear suspicious? Maybe I did. But no one had told her she was a suspect, or had even hinted she needed to stick around. And I desperately needed to get away, and it would, I thought, do her good too. So if that little voice was trying to tell me anything, I didn't listen. I slid my laptop in a bag, crammed clothes in a day pack, and dug out my passport and Tiger's rabies certificate. Jessamyn was waiting at the kitchen table, a filled duffel bag beside her.

I shook out one of my canvas grocery bags and shoved food in it. I don't like traveling without food, especially in winter. I scribbled a note to Brent and Patrick, then locked the door.

"Let's go," I said, and we were off.

Neither of us looked over as we passed through Saranac Lake, but unless you closed your eyes you couldn't avoid seeing the growing stack of ice blocks. We were nearly through the town of Gabriels before Jessamyn spoke. "We're going to Canada, I presume?"

"Ottawa," I said. "I have friends there we can stay with." I told her about Philippe and his son, Paul, nearly seven now, and the nanny-slash-housekeeper, Elise. I told her that Philippe's wife, Paul's mother, had died last year, but I didn't tell her how or why. She didn't need to know, and I didn't need to tell it.

As I drove, Jessamyn assembled ham-and-cheese sandwiches, and by the time we hit the border I'd finished two. Apparently fleeing town makes you hungry. We stopped for coffee at a Tim Hortons in Cornwall, and just over an hour and a half later were pulling into Philippe's driveway.

"Wow," Jessamyn said, looking up at the house. She'd been wide-eyed since we'd reached this neighborhood with its expensive, stately homes. I grinned at her as I pressed the button at the gate, and Elise let us in.

CHAPTER 12

Elise was sixtyish and French-Canadian, pretty much the story-book devoted housekeeper. To her I could do no wrong, because I'd rescued Paul last summer. She gave me a hard hug, and then Jessamyn. Not many people would venture to hug Jessamyn, but Elise did, and Jessamyn let her. We put our bags in our rooms, and took Tiger and Paul's half-grown puppy out in the fenced backyard for a romp. Then Elise fed us homemade brownies and milk in the kitchen, telling us how well Paul was doing. She was leaving soon to collect him from school, she said, and Philippe would be home before too long.

Jessamyn looked a little shell-shocked, but ate the warm brownies and drank the milk and took it all in, like a kid sitting in Grandma's kitchen.

"And now I must go pick up Paul," Elise said, beaming. "He will be so happy to know you are here." She took off her apron and hung it on a hook, and she was off.

Jessamyn looked around the immaculate kitchen, with its marble countertops and hanging array of shiny pots and pans.

"Are we in Disneyland?" she asked. I chuckled, and she did too, and then both of us were laughing so hard we were nearly crying.

We were still sitting there when Elise returned, and Paul launched himself at me in a hug. He paused politely to be introduced to Jessamyn and shake her hand, and in nearly perfect English began chattering about his dog and school and his new friends. He sat on my lap—he was growing so fast he'd soon be too big. I watched his bright face and smooth perfect skin and, not for the first time, marveled that he seemed to have so well adjusted after his kidnapping and the death of his mother. To the move to Ottawa, to a new school, a new language, a new life.

And then Philippe was there, and gave me a hug that felt so good I didn't want to let go. He was charming to Jessamyn, and, well, he's phenomenally good-looking, with thick dark hair like his son's, and from the look on her face I could almost hear her thinking, *Why the heck did you ever leave this?* Which in a way I'd been wondering too. Reasons that are perfectly logical don't always ring true to the heart.

After one of Elise's marvelous dinners, Paul went off for his bath and then his bedtime story from his father.

"I'm going to bed. I'm all in," Jessamyn told me. She looked ready to drop.

"That's fine. Do you need anything?"

She shook her head and went off. When Philippe came back, I told him everything that had happened.

"It just went crazy," I said. "All because of a stupid little piece on the paper's website that the wrong person saw and decided to spread."

"That's all it takes sometimes," Philippe said, nodding. He owned a marketing firm that specialized in reviving or reinventing companies' images after public-relations disasters, so he knew this stuff. "But people know Jessamyn, right? It's not like she just moved to town. They'll know she wasn't involved."

"She's been there at least a couple of years, longer than Tobin. But he knew a lot of people—he had a lot of drinking buddies who thought he was great. And Jessamyn can rub people the wrong way." The old Jessamyn, at least, could be outspoken, and didn't suffer fools well. And while her string of rejected suitors had all seemed fine with her moving on, it wasn't impossible that at least one hadn't taken it as well as he'd seemed.

"It'll be all right, Troy," Philippe said.

And maybe it would. For him, this was how it had worked after Paul's kidnapping and his wife's death. Of course it had hit him hard emotionally, and on some levels he was still reeling, but socially and professionally there'd hardly been a blip. But Philippe had picked up and moved to a new city in a new province, and wasn't an underemployed girl in a small town whose boy-friend from a well-off family had been found frozen into a lake. There was a world of difference here I didn't think Philippe was getting—maybe because he'd always had money, maybe because he didn't want to see this side of things. He had a tendency to see the world as he wanted it to be. Which may have been partly why his marriage had gone as wrong as it had.

I thought about trying to say some of this, but I was tired, and it was late, and maybe it wasn't that important. Maybe I spend too much time looking at the dark side of things. I moved closer to Philippe on the sofa and leaned up against him, and his arm went around me like it belonged there. We sat in silence a long while, and I could feel the heat of his body next to mine. My pulse quickened. Maybe something would have happened, but a loud cough came from Paul's room, and then another, and Philippe dis-engaged himself.

"I have to check on Paul," he said apologetically.

"Of course," I said. "And it's been a long day—I should go on to bed." He gave me a quick hug and a kiss atop the head, and off I went. In the night I reached out to Tiger, by my side. Sometimes it's very hard to do what you think is the right thing. And some-times it's very hard to be alone.

CHAPTER 13

It had been a good decision to come here, I thought at breakfast the next morning, looking at Paul and Philippe's smiling faces, Elise scurrying to refill coffee cups, Jessamyn looking relaxed and the closest to happy I'd seen her in a long time. We both needed this. Heck, everybody could use this once in a while.

After breakfast I went off to call Jameson, and he suggested meeting for lunch, as I expected he would.

"Bring along your friend," he offered.

I found Jessamyn in the kitchen, perched on a stool watching Elise prepare something that involved a lot of chopping.

"I'm going to meet my friend the policeman for lunch," I told her. "You're welcome to come."

She shook her head. "I'll stay here. Elise is going to show me how to make an apple pie."

I wouldn't have expected pie making to be on a list of skills Jessamyn wanted to acquire, but she seemed to be reveling in this whole homey atmosphere. She did go with me for a walk with the dogs around the neighborhood before I left, admiring the houses we passed as I worked at convincing Paul's puppy to walk politely on a lead. Neither of us brought up Lake Placid or Tobin, or anything else we'd left behind.

.   .   .

It was, of course, too cold to meet at the park bench on the Rideau
Canal, where Jameson and I had met for takeout lunch last summer, so we chose a Harvey's restaurant midway between us. He
got out of his car when he saw me pull up, and we exchanged the
clumsy, well-insulated hug you do when wearing heavy parkas,
somewhat like hugging a sofa. Then we both ordered the Great
Canadian burger. He got the onion rings; I got fries. I tried to pull
out some Canadian money to pay, but he covered it.

"So what's happening?" he asked when we sat down with
our food.

I told him all of it: the newspaper story that got pulled not quite
soon enough and had been e-mailed around, the deluge of phone
calls, the knocks on the door, the hints of killing and cover-up.

"A woman scorned?" he asked.

"Maybe. I haven't found out yet."

"Have the police been back in touch?"

"No, not with either of us. And they never asked for the
photos I took."

Jameson ate an onion ring. "Family?"

"Parents and a sister; the articles all said they weren't available for comment. The editor told me his family was on their way
to Saranac Lake. We haven't heard from them."

"Jessamyn didn't know them?"

I shook my head.

After a moment he asked: "Could Tobin have killed himself?"

"I wouldn't have thought so," I said. I'd thought more about
this after Jessamyn had brought it up. "But he lost his brother
when he was nineteen, in a boating accident—maybe he'd never
gotten over it." Maybe something had reminded him of his
brother. Maybe Tobin had gotten tired of North Country living,
tired of Jessamyn, tired of the cold. Maybe, after a night of ca-
rousing in a Saranac Lake bar and with Christmas not far off, he
had made an impromptu decision to pack it in.

Jameson nodded, and wiped his lips with a paper napkin. "Could your roommate know anything about his death?"

I considered this. I thought about Jessamyn's face as I'd told her the news, how hard she'd cried when she found out Tobin was dead. I was shaking my head even before I spoke. "No, she was really shocked when she found out."

Jameson nodded again, pushing his plate away. "Something will happen soon. After the autopsy, after the police finish interviews, after his parents weigh in." He didn't say he thought things would be fine; he didn't assure me the hubbub would die down soon. He wasn't one for platitudes. In many ways, his view of the world was even bleaker than mine.

He told me work had been busy; I told him about some of the magazine pieces I'd done. In the parking lot we exchanged another overstuffed-sofa hug, maybe the only sort we would ever be comfortable with.

When I got back to the house and Elise opened the door for me, I felt a wave of affection and warmth and nostalgia for the people who lived in this house, so powerful it made me ache. It seemed too much, too intense a set of feelings to fit into one being.

But maybe it just took some getting used to.

Jessamyn was flushed from the success of having made the apple pie, her first ever, she told us, more than once. I admired its somewhat wandering lattice top, more than once. Elise beamed proudly. *Elise's School of Homemaking.* She'd tried to show me how to iron neatly last summer, but I'd failed miserably. Jessamyn seemed a more willing and apt pupil.

I volunteered to go get Paul from school—I was still on the approved list to pick him up, and Jessamyn decided to go along.

The confident, cheery Paul who jumped into my back seat was a different child from the one I'd picked up from school last June. I had to admit that part of me missed the little boy who had needed me so much. I suppose parents go through this, watching their children grow more independent. Just when you'd gotten good at one phase, they were off to another. Philippe was doing a good job with Paul, I thought, and having the bedrock that was Elise didn't hurt.

That night after dinner, after apple pie for dessert, and after Paul was tucked into bed, the three of us retired to the library and a crackling fire. We relaxed and sipped a superb pinot noir and sampled different cheeses. Philippe chatted about Paul's school and his marketing business. I talked about my brother, Simon, my friend Baker, my roommate Zach who was in Boulder visiting a girlfriend—all people Philippe had met. Jessamyn told funny stories about tourists visiting the restaurant.

And then Philippe asked her, "Where are you from originally?"

It was a simple question, and up until that moment I hadn't really considered that in Lake Placid you don't usually ask people where they're from. Sometimes they tell you, and sometimes you figure it out from where they disappear to on holidays, if they do. But you don't ask.

There's a line in the movie *Insomnia*, something like *There's two types of people in Alaska, the ones who were born here and the ones who came here to get away from something.* You could say much the same about the Adirondacks.

But Jessamyn replied easily, though vaguely. "The Midwest, but I don't keep up with anyone."

And Philippe, bless him, just poured more wine and smiled with the right mix of sympathy and understanding, and launched into a story about one of his clients who owned a small winery. This was one of the things he excelled at, putting people at ease. And after a while he excused himself, saying he had some paperwork to do. After he was out of earshot Jessamyn leaned toward me and whispered, "What's the deal with Philippe?" I nodded toward my room—this wasn't a discussion I wanted to have in the open. She followed me, and we sat cross-legged on the bed as if we were in junior high.

"So what's the deal with Philippe?" she repeated.

I didn't pretend not to know what she meant. I told her about finding Paul last summer and staying in Ottawa to help him adjust to his new life here, without a mother, with the father he hadn't seen for months; that Philippe and I had gotten close, partly because of Paul, but had backed off for many reasons. The timing wasn't right; I was deeply attached to his son, and he was recovering from the loss of his wife. Not the best time to start something.

Jessamyn drained her wineglass. "I dunno, maybe you should just go for it, Troy. He seems to be a great guy. You like the kid, and this place is amazing."

Yeah, I know. I wasn't going to open my veins here and tell her how much I'd struggled with my attraction to Philippe and to Paul and the whole setup, and explain why I couldn't have stayed here. "I know. Maybe if there wasn't a child involved. But I didn't want to try something that was too soon or not right, and then not be a part of Paul's life. He'd already lost his mother; I didn't want him to lose me, too." It was late enough and this was enough of the truth that my voice caught.

Jessamyn thought for a moment. Her next question took me off guard. "Are your mother and father together?"

I nodded. "Yeah. I don't think it ever occurred to them not to be. They seem okay. Neither of them have much use for me, but that's just how it is."

"Mmm, kind of the same here. But no father. He took off when I was about three. I saw him again once, I think, and that was it. I don't even remember what he looked like." She shrugged. "Paul's lucky. He's lucky to have his father, and Elise, and you, and all this." She waved a hand to encompass *all this.* The puppy, the delectable meals, the fine furnishings, the house filled with love.

My throat tightened. "Yes, he is."

"I think we need more wine," she said.

"I think you're right."

We tiptoed off to the kitchen and polished off the bottle and the last of the apple pie while we were at it. We rinsed our dishes and went off to bed, comfortably full, and feeling, I think, more like friends than we had before.

CHAPTER 14

At breakfast Philippe excused himself to go to work early, but we'd be meeting him downtown later. Jessamyn said she was tired, and found a book and went off to her room to read. I fired up my laptop and sent an e-mail to my brother, telling him what had happened, because at some point in all this I might need Simon's cool logical brain.

And then I started some Googling to see if I could track down the person who had sent that article around. I had the e-mail address from George, and it didn't take long to trace it to a little-used Facebook page with a cartooned Marilyn Monroe for an avatar. Lives in: *Lake Placid, New York*. Worked at: *Price Chopper*. User name: *Marilyn Munro*. It was likely a fake name but if not, how unfortunate. I asked Jessamyn if she knew anyone named Marilyn, and she said she didn't.

Then we drove downtown to meet Philippe for a bundled-up walk and an early lunch at a bistro. Because, as he told Jessamyn, you shouldn't come to Ottawa and not at least see the Parliament buildings and Rideau Canal. It was iced over so thoroughly that some people commuted on skates to work, and little huts were set up to sell hot chocolate and beaver tails, a particularly large and sticky pastry.

When we got back I went through the voice mail messages that had downloaded into my inbox as mp3 files. Most were reporters, but not the last two, and they left me feeling queasy.

I found Jessamyn in the kitchen.

"The state police called me at home," I told her. "They were trying to get in touch with you—they want to interview you."

All the animation drained from her face. I hadn't realized until then just how much Jessamyn had relaxed here, how different she looked.

"The state police?" she asked. "Not the local police?"

I nodded. "I guess they're following up on Tobin's death."

"Do we have to go now?" Her voice was plaintive, like a small child's.

I looked up at the wall clock, and at Elise, carefully busy with something she'd taken from the fridge. "Even if we left now we'd have trouble making it by five. We can wait until morning."

The state police investigator, when I called, was none too happy, and I felt more than a trifle guilty. I hoped I hadn't made things worse for Jessamyn by whisking her out of town. I told him we were visiting in Ottawa, I'd just gotten the messages, and we'd come straight to the state police headquarters in Ray Brook in the morning. I gave him my cell phone number, and put Jessamyn on the phone to confirm what I'd said. He didn't push it—it wasn't as if they were going to extradite Jessamyn to interview her half a day earlier.

I called Jameson, who agreed that someone could be exerting pressure to bump this up a notch. "Or it's possible that all nonconventional deaths there are referred to your state police," he said. "I'd remind Jessamyn not to say anything that's not a fact, and if she gets uncomfortable, to ask to leave. Or consider getting an attorney before she goes in. And if you need me, call me."

If you need me, call me. For Jameson, this qualified as almost intimate.

Again I went looking for Jessamyn, and this time I found her sitting in her room, on the bed, neatly made. My eyes went to her duffel bag on the floor. It was plump, full. Packed. "You're thinking about taking off," I said, and I realized there was nothing stopping her. She could hop a bus or stick out her thumb and leave Lake Placid and her tiny room and her few possessions behind. Just as she'd left somewhere else to come to the Adirondacks. Her eyes darted around the room. Finally she looked at me.

"I don't want to talk to the police, Troy." Her voice was thin, tight.

"But you did once, and it wasn't so bad."

"Yes, but this is the state police—that's a bigger deal. That means they think someone did something to Tobin, that he didn't just drown."

I'd hoped she hadn't thought of this. I sat on the edge of the bed. "It's possible," I said carefully. "Or the Saranac Lake police could be uncomfortable handling it because of things stirred up by the newspaper article, or the missing truck. Or pressure from Tobin's parents."

"Or it could mean Tobin's death *wasn't an accident.*"

The words hung in the air. I looked at her full on. "It could. What do you think?"

Her eyes shifted. "I don't know," she whispered.

I spoke rapidly. "Jessamyn, if someone did something to Tobin, it needs to be found out. If you think anyone could have hurt him, you have to face this, you have to tell the police. You don't want to run from this."

She looked miserable, but she nodded.

"Do you want to talk to an attorney before you go?"

She shook her head, and on this she was adamant. In the North Country, she said, showing up with a lawyer would make everyone assume she was guilty of something. She was right about that.

I thought of more I could say, but in the end I just left her there.

That evening we had an even better dinner, lasagna with homemade noodles, an exquisite salad, fresh-baked bread. Jessamyn was more animated than I'd ever seen her, as if wringing every bit she could from one last happy evening with this family. We played a rousing game of Pictionary, roping Elise in, me coaching Paul, until it was time for Paul to go to bed. I got to tuck him in, freshly bathed in his flannel pajamas, and I read him *Where the Wild Things Are*. Paul loved this book, and the little boy Max.

"Max was *très vilain*—very naughty," he told me solemnly. "But I shouldn't like to be sent to bed without dinner."

"He was a little naughty," I agreed. "But I don't think you ever have to worry about going to bed without dinner." I thought of the months Paul had been held captive, with the closest thing to a real dinner an occasional McDonald's meal put in his room. Maybe he thought of that too. He gave me a hug so warm and tight I didn't want to let go. I felt that swell of love, so intense it nearly hurt, like I'd felt not long after I'd rescued him last summer. I'd known then I would lay my life down for this kid. That hadn't changed. I didn't think it ever would.

Afterward Philippe and Jessamyn and I sat in the library, fire blazing, and talked about anything but Lake Placid until we couldn't keep our eyes open. We went off to our rooms, and I saw Jessamyn close her door. I hoped she'd be there in the morning.

And she was. A little wan, but she was there. We left right after breakfast, taking along an enormous box of food from Elise, who thought we didn't eat well enough. She was probably right.

We didn't talk much on the drive. I repeated what Jameson had said, to just tell them facts, and to stop answering questions if it got uncomfortable. "And if you don't know something, just say so—don't make something up," I added.

"I *won't*," Jessamyn snapped. "I'm not stupid, Troy."

I guessed I did sound patronizing. I should have been surprised Jessamyn hadn't been sharp-tongued before now. In a way it was good to see her like this, more like her old self.

"I'm sorry," I said. "It's just that it's no fun being questioned by the police, and these guys are going to be pros, not like that yahoo from Saranac Lake. They can trick you or hammer at you until you want to say anything to shut them up."

She looked at me curiously. I hadn't told her the police here had considered me a suspect in Paul's kidnapping last year, and I didn't go into it now.

We drove for an hour before she spoke again. "Do you think Tobin's parents are in town?"

I thought about the parents from Connecticut, the rich parents, the parents who had just lost a second son. "I imagine they are," I said. They would, I thought, have come up to ID the body if nothing else. I didn't know if Jessamyn hoped to meet them, or hoped not to.

We got to the state police headquarters before noon and waited in not particularly comfortable chairs. It seemed there might be security cameras recording what we said and did, so we said and did nothing. Finally Jessamyn was called, and I opened the paperback I'd brought. After I'd pretended to read three chapters, she was back. She gave a shrug that seemed to say *No big deal*. The investigator turned to me.

"Miss Chance?"

I nodded.

"I need to talk to you as well."

This I hadn't seen coming. I'd been so concerned about Jessamyn, I hadn't given any thought to the notion I might be questioned. I gave Jessamyn a fake smile and followed the man. The room we entered was a regular office, not an interrogation room, but still reminiscent of when I'd been questioned in the Ottawa police station last summer. The investigator was typical of most New York state troopers I'd seen: tall, tightly muscled, white, male, with a brush cut.

"We'd like to ask you a few questions," he said briskly. Which made me want to ask who "we" were, if someone was in the closet or under the desk. But I didn't.

He asked when I'd met Tobin, when I'd last seen him, the names of his friends. And about Tobin's relationship with Jessamyn. I wasn't going to out-and-out lie, but neither was I going to throw Jessamyn under the bus.

"It seemed fine," I said brightly.

"They got along? They didn't fight?"

I shook my head. "I never saw them fight," I said, which was true. Jessamyn could have gotten that fat lip from running into a door. I've done it: walked slam into the edge of a door standing open—it hurts like heck, and you feel really stupid. Or someone other than Tobin could have done it.

"How often did you see them?"

"When Tobin was in town, he was at the house at least every other day, sometimes more."

"And what was your relationship with him?"

"Relationship? He dated my roommate. I never knew him before that."

"You never went to his place?"

I gave a short bark of laughter before I could stop myself. "No, of course not."

"So you were never in his house?"

"Of course not," I repeated.

"Do you know where it was?"

"Vaguely. It's on one of the roads off Highway 73 toward Keene. I gave him a ride home once." It had been snowing and Tobin was hitchhiking; he said he'd had too much to drink to want to drive. It had surprised me, because it wasn't rare in these towns for guys to get behind the wheel with sky-high blood alcohol.

The investigator seemed to smirk. "But you just said you'd never been at his house."

"No, I said I hadn't been *in* his house. And it wasn't a house, it was a cabin, a small cabin."

"And you never went inside?"

I sighed inwardly. This game I knew. Keep repeating the question to see if I changed my answer.

"No," I said. "I never went in. Not once. Not ever. I stopped my car; he got out and walked to his front door. I drove home. Period, end of story. I don't even know if I could find it again."

"And what is your relationship with Jessamyn Field?"

I felt like throwing up my hands. "She's one of my roommates. She's lived there since late summer."

"But you went out of town together."

Suddenly meeting the investigator before lunch didn't seem like such a great idea. I was hungry and getting crosser by the minute.

"Yes," I said, and couldn't keep the edge from my voice. "I've been known to go out of town with many different people, some roommates, some not." I pulled two business cards out of my wallet that I'd put there yesterday, possibly because a little voice in the back of my head had hinted I might need them. I set Philippe's card on the desk. "Here's the friend I was visiting in Ottawa." Then I placed Jameson's card on top. "Here's another friend I saw while I was there, a detective with the Ottawa Police Service. You can call either of them and ask them whatever you want." I stood up and started for the door. He let me go.

So much for advising Jessamyn to stay cool and calm. She was smart enough not to ask anything, and just followed me to the car. I reached into the box of food in the trunk and pulled out a turnover. I offered her one, but she shook her head. I finished it as I pulled out of the lot.

"Didn't go well, huh?" Jessamyn asked after a while.

"Nope," I said.

She started to say something else, but we were nearing the house and could see someone on the front porch, perched on the edge of the big swing.

I sighed. "We could park in the back and go in the kitchen door. I think we can get it open."

"No," she said. "I'm tired of this. Let's just go in."

We parked in my usual spot in front of the house, and the woman stood as we came up the steps. She was, I guessed, in her mid- to late twenties, trim, attractive, with brown hair to her shoulders, and stylish earmuffs instead of the thick knit hats Jessamyn and I wore. Her jeans and boots and coat were far nicer than I'd ever had or thought about having. She looked tired and cold.

She took a step toward us. I was thinking she didn't look like a reporter when she spoke. And just before the words came out of her mouth, I guessed who she was.

"I'm Tobin's sister," she said, looking from one of us to the other. "I'm Jessica Winslow."

CHAPTER 15

If Jessamyn and I hadn't just had the week we'd had, this woman showing up on our doorstep might have thrown us for a loop. But in a way it seemed the inevitable next step in an inexorable chain of events: *body found, media blitz, escape to Canada, police interview, arrival of bereaved sister.* We didn't know if she was here to blame or commiserate, and didn't ask. We just told her who we were and invited her in. I unlocked the door and led the way inside, and turned on the water for tea. We sat at the kitchen table. I opened the bag of Elise's pastries. No one took any.

The woman had Tobin's coloring, and you could see the resemblance around her mouth and jaw. I put a mug of tea in front of her, and set out milk and sugar. She poured in some of both, stirred, and took a sip, wrapping her hands tightly around the mug. It had been cold on our porch, and I guessed she'd been out there a while. We waited for her to speak.

"Call me Win," she said. Maybe she realized an already awkward conversation would be even more awkward with one person named Jessamyn and another named Jessica. "That's what my sorority sisters called me." It was a measure of how much I instinctively liked her that I didn't hold the sorority-sister thing against her.

She started talking, in that flat tone you have when all the energy has drained out of you. The police had notified her parents when Tobin had been found, she said, but she'd been out of the country and couldn't get here until now. Someone had mentioned the online article with Jessamyn's name, but she hadn't seen it. She'd asked around and had found her way to the restaurant, and had been directed here. She wasn't quite sure why she was here, in our house, she said, but she'd needed to come here. It made sense, I supposed. If my brother had died, I might be doing the same thing, visiting his friends, retracing his last steps.

"You were his girlfriend?" she asked Jessamyn.

Jessamyn nodded, her face blank.

Win turned to me. "And you knew him too, right? You wrote the newspaper article, about Tobin."

I nodded. I think her next question took us both by surprise.

"Was he happy here?"

Jessamyn's face clenched. She opened her mouth, and closed it again.

"I think he was," I said, when I saw Jessamyn wasn't going to be able to answer. "He had Jessamyn. He had friends. He did some construction work. He was healthy."

It wasn't much of an epitaph, but it seemed to be what Tobin's sister needed, at least for now. She nodded. She set down her tea and looked around.

"Are you two hungry?" she asked. "Would you like to get something to eat?"

So we bundled up and walked up to town, like three friends out on a cold Adirondack afternoon. We went to Pete's, across from the movie theater, and took a table in the far back.

It should have seemed odd, sitting there with this woman who was Tobin's sister, but it didn't. After we ordered, Win started talking again, like a toy wound too tightly. She told us about being the only girl between two brothers, about growing up with them, Tobin dropping out of college after their brother died. "Tobin took it hard," she said. "Up until then he'd tried to please our parents, tried to do everything Trey did, and after the accident he just stopped trying, and pretty much left the family." At first I heard *Tray*, and it took a moment to remember this was what rich families called sons whose names were Thirds—*trey*, for three.

"This was the first place he'd seemed to settle down." She blinked hard, the way you do when you're trying to convince yourself not to cry. "What about you two? Are you from here?"

We shook our heads. Our food arrived, and I told her about growing up in Nashville and taking the job here after university out West, how I'd loved working as a small-town sports editor but because of the nonstop schedule had quit to freelance. Jessamyn volunteered that she was from the Midwest and had lived here a year and a half, and had never been to college. She said it with a touch of defiance, but Tobin's sister wasn't in a judging mood. And maybe she wasn't a judging sort of person.

"So are your . . . did your parents come up too?" I asked.

She shook her head, her expression bland. "They're leaving it up to me," she said.

I didn't know what this meant, *leaving it up to her* . . . to identify the body, manage Tobin's affairs, close out his cabin, I supposed. We sat in silence a long moment.

"Are you staying out at Tobin's cabin?" I asked finally.

"No. The police mentioned it, out past town, right? I don't know exactly where it is. I just have his PO box number, here in Lake Placid."

Jessamyn and I looked at each other. "I found the owner's phone number," I said. "You can call him and ask if you could go out there."

Win blinked. "But I wouldn't know how to get in."

Jessamyn spoke up. "I know where there's a key."

We took my car—Win's rental didn't have four-wheel drive, and the road to the cabin wouldn't be as well plowed as the main road. Jessamyn sat up front and directed me. There were no other tracks, car or human, as we neared the cabin, but it had snowed heavily. As we got out, the sound of our car doors closing was crisp in the stillness.

It felt odd to be approaching Tobin's cabin, in a row, silently, as if in a funeral procession. On the front porch Jessamyn tipped over a dead potted plant, pried off a key iced to the base, and handed it to Tobin's sister. She pushed it into the door, hesitated a moment, and turned the key.

It was dark. Win fumbled beside the door and found the switches, and the room flooded with light. From the doorway you could see the entire place: iron bed frame, bed covered in a quilt and neatly made, clothes hanging on wooden pegs, woodstove in the middle of the room, a small kitchen, a sofa and a rocking chair, a small battered wooden desk and chair, a door opening into a bathroom. All tidy, all waiting for a man who was never coming back. Win took a deep breath and stepped inside. I looked at Jessamyn. Her face was pale.

The cabin had small baseboard electric heaters that likely put out just enough to keep the pipes from freezing. It was cold, very cold. The woodstove had a box of kindling and newspapers and a small stack of logs beside it.

"Do you want a fire?" I asked.

Win nodded, and I knelt and set to building one. The wood was dry and the stove drew well, so it took only minutes to get a crackling fire going. The stovepipes creaked as they expanded with the heat.

The place smelled vaguely of wood smoke, with a thin layer of dust on the furniture, but without that musty smell some shut-up old places have. There seemed to be nothing out of place, no powder from dusting for fingerprints, if that's really how they did it. Maybe the police hadn't even come out here. Maybe they'd already decided this was an accident, and were just going through the motions to keep the family happy.

Tobin's sister moved around the room, looking at the hanging clothes, the books aligned on the desk. She sat on the bed, smoothing the quilt with one hand. She looked up, tears trailing down her face. "I gave him this quilt when he came up here," she said. "I told him it would be perfect for the Adirondacks."

Jessamyn moved to her, gracefully, easily, in a way I wouldn't have thought her capable of, and the two of them sat there clinging to each other. I felt an interloper, there in that small space with their pain. I hadn't liked Tobin, and now I was in a room with two people who had loved him and were grieving him. I sat down in the rocking chair. I thought of the moment when Tobin had slid past me in his ice coffin, and damned if I wasn't crying too.

When the knock came on the door we all jumped. Jessamyn and Win looked at the door and then at me. The knock came again, louder. I don't know who we thought it was, but we were all scared. I looked around—no phone. My cell phone was in my pocket, but I didn't know if it would get a signal out here.

"Who is it?" I called, pulling out my cell and fumbling it open.

The voice on the other side of the door was deep, male. "It's Dean—a friend of Tobin's."

I glanced at the others and moved to open the door. I hoped this wasn't someone who hadn't heard about Tobin's death. Breaking that news to one person had been bad enough; I didn't want to be doing it again.

The man at the door was tall, wearing a heavy coat with a hood over a watch cap. As he pulled his hood back I saw he was one of the two men who had accosted Jessamyn on the street— not the semi-drunk one, but the other one. His gaze moved past me to Win and Jessamyn.

"My place is across the way and I saw the lights here." He looked around. "I know—"

"This is Tobin's sister, Win," I interrupted, gesturing to her. "And I think you know Jessamyn." I kept my tone bland.

"Dean Whitaker," he said. "I'm, um, very sorry about your brother," he said to Win. He nodded at Jessamyn, his face a touch red.

As soon as he said his last name, I realized who he was. I'd spent much of the Saranac Lake football season my last year at the paper focusing on a square jaw much like this one. "You're Eddie's brother," I said.

He looked at me, startled.

"I was the sports editor at the *Enterprise* when Eddie was quarterback," I told him.

He nodded, then moved his feet uncomfortably and looked at Win. "I just wanted to make sure everything was okay. And that nobody was messing with Tobin's stuff."

Win stood, graciously, smiling at him. "Everything is fine. Thank you for coming out."

He cleared his throat. "Tobin was a good guy," he said gruffly. He nodded again at Jessamyn, as close to an apology as she was going to get, and turned to go. "You did some good articles," he said to me on his way out the door. For around here, this was high praise.

After Dean's visit we simultaneously decided it was time to head back into town. We locked up and put the key back where we'd found it.

"Look," Jessamyn said, pointing to a trail of large oblong indentations in the snow.

"Snowshoes," I said, recognizing the shape. "Dean came on snowshoes." I hadn't thought there was another house or cabin close enough to see this one, so maybe he'd been out snowshoeing and happened to see the lights. He hadn't seemed the type to hike around in the woods on a cold evening, but who knew?

We got into the car, Win in front this time. It was her turn, Jessamyn said, to get the benefit of the seat heater.

"So you have other roommates?" Win asked as my car crunched down the road.

"Yes, Patrick and Brent, he's a biathlete, and Zach, but he's out of town now," I told her.

"Did they know Tobin?"

"They'd met him but didn't know him well," I said. Heck,

I hadn't known him. I wasn't sure Jessamyn had known him. I couldn't imagine the Tobin I thought I'd known having a sister like this, one who cared so much about him that she was traipsing around the frozen countryside with two strangers, retracing his last steps.

CHAPTER 16

On the trip back to town we formulated a plan: Win wasn't looking forward to another evening in a soulless hotel, and we had
that huge box of food Elise had sent. Win would have dinner
with us.

"You're sure it's okay with your other roommates?" she
asked. We assured her it would be. We didn't try to explain that
we didn't need to clear things with them, that it wasn't like, well,
a sorority house. Win said she wanted to stop at her hotel and
could walk back down to our house, so we dropped her off.

"She's nice," Jessamyn said as we pulled away.

"Yep. Tobin never talked about her?"

She shook her head.

This didn't surprise me. Nor did it surprise me that Win hadn't
asked us anything about how we thought Tobin had died. Maybe
the why didn't matter to her, at least not now. Maybe all that mattered was seeing some of his life here, the closest she could come
to visiting him.

I brought my bags in and the box of food from Elise, and slid
a partially thawed casserole into the oven. I put together a salad,
and set out Elise's home-baked bread and leftover brownies. I ran
upstairs to e-mail Philippe and Jameson that we'd gotten home
and that Tobin's sister had showed up.

I didn't hear the knock on the front door, but as I came down Jessamyn was showing Win into the kitchen. She had brought wine, which we poured into juice glasses and had with bread and cheese while we waited for the casserole to finish cooking. It was delicious, chicken and cheese blended with broccoli and noodles, with a spice I couldn't identify. We told Win about Ottawa and Paul and Philippe, and she told us stories of the summers she and her brothers had spent with their grandfather. When she'd gotten news of Tobin's death she had been on a cruise, and it had taken a while to get a flight to Albany. She had owned half a small real-estate firm in New Haven, she said, and had sold out her share last year, partly to spend more time with her grandfather, who had been in a nursing home nearby. But after he'd passed away, she'd decided to take a vacation and head somewhere sunny.

I winced. "I'm sorry," I said. I was sorry her grandfather and her brother had died, but sorry too she'd left her warm vacation to come here to subfreezing temperatures.

"I'd like to see more of Tobin's friends here," she said. "Do you know how I could meet them?"

Jessamyn glanced at me, and up at the clock on the wall. "I could take you out," she said. "A bunch of them will be out before long."

"Oh, I'd like that," Win said brightly.

I gave Jessamyn a look. She looked back, wide-eyed and innocent. I could have throttled her.

"Jessamyn, you can't let her walk into this cold."

Win looked at us, confused. Jessamyn gave me a *whatever-do-you-mean?* look. Maybe this was her way of paying me back for the newspaper debacle. I hadn't thought she'd blamed me for it, but maybe she had. Or maybe this was just how she dealt with stuff: stir things up, and sit back and see what happened.

"That newspaper piece online that mentioned Jessamyn, the one that got pulled," I told Win. "Someone sent it around to a bunch of people and people started harassing Jessamyn, saying she had something to do with Tobin's death."

Win's face was blank. "I don't understand."

This would be easier to show her than to explain. I held up a finger in the universal just-a-sec gesture, ran up to my room, and got the printout I'd made. Back downstairs, Jessamyn was looking anywhere but at me; I think she was regretting how she'd played this. Like a kid, I don't think she'd thought it through.

"The reporter substituted this for another piece," I said as I handed the paper to Win. "It was never in the actual paper, but someone saved a copy and sent it to everyone they knew and just about every news outlet around. Things went nuts—reporters calling and coming by. That's why we went out of town for a few days."

Win read the piece and looked up, frowning.

"This is ridiculous. So what if Jessamyn had a tiff with Tobin? I had plenty of them, and I never shoved him into a lake. And maybe Tobin had cash on him that night—what, the reporter's suggesting Tobin was killed for his money? So was it an angry girlfriend or mugger or drug dealer?"

Her voice was almost imperious, and at that moment it was very clear that Win had grown up with money, that she was used to making things happen. I no longer wondered how she'd managed to build up and sell a real-estate firm before she was out of her twenties.

Jessamyn grinned. "I like this woman," she said. I grinned too, and after a moment Win relaxed.

"Of course it's ridiculous," I said. "But the media jumped all over it. And you need to know that if you go out tonight, things may get ugly."

She straightened. "Dangerous?"

"No, not dangerous, but maybe unpleasant. Tobin had a lot of friends, and they seem to want to blame someone. And it's possible the person who sent this piece around will be there, a woman named Marilyn, we think."

"This was my brother," she said, jaw set. "I'm not letting an idiotic article by a bad writer keep me from talking to people who knew my brother."

So she and Jessamyn bundled up to go out. I begged off. I'm never entirely comfortable in bars, where it seems a language is spoken I don't understand. They're dark and noisy, so you can barely hear anyone, and the purpose of being there night after night, I don't get. But I don't drink much or see the point in that, either, so I'm not likely ever to get it. Maybe it's just someplace to go when you don't want to go home.

And for now, I thought, it was best to leave me, the reporter, out of the mix.

I did the dishes. Patrick came in and cooked a vat of spaghetti; Brent ventured down to the living room to watch TV. I told them Tobin's sister was here and that she and Jessamyn had gone out. I took Tiger for a walk, partway around the lake and back rather than all the way around—I wasn't in the mood to face the lights and people on Main Street.

I went on to bed. I didn't hear the others come in. My phone rang once, but when I fumbled it to my ear, there was nothing but a dial tone. Wrong number. Or maybe, I thought, as I curled back under the covers, I'd only imagined hearing it ring. I've done this before, been jolted out of sleep by what I thought was a phone ringing or alarm clock buzzing, only to realize I'd dreamed it.

CHAPTER 17

As soon as I rolled out of bed in the morning I checked e-mail:
only a few new Google Alerts about Tobin. But there was a cryp-
tic message from George that he needed to talk to me. This made
me uneasy. Maybe he, like Jessamyn's boss, was going to tell me
he couldn't use me anymore. Maybe this whole thing was going
to make both of us persona non grata.

I was surprised to see Win at the table when I went downstairs, sipping a cup of coffee from Stewart's up the street. She
smiled when she saw me—her smile was Tobin's, and suddenly it
seemed his ghost was in the room.

"Hi," she said. "It was late when we came in and I'd been
drinking and didn't want to drive or walk back to the hotel, so I
borrowed your guest room. I hope that was okay? Jessamyn said
it would be."

"Sure," I said. "That's what it's there for."

Their outing had been fine, she said. Someone told them the
woman who sent around that article was out of town. Dean, who
we'd met at the cabin, had been there, and Brent had come up.
I blinked. I'd never known Brent to go to the bars.

"Some people were a little strange at first," Win said. "But I
told them it was absurd to think that Jessamyn had anything to

do with Tobin's death, and that the person who wrote that article needed his head examined."

I could imagine her setting them all straight, then buying everyone a round, comfortable in an unfamiliar setting with a bunch of strangers in a way I could never be. She seemed to have that skill, to fit in anywhere. The crowd had probably transferred their loyalty straight to her and, by extension, to Jessamyn.

"Well, good, that'll take some of the pressure off Jessamyn," I said.

"Do you think she's gone to work? I heard someone leaving."

I shook my head. "Probably one of the guys going out to ski. I imagine Jessamyn's still sleeping. She's not working now; she got laid off."

Win raised her eyebrows.

"Because of the thing with Tobin, because of all the news coverage."

She frowned. "Her employer can't let her go because of that."

"Well, he did. They said business was slow, but it isn't, not this time of year, and she was one of their best waitresses." I didn't try to explain that business owners here basically did what they wanted. If people wanted to fire you, they fired you. You either found another job or moved on. There was always someone willing to take your place.

Win was silent a moment. "Troy, do you think you could . . . would you mind taking me out there?"

My confusion must have showed.

"To the lake, to the ice palace."

It didn't surprise me. I guessed it's what I would need to do, if it had been my brother who had died.

On the way she asked if we could stop at the restaurant where Jessamyn had been working. I didn't ask what she wanted to do, because I had a pretty good idea. She hadn't liked Jessamyn losing her job, and she had decided to fix it. She did it masterfully, car-

rying off that person-of-importance thing Philippe did, possibly
even better than he did. Win was pleasant and charming, and by
the end the manager was in wholehearted agreement that not em-
ploying Jessamyn during this time of bereavement just wouldn't
do. I suspect he was on the phone before we were out the door,
offering Jessamyn the best shifts. Someone would be annoyed at
being bumped to afternoons.

We fell quiet as we neared Saranac Lake. We parked behind the Lakeview Deli and walked across the street. Men were
at work, cutting ice blocks, moving them with a forklift. A half
dozen rows had been set into place, starting to reach toward the
sky. You could see the footprint of the palace, a hint of what it
would become. This felt more than a little unreal, as if I were re-
playing the last time I'd been out on this ice, before Tobin's body
had been found, before this had all become like a bad dream.

"You're sure you want to do this?" I asked Win before we
stepped onto the ice.

She nodded.

Matt Boudoin saw us, and didn't manage to hide his surprise.
I introduced Win, and he shook her hand.

"I just wanted . . . wanted to see where Tobin was," she said.
His face reflected the pain on hers. Probably mine did too.

He nodded. "Anything I can do, let me know."

I took her over to the wooden blockades set up around the
hole. She walked to the edge to look over, and, I think without realizing it, reached out toward me. I grasped her hand and she held
on while she looked down at the hole in the ice. Water had seeped
in, and it was starting to freeze.

Win pulled back and walked a few paces away, staring across
the ice at the homes across the lake, blinking hard.

"What was he doing out here?" she said, her voice faint.

I shook my head. "Maybe just taking a walk, and went out too
far." She didn't need to know the other things I'd thought of. Not
now, maybe not ever.

"It would have been dark then."

"Moonlight," I said. "Just moonlight."

"It's so cold." I didn't think she was referring to how cold it was now, but how cold it had been the night Tobin went missing, when he had gone under the forming ice of this lake. It didn't seem that anything I could say would help, so I said nothing.

We went back to the deli and bought cocoa, and drank it down like we were trying to warm our souls. A beep from my pocket told me I'd missed a call. I took my phone out and glanced at it: George. Might as well get this over with.

"Listen," I told Win, "the editor of the newspaper has been calling me. It's just a few blocks from here and I'd like to stop in to see him. Do you mind? You could wait here. Or come with me."

Coming with me suited her, and she wanted to walk. By the time we reached the newspaper building the warmth of the cocoa had long since left us.

I stepped into the newsroom, leaving Win on a chair in the front lobby. George was at his desk, punishing his keyboard. He didn't look up for a few moments, and when he did he nodded and kept typing. When he finished, he pushed back from the desk.

"Got your messages," I said. "What's up?"

"Let's go in my office," he said, standing up. I'd only been in his office once or twice—it was for business meetings, paperwork, and the rare occasion when someone was in trouble.

I loved this place. I loved the newsroom and its vague smell of dust and newspapers and ink, its old desks and battered computers, the break room with the rickety table and chairs. I loved how the paper covered the parades, the births, the softball games, all the minutiae that made up this town, kept it from seeming like just another Adirondack village. If George was going to cut me loose, it would hurt—losing my connection to this paper would be like being shunned from the first place I felt I belonged. There was an odd taste in my mouth.

Win looked up as we approached, and I introduced her to George. He shook her hand and muttered condolences, and led me into his office and shut the door.

He pointed to an ugly metal chair. I sat.

He cleared his throat. "Troy," he started, then stopped. A lump grew in my throat. "Troy, I don't know if you know, but there's been some rumors." He stopped again.

I prompted him. "About Jessamyn and Tobin?"

"Mmm. Sort of. More about them and you."

My expression told him I had no idea what he was talking about.

"It was the kid I fired. You were right about him, Troy. I never should have given him a big story, but I took a chance on him. He had no judgment and no ethics. But because you took Jessamyn's name out of his article he started a rumor that you, well, that you were mixed up with Jessamyn."

"Mixed up with?" I was confused.

George's face was red. He cleared his throat. "*Involved with*," he managed to say. "And that Tobin was knocking her around, and that—"

I stared at him, trying to take this in. "That we bumped him off? Or I bumped him off?"

He nodded. So this was what the state investigator had been hinting at, although he'd seemed to be fishing as much as anything.

George cleared his throat again, now all business. "Here's what I want, Troy. I want you to do a series of articles on Tobin, three or four of them, in-depth, magazine-style. On him, his life before he came here, what his life here was like, how his death has affected people, how he died, whatever the police find out. And cover the piece that got on the Internet and the effect it had. I can put you on salary, or pay a flat rate per piece, your choice. You'll own all but the first publication rights, so you'll get the income if other papers pick it up or if you sell it to a magazine."

I stared at him. He was proposing a series that a *New York Times* or *Washington Post* reporter would do, not something that would run in a small-town paper with a circulation of six thousand. This would take time and energy and a lot of emotional resources. You couldn't write this type of thing without digging deep.

"George, are you sure?" This would stir things up for the paper, the town, for everyone involved.

He nodded. "This is a good paper. This is a good town. We don't deserve to be dragged through the muck—and neither do you or Jessamyn. I'm the one who hired the kid who started this, and I'm the one who let him try this story."

"I'll need to ask Jessamyn and Tobin's sister—it would involve them both, his sister the most."

"Bring her in," he said.

He explained it to her, succinctly and without the embarrassment he'd shown when talking to me. At the end she nodded.

"I think it's a great idea. I'll help out however I can. And I think Jessamyn will be fine with it."

And, just like that, I had the biggest assignment of my writing career.

He paused, and then pushed back from his desk. "Look," he said. "This made the paper look bad. It made the town look bad. It made Tobin and everyone involved look bad. It's my responsibility to set this right."

I looked at George. He knew what he was doing, I realized. In a way this assignment was a gift, a gift to make up for the article that had been sent around, the gossip, the effect this had had on me and my roommates and everyone involved. He knew this could win some acclaim for the paper, but it would also be my chance to set the record straight, to show the town and its people for what they were, to tell Tobin's story, whatever it may be.

It was a huge responsibility, and I had no idea if I was up to it. I took a deep breath.

CHAPTER 18

My mind was buzzing, firing on cylinders I hadn't known I possessed. I could see the articles, the words on the page. I could see the arc of the story: the portrait of a young man's life, of this town and its people and how their confluence ended in a death.

"This could have a lot of repercussions for you and your family," I told Win as we walked back to my car. "Do you want to talk to anyone? What about your parents?"

She shook her head. "No, I think this is good. Maybe it's time to air the linen."

I wasn't sure what she meant, but I was thinking what I'd need to do, who I'd need to talk to. First on the list would be to tell Jessamyn. I'd mentally leaped past asking permission to wondering, *How is she going to take this?*

As we were getting back into my car, Win turned to me. "I think I'd like to stay out at Tobin's cabin while I'm here."

"What?"

"His cabin. I want to stay out there. I just . . . it may sound silly, but I want to stay where Tobin stayed."

I glanced over at her. "I don't think it's silly at all, Win. I mean, it was your brother's home. But it's kind of desolate—do you think you'll be all right out there?"

"I think so. I'll have my cell phone. And that fellow Dean lives nearby, right? So it's not like I'd be completely isolated. I'll ask the cabin's owner if it's all right with him."

She made the call as we drove, and I could tell it was going her way. "He knew Tobin at Princeton," she said as she hung up. "He said he used to use the cabin all the time, but with a wife and new baby he never gets up here anymore. So it's fine with him for me to stay there. Maybe in a year or two, when their baby is bigger, they'll start coming up again."

"Do you want to go out there today?" I asked as we pulled up to the house.

"I think so," she said. "I'll tell Jessamyn about it, make sure she's okay with it. And I'll tell her about the articles, too, if that's all right. Then she'll know it's fine with me."

I nodded, and she went upstairs to find Jessamyn. They came down a few minutes later, Jessamyn happily telling us the restaurant owner had called and asked her back to work. Win didn't mention her chat with him, and neither did I. They went off together, to shop for things for the cabin.

I went up and sat at my desk. To say I was overwhelmed would be putting it mildly. I was going to have to interview people about a friend who had died, try to talk to Win's parents, deal with bereaved sister and girlfriend, sort through rumor and innuendo, and weave it all into articles that were neither too maudlin nor too detailed. And do it all relatively quickly.

I picked up the phone and called Baker.

"What are you the most worried about?" she asked.

"That I can't do it," I said promptly.

"Of course you can," she said just as promptly. "What else?"

I thought. "That it will be really, really hard."

"That's never stopped you, Troy. You didn't know anything about team sports when you came here, and you were the best sports editor the paper ever had."

I thought more. "Afraid of what I'll turn up."

"That you can't help," she said. "But you'll deal with it."

I felt calmer when I hung up. But what I hadn't articulated ran deeper: the fear that I would like this, too much—that I'd want to keep writing pieces this involved and difficult, and would no longer be content to write about rugby tournaments and sled-dog races and three-day canoe events.

The phone rang. Baker again.

"Mmm?" I said, meaning *What's up?*

"What's Tobin's sister like?"

Baker never asked anything without a reason. "She's nice, really nice. Sad, but not over the top or anything. Rich, I think."

"The guys are having a thing tonight at the Waterhole, sort of in Tobin's honor. Matt Boudoin told people his sister was in town and they want her to come."

"Something organized?" I tried to picture the guys standing up in the bar, giving testimonials between rounds.

"No, just the guys getting together. Talking. Drinking."

"So—I should take his sister."

"I think so. It'll be good for the guys. And maybe for her."

And I can get some reactions, quotes to use in the articles. I didn't say it out loud. Sometimes I hated it that my brain did this, went right to figuring out pragmatic things. And, I thought as I hung up, if there were any hints of rumors about me and Tobin or Jessamyn, it wouldn't hurt for me to show up with Tobin's sister.

I checked the time. Jessamyn would be working, so I wouldn't have to avoid asking her. I knew enough guys in Saranac Lake to introduce Win around, but they likely didn't know Jessamyn. I figured they could handle meeting Tobin's bereaved sister, but his girlfriend would be one bereaved female too many.

I sent Win a text from my computer, which you can do if you know the person's cell phone provider: *Can you stop at the house before you go to the cabin?*

Sure thing, she texted back.

.   .   .

Win was in good spirits when she showed up. She and Jessamyn had made the rounds of the town shops, getting new sheets, groceries, warmer clothes. She showed me her thick mittens and insulated boots, more suited to the weather here than the ones she'd arrived with.

"The guys in Saranac Lake are having a thing at the bar tonight," I told her. "Sort of a get-together in Tobin's honor. Nothing formal, just guys getting together. They told my friend Baker they'd like to meet you."

"Sure," she said without hesitation.

"It would be around seven. I could take you over there and introduce you."

"That would be great," she said. "I'll run out to the cabin and set things up, and then come back here—say, six thirty?"

I nodded. "Listen," I said as she rose to go, "do you know how to use a woodstove?"

She stopped. I could see her thinking, realizing it wasn't like a gas fire where you just turned it on.

"I'll come out and show you," I said. You can't explain a woodstove to someone; you pretty much have to show them. I led the way to the cabin, Win's rental fishtailing slightly in the tracks my car made.

It didn't take long to get a fire going. I showed Win how to open the damper and vent, how to lay a fire and feed it, how to monitor the temperature gauge.

"When you get too many ashes, you scoop them into the bucket." I pointed to the metal can beside the stove. "But that takes a while." I didn't figure she'd be staying that long.

"It heats up fast," Win said as she moved away from the stove. She opened the small fridge and frowned at the contents. I could see it held little besides a bottle of ketchup. I suppose she expected to find curdled milk, withered fruit, dried-out containers of takeout. "I would have thought Tobin would have had some food here. I guess someone cleaned it out."

"I imagine so—maybe Jessamyn emptied it when she came out here a while back. Or Tobin's friend Dean."

She nodded. "I'd like some coffee," she said. "How about you?"

"Sure," I said. I could see a gleaming coffee maker in the corner, a fancy one, and Win rooted around in the cupboard before triumphantly pulling out a canister of coffee beans and a grinder. She smiled. "Tobin was insistent about fresh-ground coffee. I gambled that he'd have things here—I didn't even buy coffee." She buzzed the beans through the grinder and set the coffee to brewing, then served it in Tobin's heavy white mugs, with half-and-half, and some thin Pepperidge Farm cookies on a plate.

"Roughing it in style," I said, raising the mug in a toast.

She clinked mugs with me, and made a sound that was half laugh, half sob. "That was Tobin. He loved his coffee. I used to tease him about it. It was one thing he would never economize on."

She buried her face in her mug, and it was a moment before she spoke again. "Troy, I want these articles to show Tobin's life, good, bad, whatever. I want them to show who he was and what he could have been."

"I'll do my best," I said. I tried not to show that this rattled me—she was taking an enormous amount on faith. As far as I knew she'd never read any of my articles, just that one report on Tobin's death. I spoke up: "Win, this may turn up stuff you don't like. I'm going to have to ask a lot of personal questions. This isn't going to be easy."

She gave a half laugh. "I know," she said. I hoped she did.

It was warm now in the cabin. I showed Win how to add wood to the stove, how to poke the logs and keep the fire going.

"You'll be okay here now?" I said. She nodded, and I left for home. I wasn't entirely sure her staying out there was a good idea, but she seemed determined.

CHAPTER 19

Win showed up at six thirty on the dot. It was starting to snow, so we took my car. When I first moved here I didn't have four-wheel drive, but before the end of that first winter I sold my old Datsun and used a chunk of savings to buy a used Subaru. Every snowfall since, I'd been glad I did.

These Saranac Lake bars I'd been in occasionally for work, snapping photos of the winner of a darts tournament, interviewing players after a softball championship, attending a celebration for someone at the paper. And many of these guys knew me—I'd taken photos at their ball games, covered the sporting events of their kids or younger siblings. They seemed happy to meet Win, to like talking to her about Tobin, to tell her how sorry they were. No one treated me any differently than they ever had, so any rumors the fired reporter had tried to start up had fallen flat. I should have known he hadn't been here long enough to have any traction.

After a while Win and I veered apart, chatting with people on different sides of the room. The guys had warmed up to her easily. She was listening intently to one man, then laughing at something another one said. Her smile was Tobin's, I noticed again, and I wondered if I was the only one who felt that Tobin's ghost was in the room.

In a corner I saw Eddie, Dean's younger brother, grin flashing, looking much as he had on the Saranac Lake football team a few years ago. I didn't think he was twenty-one yet, but around here getting a fake ID was a rite of passage, like hanging your first deer in your yard. I chatted with some of the guys who had been on the ice-cutting crew that day, and then sat down by an older fellow named Armand. He tipped his head to acknowledge me. We sat in silence for a bit.

"You were taking pictures, weren't you?" he asked. "The day Tobin was found."

I nodded.

"It was damn cold out there."

"Yes, it was," I agreed. Something told me he wanted to say more. He ordered another beer and raised his eyebrows to see if I wanted one. I shook my head.

"Not a good sight," he said, after taking a long drink. "You knew Tobin?"

"Yeah, he dated my roommate."

"Mmm. Tough on her."

I agreed. When he spoke next I had to lean in to hear him.

"No one should die that way."

I wasn't sure what he meant. "You mean drowning? Freezing?"

"Cold," he said. "Cold and alone." A long pause. Sometimes, he said at last, looking into his beer, he saw Tobin's face under the ice, at night when he tried to go to sleep. I didn't know what to say. I just sat there while he finished his beer. Maybe that's every Adirondacker's secret fear, dying cold and alone.

By now more people had arrived; more beers had slid down throats, and people were becoming more garrulous. I saw Moose, who worked in the press room at the paper, and others I recognized. Most of the guys in Saranac Lake have nicknames, some so long-standing that few people remembered their real names or where the nickname had come from. When I was reporting local softball stats, I'd given up on listing real names of locals, and just used the names everyone called them.

I asked if anyone had been around that night Tobin was last seen, and if they'd seen the supposed wad of cash.

"Nope," a guy called Major told me. "Sure, he bought some drinks, but Tobin did that now and then. He was a good guy." Out of the corner of my eye, I saw two men to our right get up and move to the back of the bar. They resembled each other more than a little and moved the same way—brothers, I thought. Not everyone, it seemed, wanted to talk about Tobin.

None of them knew the woman who had sent around the e-mails, which wasn't surprising—these guys hung out at Saranac Lake bars, not ones in Lake Placid. Some of them had known Tobin had been seeing someone from Lake Placid, and Major had met Jessamyn once. He scoffed at the notion she might have been involved.

"That tiny thing? Not likely. And if she'd had someone do something to Tobin, everyone would know about it."

He was right about that, but that didn't mean they would tell anyone. This was Saranac Lake, not Lake Placid, and Adirondackers could keep things to themselves if they wanted to. Drunk or not.

I didn't know if Win was asking any questions, asking if anyone knew what had sent Tobin out onto that ice. Maybe all she needed was to visit this place, walk where Tobin had walked, chat with his friends, drink a beer or two in his honor.

But I could ask, and I did. Most people shrugged. But a dark-haired guy called Chowder told me he'd seen Tobin go out and hadn't seen him come back. "He said his head hurt a little. He said he wanted some air."

No wonder, I thought. The air in here was dense, and between the buzz of conversation and the background music, my own head wasn't feeling great. "So you think he left? Just took a walk?"

"Must have."

That could have been all it was—a headache from the noise, the booze, the late night; a walk onto the lake and onto thin ice. The police would close this, I thought, once the missing truck was found and the tox results were back. I'd write my series about Tobin, his life and his death, and Win would head home.

We made our farewells, and we were quiet in the car on the way back. "That was good," Win said when she got out. I nodded, and waited to make sure her car started before I went inside.

Jessamyn was at the kitchen table, with a bowl of cereal she was more playing with than eating. She glanced up.

"So you've been out with Win," she said. She must have seen Win's car here, or saw us drive up. There was an edge to her voice that took me aback. No one here paid much attention to anyone's comings and goings, and Jessamyn had never commented about anything I did.

"Uh, yeah," I said. "I helped her get her woodstove going, and we went to this thing in Saranac Lake."

"Oh, you guys are best buds now."

This was a tone I'd never heard from Jessamyn. Even I could tell it was jealousy, although I didn't understand it, not in this context. But this had been one heck of a week, and Jessamyn did sometimes lack the filter most people have.

"Jessamyn, she needed help with the woodstove. I needed to see the guys in Saranac Lake, and they wanted to meet her. What's the matter?"

She shrugged. She'd set the business cards we'd collected from the door on the table, and was pushing them around. "Do you think any of these guys would pay me for an interview?"

I stared at her. Now she was trying to make me angry. I kept my tone even. "I have no idea. You can call them and find out."

"Just joking. Hey, look at this one." She pushed one card toward me. "Maybe Win sent him."

I picked it up. It was the card from a private investigator. "I doubt it; I think Win came here as soon as she got back from her cruise. I guess it could be her parents." I watched her shuffling the business cards. I'd never seen her like this. "Jessamyn, what's wrong?"

She dropped the cards, and her mouth twisted. "It's just that we had a lot of fun in Ottawa, and then you go off with Win. And I found out she's the reason I got my job back—Miss Rich Do-Gooder fixing things up for her brother's poor girlfriend."

I took a deep breath and sat down. This was one reason I didn't usually have female roommates—you had to worry about hurting their feelings.

"Jessamyn, Win didn't think it was fair you lost your job. And look, obviously Win has money. So does Philippe. That doesn't make them bad people. No one is putting you down."

She rubbed at the plastic tablecloth with one finger. "I know. It's just . . . I'm not used to having friends like you guys."

"Well, then, don't be a jerk."

This was apparently the right thing to say. She grinned, poured her soggy cereal into Tiger's food bowl, and went down the hall.

I let Tiger out, trudged upstairs, and fell into bed. I was nearly asleep when the phone rang—maybe Baker, I thought groggily, but she wouldn't call this late, and suddenly I was afraid something had happened to Paul. I grabbed up the receiver. "Hello?" I said. There was no answer, and for a moment I thought it was a hang-up like the one I may have dreamed a few nights back. "Hello?" I said again, louder. This time someone answered, and I didn't immediately recognize the voice.

"What?" I said, in the tone that means *I didn't understand anything you said.*

This time the words were slower, and I could tell it was Win.

"Troy, somebody broke into the cabin."

PART TWO

ICE CAN FORM IN FIFTEEN SEPARATE KNOWN PHASES,
DIFFERENTIATED BY THEIR CRYSTALLINE
STRUCTURE, ORDERING, AND DENSITY.

CHAPTER 20

Win had retreated to her car and was calling me from there. She'd called 911, and had tried Dean but reached his voice mail. I told her I'd ring the Lake Placid police—the 911 folks are way downstate, in Albany, I think. I'd feel better calling directly.

"You don't have to come out," she said, but of course I was going to.

She was in her car when I got there, engine running. The police hadn't arrived. She unlocked her passenger door to let me in. It was snowing lightly.

"How bad is it?" I asked.

"Oh, it's been trashed," she said. "I didn't go all the way in, but I could see from the doorway. Things are dumped out and turned over, and dishes broken."

"Your computer?" I asked.

She gestured toward her back seat, where I could see her computer bag and a fat brown binder envelope. "I carry it with me, plus a file of things I've been working on. That's all my important stuff."

"Did you call the owner?"

She nodded. "I left him a message."

We heard the police car approaching before we saw its headlights. There was one officer behind the wheel. For a moment I feared it would be the one who had come to the house, the one I'd annoyed, but I remembered he'd been on the Saranac Lake force, not Lake Placid's.

We got out and he shone a flashlight on us, and I knew how a deer felt in the headlights. Win told him who she was and who I was, and he told us to wait while he went through the cabin. He scrutinized the snow near the porch before entering, but to me and probably to him, one blob of trampled-snow-melted-and-refrozen-into-ice looked like another. He was inside maybe five minutes, long enough for us to reach that almost-shaking-with-cold phase. But neither of us made a move to get back in the car, as if standing there shivering was somehow helping. Finally he came out and beckoned us to the open doorway, and we stepped inside.

"Does anything seem to be missing, anything that you can see?" he asked Win. "Television, microwave, anything like that, things that might have serial numbers?"

It looked like a cartoon scene, every drawer opened and emptied, every kitchen cupboard cleared out, and all of it on the floor. The oven stood open. The lining of the box springs was ripped loose, the sofa cushions pulled off and sliced open, the sofa overturned. Win's suitcases were opened and the contents dumped in a pile.

Win looked around, surveying it all, then shook her head. "I can't see that anything is gone. I had my laptop with me, and my purse."

"You've been up here just a few days, right?" he asked Win.

She nodded—I don't think she'd realized quite what a small town this was. People pretty much knew who did what with whom and where. Now I recognized the policeman as the father of twins who had been on the Lake Placid High School hockey team. I'd seen him at games several times, once in uniform. I'd gotten a great shot of the twins, intent on chasing the puck down the ice, and had given them a print. His nod told me he'd recognized me as well.

"This cabin's owned by a fellow downstate, right?" he asked Win. "You know his name?"

She nodded. "I called and left him a message."

He pulled out a pad and took down the owner's info. "Your brother used to live here?" he asked. "Your, er, deceased brother." He looked uncomfortable, and I liked him for that.

"Yes, he did. I came up here after his body was found, and the owner let me stay here."

"Would your brother have had anything valuable here? Anything in particular someone would want to steal?"

Win shook her head. "He had an old watch of our grandfather's, but I don't think much else."

He waited, as if expecting her to say more, but she didn't. "The door wasn't damaged. You left it locked?"

When Win nodded, he asked, "Do you know who else has a key?"

I thought, not for the first time, of the key that had been stored under the flowerpot—which anyone could have had copied at any time.

"The owner, and of course my brother did, and there used to be one kept on the porch. Otherwise, I have no idea."

He wrote more in his notebook. "You'll want to get that lock changed. And you shouldn't stay here tonight," he told Win, and then looked at me, in a sort of turbo-charged hint.

"Of course, she can stay with us," I said. Which I would have assumed she would. I wasn't leaving her in this mess.

Win hesitated. "I don't really want to leave the place like this—and with someone having a key."

I was shaking my head without realizing it. "Win, you can't stay here. And you don't really think they're going to come back tonight?"

She looked around. "There are papers and things here I don't want to lose."

"Well, you can't stay here until you get a new lock and we get it cleaned up. Not even if I left Tiger with you. Look, try Dean again and ask him to keep an eye out, and we can leave your car or mine here so it'll look like someone's here. If there's anything you're really worried about, bring it with you."

The policeman was watching us. Win looked around the room again, and I think she realized that she couldn't stay here, not now. She stepped toward the mattress and pulled at something, and when she turned she had the quilt she'd given her brother in her arms. She handed it to me, then moved toward an opened suitcase, pushing inside whatever fit in one brisk motion, grabbed up papers from the floor and dumped them on top, then snapped it shut and stood. "It's okay to go in your car?" she asked me, her fingers gripping her bag tightly.

I nodded. "Sure."

We locked the door of the cabin behind us, however pointless that might have been. She retrieved her things from her car, and got into mine. We followed the police car down the road to the highway. We didn't talk on the drive.

No one was downstairs, and the house was quiet. I showed Win into the downstairs bedroom. I'd realized she'd need clothes and toiletries, and had brought in my emergency bag from the car for her. "There's sweats and stuff in there," I said. "In case you don't have what you need." I nodded at her suitcase.

She grimaced. "Thanks. I won't be wearing any of those until they're laundered, anyway."

I nodded, and heard her close her door and snick the lock shut as I walked down the hall. Not a bad idea, I supposed. As I went upstairs I closed and locked my door.

It was cold when I got into bed. As I lay there waiting to warm up, I began to think that there had perhaps, after all, been more to Tobin's death than a tipsy late-night ramble across a lake, on ice too thin, in weather too cold.

CHAPTER 21

By the time I got downstairs in the morning, Win had wheeled the portable washing machine to the sink, figured out how to hook it up, and had a load of wash going. She was wearing some of my old clothes from the emergency bag, jeans I didn't like and a ratty sweatshirt. Somehow they looked elegant on her. Somehow very little seemed to look elegant on me, or stay that way for long.

I asked if she'd like to try cornmeal pancakes, and she thought that would be fine. I melted butter in my cast-iron skillet and within five minutes slid a plateful of corncakes on the table, and set out my blackberry preserves from Nashville and the crunchy natural peanut butter I bring back from Ottawa. This I never would have done with my own sisters—they would have been highly disapproving of the picnic table used as a dining table, never mind the plastic-coated tablecloth. Not that they ever would have visited me.

"I don't have syrup, sorry," I said, but Win spread the crispy corncakes thinly with jam and even tried one with peanut butter, and said they were delicious. The trick is using butter instead of oil, and not using a packaged mix—it's not as if mixing flour, sugar, salt, and baking powder takes a lot of skill. Patrick ambled in, and I convinced him to help me out by taking one of the too-brown corncakes.

Win asked if I knew a locksmith.

"I imagine there's one in the phone book. Or you could buy a new lock or take the cylinder in yours to be rekeyed. Either would be cheaper and faster than getting a locksmith out there. They're easy to install. I could do it."

She thought about it, and decided a new lock would be best—the owner had told her she could do what she wanted.

"So you heard back from him?" I asked.

"Yes, he called back. He says that key's been under that flowerpot for ages, and anyone could have made a copy. Of course, I didn't leave it there when I moved in, but I didn't think about getting the lock changed."

"Do you know . . . were Tobin's keys found with him?"

She was quiet for a moment. "They told me his wallet was in his pocket. But no, no keys."

I could see the keys in Tobin's hand, see him jingling them, sliding them into his pants pocket. "He carried a ring of them, maybe four or five. In his right front pocket."

"That sounds about right. He would have had a key to the cabin, one to his truck, his post office box, one to my place. You're thinking someone could have used his keys to get in."

I shrugged. "Maybe," I said. Of course, then that person would now have a key to Win's home. Her brain was trekking along the same path.

"I had a deadbolt installed on my door at home," she said. "Tobin didn't have that one yet."

"Probably his keys just fell out of his pocket in the lake." This had happened to me when I'd dived into Lake Champlain last summer to rescue Paul. But I wasn't going to discuss the forces of water and current and the deepness of Carhartt pants pockets.

Win sat up straighter. "I'd like to go talk to the state police. I haven't been able to get answers over the phone, and I'd like to go in person. I wondered if you might like to go, although I know you have a lot to do."

Sure, I had lots to do, but I wasn't going to pass this up.

"Do you . . ." I stopped, then started again. "Do you know why the state police are investigating?"

"My parents may be pushing it. They may want someone to blame."

"Blame . . . as in, it's an accident someone had something to do with? Or that someone did it on purpose?" It's a common refrain with parents—their child couldn't be at fault. *My boy never would use drugs . . . cheat on his exams . . . haze his fraternity brother . . . drink until his blood alcohol level was so high he could hardly walk.* But somehow, they did.

"They won't discuss it. I don't know that they've thought it through, just that Tobin moved to this town, where no one he knows lives, and he died—so someone has to be at fault. But I think it likely would have been declared an accidental death if not for that article, and maybe my parents."

"And the truck," I said without thinking.

"Yes, the truck. That's the thing that doesn't make sense— unless someone hid the truck so no one would realize Tobin was missing." She saw the expression on my face. "Yes, I've thought of all kinds of possible scenarios."

So Win wasn't just here to grapple with loss and walk in her brother's footsteps. I cleared my throat. "I didn't know if you had thought about that. You've had a lot going on."

She gave an odd smile. She was smart, very smart, I realized, and her brain worked at things whether she mentioned them or not. Sort of like me.

"Oh, I've thought about it," she said lightly. "I've thought of all kinds of things."

I spoke impulsively. "You know I have no idea what happened to Tobin."

This time her smile was wry. "I know you don't, Troy. You wear your honesty on the outside."

And this left me with nothing to say. I went up and sent a quick e-mail to Jameson, telling him about the break-in. And then we headed off to the state police headquarters.

Win had deliberately not called ahead, but we didn't wait long, and someone brought us coffee. When Jessamyn and I had been interviewed, mind you, we hadn't been offered anything. But Win had that manner that made people pay attention, and she was the sister of the victim, and not a suspect.

I could tell the investigator thought it was odd I was there with Win, but he didn't object. She told him we were friends and that I was writing a series of articles on Tobin. His look said he was well aware I was writing a series of articles on Tobin, and wasn't entirely happy about it. But his letting me sit in pretty much told me they didn't suspect me of anything.

He went through the basics quickly: No, they hadn't yet gotten all the toxicology reports. Yes, the preliminary findings showed water in the lungs, indicating drowning, and some bruising that neither definitively indicated foul play nor the lack thereof (he actually said the words *foul play*), which could have been caused by a fall onto or into the ice, or in the water. No, no keys were found with Mr. Winslow, only his wallet. He brought it out in its plastic bag and let Win look at it, take it out and thumb through it, glance at the bills inside, remove every crumpled and dried-out scrap of paper that had been put in there by her brother's hands.

Win looked up at the investigator. "Could I have a photocopy of everything that's in there? Not the money, of course, but everything else."

Now he blinked. He'd been prepared to tell Win she couldn't have the wallet, but apparently hadn't anticipated this. Then he nodded, took the wallet and its contents, and started out of the room.

"Everything on one or two sheets is fine," Win said as he reached the door. "I don't need each thing on a separate page."

He smiled then, what seemed like a genuine smile. It was almost impossible not to like Win. Then he was back, waiting for Win's next question.

"Someone supposedly said that Tobin had a lot of cash that night—but this was all the cash found on him?" she asked.

He nodded.

"Did you find out anything from the people in the bar with him that night?"

Yes, a number of people had been interviewed. No, Mr. Winslow apparently hadn't done or said anything out of the ordinary. No one had reported seeing him after he'd been at the Waterhole.

Chowder saw him leave, I thought, and wondered if he'd told the police.

"So do you think his truck was stolen? Abandoned? Is there a chance it's in the lake?" Win asked.

"No, if a truck had been driven across the ice and gone through, almost certainly people would have seen tracks in the snow and a large opening, even the next morning."

A woman came in and handed him several sheets of paper and the plastic bag with the wallet. He thanked her, and handed the papers to Win. She smiled her thanks.

"Miss Winslow, I understand you had a break-in last night."

So they were paying attention; this wasn't just paint-by-number.

"Yes," she said. "I'm heading there now to clean up."

"You have no idea who would have done this?"

She shook her head.

"Who do you know here?" he asked.

"Troy and Tobin's girlfriend, Jessamyn, and their roommates Brent and Patrick," she said. "And Dean"—she looked at me, and I supplied his last name, *Whitaker*—"Dean Whitaker, who was a friend of Tobin's and lives near him. And I've met a few other of Tobin's friends here, just briefly."

"Would Miss Field have any reason to resent you? Or to want to look for something at Mr. Winslow's cabin?"

Win shook her head. "No, we're friends, and she would have had months to search his cabin before I showed up. And she was with me all afternoon until she went to work."

His eyes turned to me. "You as well, Miss Chance?"

"No, but I was out with Win all evening. And I have no reason to search Tobin's cabin. If I want something for the newspaper articles, all I have to do is ask Win—she's been very helpful."

Somehow I kept getting myself in the middle of these situations, and not managing to keep my mouth shut. This was just the sort of behavior that makes the police think you might be involved. Like firebugs who set fires so they can help put them out, and nuts who commit crimes and show up afterward and want to be helpful.

He started to rise, the signal, I figured, that this interview was over. But then he turned to Win. "Your older brother drowned as well, correct?"

Her face blanched. I'd thought of Win as extraordinarily tough, but suddenly she seemed fragile, the bones in her face prominent, and you could see what she would look like as an old woman. It seemed a horrid thing to ask and a horrid way to ask it. But Win pulled herself together and said calmly, "Yes, he did," recited the date and place of her older brother's death, and then she stood and we were on our way out the door.

In the car, I spoke first. "I knew I didn't like that guy."

Win gave a shaky laugh. "He was blunt, wasn't he? I guess he was implying that Tobin decided to drown himself because his brother did, or that I'm bumping my brothers off so I can inherit their share of our grandfather's trust fund—which I suppose I will, actually." She tried to laugh again, but her voice broke. I looked away while she regained control.

"Hardware store," she said. It sounded like an order, but I knew it was all she could get out. I drove to Aubuchon, where she picked out the most expensive and sturdiest deadbolt keyed lock they had, heavy trash bags, and cleaning supplies.

When we reached the house, Brent and Jessamyn were in the front hallway, putting on jackets. Jessamyn was wearing ski boots, and two sets of skis and poles were leaning against the wall. It took a moment for it to sink in that Brent was taking her cross-country skiing—Jessamyn, who had probably never done a voluntary bit of exercise in her life.

"We're going skiing," Jessamyn said, unnecessarily, and with no trace of her animosity of last night. "Where have you guys been?"

"Long story," I said. She didn't need to hear now that her former boyfriend's cabin had been trashed, and I didn't feel like telling it. "I'll tell you later. You going to Hoevenberg?"

She nodded.

"Have fun."

She gave me a curious look. Another time I would have ribbed her unmercifully, asked if she realized that skis didn't come with little motors, that there were no ski lifts to go up hills. I forced a smile, and she picked up her borrowed skis and poles and out they went.

I was glad she was going, glad she was trying something different, glad she was becoming friends or whatever she was becoming with Brent. But it gave me an odd feeling, as if I was the one stuck in the past. Me and Win. The last Winslow child.

Win followed me up to my rooms and I scanned in the copies the police had made for Win of the items in Tobin's wallet. She told me to keep a copy, in case there was anything I could use for my article.

"You ready to go get started cleaning the cabin?" I asked when I was done.

She made a sound that was half laugh, half exclamation. "This isn't your job, Troy. You have articles to write."

"Win, you can't do this alone. My stuff can wait a few hours."

She brushed away a tear and stood. "Okay, then," she said. Maybe at home she would have hired a cleaning crew, but not here, not for this.

Downstairs, Patrick came in when I was gathering up rags to take along, and when he heard about the break-in, surprised me by saying he had nothing to do and might as well come with us. So we loaded up tools and bucket and rags and the three of us got into my car.

CHAPTER 22

We stood for a moment in the doorway of the cabin, taking it in. I was glad Patrick was there, because otherwise we might have sat down and cried. It looked worse in daylight, and the sense of invasion was overpowering. I took photos. The owner had told Win he wasn't going to bother with an insurance claim, but it seemed we should document this. Then we got started. I spun out the screws to remove the old lock and put the new one in place. Patrick grabbed a broom and started sweeping up broken glass while Win carried anything washable to her car—sheets, mattress pad, towels, clothes. Next I got a bucket of hot water and Pine-Sol and started scrubbing the floor; Win picked up papers while Patrick ripped off the dangling bottom of the box springs and put the bed back together, then she doused it with a liberal spraying of Lysol. Guaranteed to kill intruder germs.

Patrick moved on to tackle the bathroom, and Win and I surveyed the sofa and its slit cushion covers.

"We could fix the covers, then turn them over so the patched area doesn't show," I said. "Do you think it's worth salvaging?"

She thought for a moment and then said, "Let's do it. I don't want to feel that these people destroyed anything, even an old sofa." So we wrestled the foam cushions out of their zippered covers and added the covers to the pile in the back of her car, and moved on to the kitchen.

We wiped down the countertop and then the cupboards and drawers, washed the dishes that hadn't broken, and started to put it all back together, like a film running backward. Win began scanning the kitchen area.

"Where's the coffee maker?" she asked.

I looked around. There was the grinder, lying on its side under the table. But no coffee maker.

I handed Win the grinder, and she set it on the countertop. "I'm really upset that they took Tobin's coffee maker." She sounded almost prim. Her lips were quivering and she sat in one of the kitchen chairs. "They took his coffee maker," she said, her words punctuated with sobs, like hiccups. "They took Tobin's coffee maker."

Patrick glanced out of the bathroom, and retreated—it was going to be a spectacularly clean bathroom. I sat beside Win at the small table. "I know," I said. She didn't need to hear that she could buy a new coffee maker. She needed the one that had belonged to her brother who had lived in this rustic cabin far from family, but still wanted his fresh-ground coffee every morning.

When her sobs slowed, Win dried her face. She looked around at the kitchen, and decided this was enough cleaning for now.

As we filed out, she locked the front door behind us. I handed Patrick my keys and asked him to drive my car so I could ride with Win, and climbed into her passenger seat.

When we pulled up at the house she seemed calm. "Thank you so much, and please thank Patrick again for me—I want to head on to the Laundromat, and the store to pick up some things and dump the trash."

"Want company?" I asked.

She shook her head.

"Stop back here when you're done," I said, and she agreed.

I watched her drive off, then collected my car keys from Patrick and headed upstairs to my computer. I e-mailed George about the break-in, then my brother.

The phone rang almost immediately. It was a 613 area code, Ottawa. I answered: Jameson.

"I e-mailed you this morning," I said, surprised.

"Yes, I know." This was his deliberately patient tone. His *you're-telling-me-something-I-already-know* tone. "The break-in. Tell me about it."

So I did. I told him we'd gotten things cleaned up, a new lock installed. That we'd just been to the state police.

"Nothing stolen?" he asked.

"Nothing to speak of," I said. "I mean, just a coffee maker. A really nice one, but that's all."

"You got this newspaper assignment what, yesterday? And you met Tobin's sister the day before?"

It seemed longer ago, but yes.

A long pause. "I don't like this, Troy. Is she going to stay out there?"

"I don't know—maybe this will scare her off." I didn't say the obvious, that maybe that's what it was meant to do.

"Mmmm," he said. "Keep me posted. And the next time something happens, call me, don't e-mail."

I promised.

Win arrived back, laundry finished, reporting that she'd found someone at a yarn shop who would repair the sofa cushions, and had gotten more groceries.

"So you're going back out there?"

She nodded, and I gave her a look.

"We have the new lock," she said stubbornly. "I can call Dean if I need to. And my cell phone works there just fine."

"Okay," I said. "But I'm coming out too, until you finish getting it set up. And I'll leave Tiger with you for a night or two."

"You don't need to do that—"

I stood. I think she realized I was as stubborn as she was. We drove out in tandem, and I helped carry in the clean bedding and towels. We worked in unison, putting sheets on the bed, towels in place, food in the fridge. She'd picked up a new coffee maker, a cheap one she could leave behind without a second thought. Tiger lay beside the woodstove, watching.

"You have some questions, for the article," she said.

"Sure. You mean now?" I was startled.

"Why not? You probably want to get started as soon as you can. And this certainly slowed things down for you."

I looked around. I didn't even have a pad of paper. "I didn't bring anything with me—I usually use a tape recorder or take notes on my computer."

"You can use my laptop. It's right here, and I have extra flash drives." She pulled her computer out of its small bag and set it on the kitchen table, and handed me a flash drive.

This felt odd and it wasn't how I'd planned to do this, but one thing you learn as a writer is to talk to people when they want to talk. You never say *Maybe later.* And I'd passed normal journalistic boundaries some time ago: I'd known the victim, lived with his girlfriend, and was becoming friends with his sister.

I started with basics: date of birth, names of schools. As we went, Win began talking faster and faster, anecdotes spilling out between names and dates and places. I can type just about as fast as most people talk, if I don't capitalize or punctuate or try to spell correctly. I didn't look down, just let my fingers dance across the keys. Finally she paused.

The room had gotten chilly, and I got up to put more wood on the fire. Win started poking around in the kitchen. "I think I'll see about fixing something to eat," she said. "Are you hungry?" I nodded and she got out cheese and bread and butter and tomato soup, the fancy kind in boxes, and made toasted cheese sandwiches. She asked if I thought Tiger would like the can of beef stew she'd found on the shelves. Tiger did—apparently Dinty Moore beat Purina One all hollow. We ate the crispy cheese sandwiches and sipped the soup, in a companionable silence.

Then she started talking again, and I went back to typing, page after page, getting it down nearly verbatim. Some of this was background: Tobin's favorite books, the stuffed rabbit he kept on his bed, the first time he picked blackberries on a visit to their grandfather. Some of it was her painting a picture of their childhood, a picture she needed to paint: parents who seemed detached, a grandfather the kids adored, how it all fragmented after Trey drowned. She didn't say what had brought Tobin to the Adirondacks, why he dropped out of college after their brother died, what happened in the years between. But she was telling the story she needed to tell in the way she needed to tell it, and I wasn't going to push. Not now. Eventually I stood and stretched, and went to take Tiger out and bring in more firewood. It was snowing, and snowing heavily. Win held the door open as I carried in an armload of wood and looked out into the darkness.

"I should go," I said. "The snow's starting to come down fast."

Win shivered. "Troy, you're going to think I'm the biggest baby in the world, and I'm sorry, I'd thought I would be okay . . . but is there any chance you could stay here tonight? After the first night, I'm sure I'll be fine."

It was dark, cold, and late. I wanted to be in my own bed, with Tiger nestled in the crook of my knees. I wanted to check my e-mail and my phone messages and see if I'd heard from Jameson or Philippe, or anyone from the outside world. I looked at the sofa. It looked uncomfortable.

"Sure," I said. "I have a sleeping bag in the car."

I brought it in, plus my bag of spare clothes I'd repacked. Win kept talking after she'd gotten into bed and I was in my sleeping bag on the sofa, disjointed fragments of her and her brothers' lives. I typed on in the darkness, so tired I was scarcely aware of what I was typing. I'd become a weary dictation machine.

When I woke, I was stiff. By the time I pulled myself out of the sleeping bag Win had coffee brewing and had let Tiger out. We dined on cinnamon toast and bacon, and heard the snowplow rumble past as we were eating. She handed me the flash drive with my notes. She'd decided, she said, to make a quick trip home to check on things, and change her rental car for one with four-wheel drive. I agreed this was a good plan—I'd seen that car slipping on this road. What I didn't say was that I figured once she got home, she'd stay there, and do her best to forget this Adirondack village where her brother had died.

Cleaning the snow from our cars took a good ten minutes. Then she followed in my tracks, slipping a bit here and there until we reached the cleanly plowed Route 73. There she turned left toward Albany, and I turned right for home.

CHAPTER 23

The house was quiet. I climbed my stairs and flicked on my computer and plugged in Win's flash drive. To say I was in an odd mood was putting it lightly. Too much had been happening too fast. There was a message on my machine that my brother had called. I called back, but he wasn't in.

I uploaded my notes from last night and started cleaning them up, correcting the typos and spelling out abbreviations. I've learned the hard way if you wait too long, some words you can never figure out.

I looked at some of my typed notes, things Win had said:

Our father wasn't tolerant of children and the things children do.

He didn't appreciate Tobin the way he should have, and he put too much pressure on Trey.

After Trey died, he wouldn't engage at all. He never wanted to hear Tobin's name and he shut me out too.

If only parents could appreciate the children they have, instead of wanting them to be someone they're not.

There was more I could do on this article now—I could look up Tobin's schools online, study the places he grew up, start trying to contact his parents. Instead I pulled out the copies Win had given me of the things in her brother's wallet when he'd died. One looked like half an index card, with a phone number on one side, and more numbers on the other. The phone number had a 518 area code but wasn't local—Albany, I thought. I took a deep breath and dialed.

"Johnstone Law Offices," said a woman's voice.

I don't know what I'd expected, but it wasn't this. I told her I was calling on behalf of Jessica Winslow, whose brother Tobin had recently been found dead, and we'd found this number among his personal papers.

"I'm so sorry," the woman said automatically. "Was Mr. Winslow a client here?"

"I'm not sure—that's sort of what we're trying to find out."

She asked me to hold, and when she came back told me Mr. Johnstone wasn't available, and could I leave my name and number. Of course I could, and did, but didn't have high hopes I'd hear back. Win, as next of kin, might have to follow up on this.

I also wanted to check out something on Tobin's truck: Win had found an outdated copy of its registration in the debris at the cabin, so I had the VIN, the vehicle number. I looked up the Department of Motor Vehicles in Elizabethtown, and called. I told the woman my friend had sold his truck, but we didn't think the buyer had transferred the title yet and wanted to see if it was still in his name. I was only a little surprised when she looked it up for me. Yes, the vehicle was still registered to Tobin W. Winslow, and the registration and tags were valid through March. Which didn't tell me a lot, I realized. Just that Tobin hadn't sold the truck, and that no one had reregistered it.

And I was still wondering about the woman who was responsible for e-mailing that article around. If Tobin's Lake Placid bar buddies had known about her, then his friend Dean likely would. So I put in a call to him, and he said he'd try to track her down for me. Then I heard slow footsteps coming into the kitchen and went down—it was Jessamyn, walking tentatively.

"Hey," I said. "How was it? The skiing yesterday."

"Oh, yikes, it's hard," she said. "I sort of got the hang of it and I only fell twice, but it's really hard going uphill. My legs are killing me."

She looked outraged. I grinned. "Well, that's the disadvantage of skiing in the woods—they can't exactly put in little chairlifts."

She sat down. "Troy, you don't care that I'm doing stuff with Brent, do you?"

The question surprised me. "Gosh, no, Brent is great. And anyone who can get you doing something outdoors has amazing talents."

"I just thought . . . you seemed funny this morning, when you came in."

"No, that was just . . . you didn't see Patrick or Win, did you?"

"No," she said, puzzled.

"Tobin's cabin was broken into last night and we were about to head out there to clean it up. I didn't feel like talking about it then. I'm sorry, I didn't realize no one had told you."

Her eyes went wide. "Someone broke into the cabin?"

"Yep." I told her about the place being trashed, nothing really stolen.

"Did they break in the door?" Jessamyn was indignant.

I shook my head. "No, they must have had a key. Win put in a new lock."

"That sucks, that someone did that. Maybe someone thought she had a bunch of money there."

"I suppose so." Most people I knew with money didn't leave it lying around in a cabin in the woods. Although I knew of one fellow who built a stash into the walls of his bedroom closet and forgot about it until after selling the house and moving. Me, I couldn't imagine forgetting a wad of cash stashed behind the Sheetrock.

I told her Win had gone home for a few days. I didn't say that I doubted she would come back.

Then my phone was ringing, and I went up to answer it: Simon, my brother, the policeman.

"So you've got a lot going on," he said.

"Um, yeah." Sort of an understatement.

He had me go through it: Jessamyn and Tobin and Win, the break-in and all the rest. He didn't like my notion that Tobin had simply taken a walk on a late cold night and drowned. "With the truck missing, it's not nothing, Troy. This guy didn't just wander out on the ice and fall in. What about the sister?"

"Um, I kind of doubt she has anything to do with it—I don't think she's ever been up here before." I couldn't envision Win surprising her brother on a visit and then deciding to bump him off by luring him onto the thin ice of Lake Flower, and said so. And if she had, I doubted she'd be up here now, waltzing around, meeting everyone.

Simon paused a half beat. "Troy, you know the main suspect has to be the girlfriend."

"No," I was saying almost before he finished. "Simon, Jessamyn was crazy about Tobin, and I saw her when she found out. She was devastated."

"Yeah, we've all seen people on TV devastated that their spouse or significant other was missing or killed, and then we find out they hacked that person into little bits and buried them behind the garage—but they certainly seem heartbroken."

His vehemence surprised me and for a moment I couldn't respond. I think he realized he'd gone too far.

"I'm sorry, Troy. But don't fool yourself here. You know your loyalty can be your blind spot."

This stung, but I didn't say so. No one likes being reminded of their blind spots. We ended the conversation congenially, if awkwardly, but it left me unsettled. Usually Simon was deliberately neutral; even last summer he hadn't told me what to do. I hadn't asked him to dissect this—his big-brotherness and his cop instincts had kicked in, right where I hadn't wanted.

But I could not envision Jessamyn involved in this. Sure, she had jerked me around a little, making me tell Win about the article that night, and had gotten into a fit of pique later. But her moods were ephemeral and slight—very different from plotting to kill a boyfriend and stash his body under the ice.

And if she had mentioned to someone that her boyfriend had roughed her up, someone who might have confronted Tobin over it, it would be preying on her mind, and that I didn't sense at all.

I had an article to do. For now I had to put this out of my head, forget about Tobin's death and concentrate on his life—his childhood in particular.

I had my notes, with names of schools and people to contact. And by the time I'd gone down to get something to eat and taken Tiger for a quick walk, Win had gotten back to me with a comprehensive list of people and contact information, all of whom she'd called or e-mailed to tell them I was writing an article on Tobin's life.

It was odd to be essentially preapproved to interview these folks, but not, I told myself, that much different from a PR person arranging an interview or a friend of a friend passing on a contact. It would save a lot of awkward cold calls, and people possibly refusing to talk to me.

I took a deep breath, and started calling.

CHAPTER 24

I'd been waiting in this office a quarter of an hour, but it felt longer. My clothes had been neat and fresh this morning when I'd left Placid, but they'd gotten crumpled and tired during the nearly five-hour drive. I should have brought my nice clothes and found a place to change. Maybe I should have done a lot of things.

I hadn't planned to do any of these interviews in person, but a batch of them were clustered near Greenwich, and George had thought it worth the time and gas money. My time, his money.

So here I was. Sick at my stomach, about to do my first interview with one of Tobin's friends. I'd interviewed famous sports figures, but that was for feature articles and profiles. Talking to someone about a friend who had died was going to be different, very different.

This man, a former high school classmate of Tobin's, worked in an investment firm where, judging from the waiting room and its furnishings, the usual clientele had plenty to invest. I imagined genteel meetings between Very Rich Clients and the Guys Who Managed Their Money. Maybe they served tea, in thin china cups, with exquisite butter cookies on a tray. Or maybe I'd seen too many BBC programs.

Finally the receptionist spoke. "Miss Chance, Mr. Butler is ready to see you."

The man in the office I was led to wasn't quite what I expected. He was impeccably dressed and well-groomed, but on the chubby side, and not just that layer of flab men get when they're working in an office. He was heavy, like he'd always been that way. When he shook my hand his grip was firm, and if he noticed I wasn't anywhere near as well dressed as his usual breed of visitors, he didn't show it. He looked me full in the face, and the friendliness of his greeting seemed real.

"You were a friend of Tobin's family?" he asked pleasantly.

"Oh, no. I knew Tobin in Lake Placid—he dated my roommate—and I know his sister now, that's all."

This didn't seem to dim his friendliness. I repeated what I'd told him on the phone, that I was doing a series of articles on Tobin, the first one on his growing-up years.

He sat back in his leather chair. "I didn't know where Tobin had ended up."

"You knew him from prep school, right?"

He nodded. I pulled out my notepad and little recorder. I raised my eyebrows to ask *Is it okay to record this?* and he nodded again. Recorded backup can come in handy; you never want someone coming forward later and insisting they hadn't said what they did. Some people apparently either have no idea what comes out of their mouths or regret it so thoroughly they erase the memory of having said it. I've learned that people can lie to themselves even better than they do to others.

Usually I start with mundane questions to start things rolling, but something made me decide to jump right in. "What was Tobin like?" I asked.

He answered without hesitation. "He was a funny one. He looked like everyone else. He dressed like everyone else. He partied like everyone else. But he was different."

All my senses went on high alert. You almost never get this degree of frankness this early in an interview. Almost always it comes right at the end—that hand-on-the-doorknob moment—and the person talks fast and you write like mad and hope your recorder is working so it gets what you can't. I kept my eyes on his face, pen poised.

I didn't say anything. I didn't think he would start this and not continue. I was right.

"I was the fat kid. In a place like that—maybe in any school—being different is like wearing a brand. The in-group, the popular kids, they have to have someone to torment. If my parents had been rich enough I might have been able to carry off being over-weight, but they weren't—they just barely managed to send me there. So I was the target."

The words were stark in this elegant office. He said it simply, but I guessed it had been brutal. I imagined he'd thought about running away or begging his parents to let him transfer.

He looked straight at me. "My parents were so happy and proud I'd gotten into that school, I couldn't tell them how bad it was. I didn't know what I was going to do. But Tobin put an end to it. He'd seen it go on, the day-to-day stuff, and hadn't said any-thing. Then, one day in the locker room, he stopped it. He just walked over and looked at the group of them like they were scum and said, 'Don't you assholes have anything better to do?' and that was it. It was over. It wasn't like I suddenly got popular, but from then on they left me alone. They left me alone, and I sur-vived the next three and a half years."

It took me a moment to process this. "Did something happen, something that triggered his reaction?"

"No, and what they were doing wasn't the worst they'd done. It was as if he suddenly had enough and just spoke up. Reached his tipping point."

"Did you ever ask him about it?"

He shook his head. "That's one of the reasons I wanted to do this interview. I never thanked him. I thought about it, especially once I went away to college, but I never got around to looking him up. He saved me that afternoon, and I want people to know it, to know that side of him."

I raised an eyebrow.

"Tobin on the surface was one of them," he said. "Popular, good at sports, smart enough to get by in class without doing much work."

He talked another ten minutes while I took notes: anecdotes about Tobin, clubs he'd been in, sports he had played. I don't look down when I write, because a break in eye contact can mean a break in conversation. When the person you're interviewing talks, you write fast, and try not to blink. As he started to run down, his phone buzzed, and the receptionist told him his next appointment had arrived. I clicked off my recorder, shook his hand, and turned to go.

"Good luck with your series," he said. "Just . . . just remember that everything has more than one side."

I turned back to look at him. He straightened the items on his desk, and when he looked up I could see what he hadn't let me see before, the agony of the fat boy who had been tormented: shame and rage and hopelessness intermingled. You never completely escape things like this; you just try to never let people know about it. Maybe in a way it fuels you, helps you succeed. Because you need to prove that your tormenters didn't win.

He cleared his throat. "After his brother died and Tobin dropped out of college, dropped out of the whole way of life, it was as if he'd broken their rules and suddenly he was the odd man out, on the outside. Once he wasn't competition, once he wasn't someone who could have the cutest girl or own the company they might be working for someday, they turned on him. Tobin didn't do anything in school they all didn't do—girls, drinking, getting high, skipping classes. Maybe he did it better than them and got away with it more often, but they admired him for it. Now they talk about him like he was a derelict."

He opened the door for me to leave. The conversation was over. He'd spilled as much as he was going to. In my car in the parking lot I wrote down as much of what he'd said at the end as close to verbatim as I could—I wouldn't quote him, but I needed to get it down.

Then I sat there. Something crucial had just happened. Even if it had been only a fleeting moment of conscience that had driven Tobin to intervene, intervene he had. I'd thought Tobin was manipulative and lazy, and in a way I had disliked him for the wealthy background I'd guessed he'd had. I'd expected Tobin's classmate to be either a supercilious rich jerk or at best distant, reserved, and superior, and to confirm that Tobin had been a poster boy for privilege. But he hadn't been. Neither of them had.

None of this, of course, meant that Tobin had been an angel or hadn't become someone who slid through life and smacked around his girlfriend. But I'd broken the cardinal rule of journalism, bringing my preconceptions with me. Without this encounter, I might have skewed all the rest of the interviews, heard only what I expected or wanted to. Which would have been an enormous disservice to the newspaper, to Win, to me—and to Tobin.

I stopped at a Wendy's, where you can get a pretty decent meal off the dollar menu, and still got to my next appointment early. Classmate 2 was more of what I'd expected: Mr. Preppy grown up, pleasant but bland at the same time, with the apparent depth and perception of a punch bowl.

This fellow told stories of Tobin playing pranks at school, Tobin acing his exams without studying, Tobin being able to talk his way out of just about anything, Tobin with any girl he wanted. He talked about the older brother, Trey, who had been good at sports, good at school, with a steady girl and a job waiting for him when he died. Despite my efforts to nudge him off this track, he stuck to the company line: *It was a lovely family, Tobin was a great guy, his sister was a doll, Trey's passing was a great loss.* Only when I gave him a slightly odd look did he hasten to add: "And Tobin's death is an awful loss as well. Such tragedy for one family."

Some of this was background, like the scenery behind the actors on a stage, but none of it particularly illuminating. I would have loved to ask what three words he would use to describe Tobin to see if he could come up with anything besides "great," but that would have been almost cruel.

By the time I got to Classmate 3, I was tiring and my guard was down. So of course this one was exactly what I'd expected the other two to be. If you had made a request to central casting for "private-school snob, Caucasian," this fellow would fit the bill: thinnish face with a seemingly permanent sneer, hair carefully styled, cut a little too long. And I wasn't imagining the disdain in his tone.

"So you work for a newspaper up in, where was it, Saranac, wherever Tobin went off to."

I didn't correct him about the name of the town, just said, "Yes, we're doing a series on him and his life."

"Found frozen in a lake, right? What an asinine way to die— falling through the ice."

It was, if that was all there had been to it, but I knew this guy wouldn't be talking this way if Win were sitting here. But to him I was inconsequential and he could say whatever he liked. If I reminded him I knew Win, that she would be reading this article, he'd likely change his tone, but I figured playing the meek, mild-mannered reporter was my best bet. I was right.

"Such a loser," he said, tone derisive. "He skated through high school, then dropped out of Princeton and became a bum. His brother, now, Trey was the best. All-star on just about every sports team, class president, you name it."

I carefully wrote *all-star* and *class president* with my smooth gel ink pen. "So Trey wouldn't have dropped out of college if Tobin had died, you think. If the situation had been reversed."

He looked at me sharply. But I'd kept my face pleasant and my tone neutral.

"You're damn straight he wouldn't have dropped out—he would have sucked it up and kept on going, done even better because of it."

I smiled and nodded and wrote *would have sucked it up.*

"You knew his sister, his family?"

"Oh, yes, his parents were great, I've been to their house." He rambled on about their accomplishments, their insurance business, their standing in the community.

Time for something more direct. "Do you have any idea why Tobin had been estranged from his parents?" I asked.

His answer was so swift and vicious it surprised me. "Well, the 'accident' "—and I wasn't imagining the verbal quote marks around the word—"when Trey died. No one believes Trey was at the wheel of that boat. He never would have crashed it, not in a million years. But Tobin would have. And nobody saw him sobbing at the funeral, that's for sure."

It seemed the air in the room had changed. I chose my words carefully.

"So . . . you think Tobin didn't miss his brother?"

He shrugged. "Who knows? Trey was the one who was going to take over his father's business. Tobin was always going to be the underling, the hanger-on."

"And the accident . . . it was Tobin's fault?" I asked.

"Of course it was," he said, his face ugly now. "Tobin was a screw-up. And everybody knew there was only one life jacket on that boat, and guess who was wearing it?"

The words seemed to resonate in the office, bounce off the walls and around the room. Even he seemed to realize how harsh this sounded, and he backpedaled, muttering about how lovely the family was and finishing with the party line, *I send my deepest condolences to the family, and to his sister.*

When I pulled away from his office I had to concentrate to follow the directions to where I was staying for the night, with a couple I'd found on Couchsurfing.org, a website that lists people willing to take in travelers for a night or two. It does sound a bit like a shopping arena for sociopaths, but you read input from other guests, and see photos and descriptions. And sometimes your hosts will feed you.

That's what this couple did. They were in their mid-thirties, she a paralegal in a law firm, he a department-store assistant manager. In another time or place they might have been backpacking around the planet, but now they did their traveling vicariously, through their guests. I told them about being a freelance writer in Lake Placid and what I was working on—they knew about the Winslow family, and had heard about the elder son's death. They fed me a thick lentil stew and crusty bakery bread, with rich, creamy ice cream for dessert, and put me up on a comfortable sofa bed.

I pulled out my laptop and sent quick e-mails to Philippe and to Jameson. Then I sent Win a text message. *All is well; how are things going?* A few seconds later she texted back: *Getting back tomorrow. Will borrow Tiger as you suggested—thanks.* So she was coming back, and she was going to stay at the cabin. She was a brave woman, or stupidly stubborn. Or both.

After I curled up under the covers, my door creaked slightly, and a sudden weight on the bed told me the couple's cat had jumped up. She ventured up beside me and, purring steadily, settled down and kneaded away. She was warm and alive, and I reached out and stroked her. I was glad she was there.

CHAPTER 25

In the morning the couple gave me steaming hot cereal, something munchy with several varieties of grain. I packed my bag and folded up the sofa bed while they bustled about getting ready for their jobs. We left at the same time, exchanging little hugs at the door. I'd given them my contact info, and invited them to visit. But if they came up, I thought, they might never want to leave—they'd want to find a battered old drafty house in Lake Placid and odd jobs and spend every spare minute hiking or skiing. But almost no one steps out of the life they think has been selected for them unless something pushes them from it. Tobin had, and at some point as I wrote these articles I wanted to get a better grasp on why.

Today I would be meeting with a man who'd known Tobin since kindergarten, and then the nanny who'd been with the family throughout Tobin's childhood.

My first interviewee was an accountant with a private office connected to his home, a stately brick affair. No answer when I rang the doorbell. I checked the address, checked the time on my cell phone, waited five minutes, and tried again. Still no answer. I called both his numbers; both went straight to voice mail. I waited another fifteen minutes, then wrote a note and folded it neatly and wedged it in the door, and called to see if it was all right to move up my appointment with the nanny. It was.

She had been with the Winslow family sixteen years, and had left them over a dozen years ago. I was expecting an apple-dumpling of an elderly lady, but she was barely middle-aged and carried herself erectly, with the demeanor of a businesswoman. She must have been very young when she'd started working for the Winslows.

She met me in the kitchen of her current family's home—a bright, cheery room with photos of smiling children stuck to the refrigerator. They were off at school, she told me, the young-est now in first grade.

"Were the Winslows the first family you worked for?" I asked. I didn't know the right terminology: *worked for? nannied for? lived with?*

"Yes, other than babysitting. I'd been at college and was tak-ing the year off, and the Winslows were about to have their first child and needed help. So I took the job, and at the end of the year Trey was just starting to learn to walk and I decided to stay on, and then, well, this just became my work."

I looked around the kitchen. "So then you came here?"

"One other family in between, with children already in school, then once they got older I came to this family. They'd tried an au pair, but the little ones don't like having a new one every year, because they get attached, you know." She smiled.

Yes, children got attached, and of course she, too, got attached. It would be like being a rent-a-mom who could be returned when no longer needed. I couldn't imagine it: seeing a set of children into teenagerhood and then starting over with another set of children, over and over, until you became too old. Suddenly I wondered what Elise would do when Paul was older—but Philippe would, I thought, keep her on as a housekeeper, as he had during the months Paul had been missing. And then she would retire and visit as a grandmother would, or keep living in her attached apartment. And never have to shift to a new family and start over.

"They're lovely children," I said, glancing at the photos.

Now her smile reached her eyes. "They are all lovely children. Every one of them. They all develop differently, but they're all lovely." She said it like she believed it, which in my view pretty much made her the perfect substitute parent.

"You know that I'm writing articles about Tobin, about his life, starting with his childhood," I said.

She nodded.

"Can you tell me what he was like, what you most remember about him?"

I didn't have high hopes for this interview, other than some background color. I knew from Elise that proper nannies didn't gossip about their families. Maybe some did, to other nannies, but not to outsiders. I'd figured out more from what Elise hadn't said than what she had.

She smiled again. "Tobin was a good boy. Smart, funny. He learned to read when his sister did, when he was just four. He learned to walk early, probably because he wanted to keep up with the other two. He always wanted to do whatever they were doing, particularly whatever Trey was doing."

"Were he and Trey alike? I know Tobin was four years younger."

"Tobin was more rough-and-tumble, more stubborn, more headstrong. But that's common for a younger child, especially a younger brother."

We talked about childhood likes and dislikes, favorite games and books and foods, how Tobin had done in school. Then I asked, almost offhandedly, "Did he have pets, one in particular he liked?"

Her face got a bit pinched—like Elise's when she didn't want to tell me something. I waited. Finally she spoke, and her voice was thin and tired.

"Tobin had a dog. He always wanted a dog, and finally his grandfather got him one, the year he was six. Oh, for all of the children, of course, but it was really for Tobin. A chocolate Lab—he called it Bunny, because it was the color of the stuffed bunny he kept on his bed. But puppies are puppies, and Lab puppies, you know, they're a bit, well, energetic." I nodded. She went on.

"One evening the puppy got into their parents' bedroom and chewed some expensive shoes, and Mr. Winslow got angry, and said it had to go. The children pleaded and Tobin said he would save up money and buy more shoes and always eat his vegetables and be the best boy in the world, but their father said it had to go, the next morning." Her voice was expressionless.

She paused. "I think he would have dropped the dog on the street or had her put down, so I told him I would take her to the shelter. Instead I took her to my brother, and he kept her. She was a good dog."

I forced myself to speak. "How did . . . Did the children get to see the dog?"

She shook her head. "Tobin cried for days. I told him the dog was in a new home, that I could take him to visit sometimes if he wanted. He thought about it but said it would be too sad. But . . ." Here her reserve faltered and her voice almost broke. "But at night, once a week, he'd want me to tell him a story about Bunny. I'd either tell him something my brother had told me the dog had done or I'd make something up, and I'd tell him that Bunny never loved another little boy, and never stopped loving him even though she never saw him. I was never sure if that was the right thing to do. But it seemed to help." Her clear blue eyes focused on me.

"I think it was," I said past the lump in my throat. "I think it was the right thing to do."

The air seemed to hang heavy in the room. She spoke through it, trying for a return to her former briskness. "His sister is a lovely young woman," she said.

"Yes, she is."

"These articles your paper wants, I think they will do her good. She needs to have her brother's life told, on paper, all of it."

I waited, but she didn't say anything else. She was, I thought, telling me to tell about the lost dog and the lost brother, and maybe more I hadn't found yet.

"Do you know of anyone else I should talk to?" I asked.

She thought for a moment, and then looked in a small address book and wrote down names and contact information for me. "These first two were some of Tobin's favorite teachers, and this one was his girlfriend in college. They dated sisters, you know, he and Trey. They used to joke about having a double wedding someday."

"So you kept in touch with the Winslow children?"

She nodded. "They called me. I'd see them once in a while, in the summers, once they could drive. They'd meet me somewhere when they could."

I looked at her face. "It was hard to lose them," I said softly.

She blinked once. "Yes," she said. "Yes, it was."

"Did you know . . . did Tobin ever talk about the accident, with his brother?"

At this her face tightened, and it took her a moment to speak. "It wasn't something Tobin wanted to discuss," she said at last.

She took my e-mail address and phone numbers and gave me hers, and shook my hand crisply. I thanked her, and felt hollow as I got in my car and drove away, away from the cheery house that was her home only until this group of children grew up. It was like a reverse Neverland, being in a world where everyone grew up around you, leaving you behind.

But at least she has them. At least she has those families for a time, I thought, those children to rear and influence and love.

On Google Maps I'd zoomed in on the street where Tobin had grown up, the park where the nanny had taken them to play, the grounds of his private school, the club where his senior prom had been held. I'd told myself this was enough, that I didn't actually need to go look at these places. And maybe I didn't, but here I was, with time to spare. I pulled out the maps I'd printed from Streets & Trips—the poor person's GPS—and found my way to the park where Tobin had played with his sister and brother. I walked around, envisioning the young nanny with the three children she'd loved, the ones she'd taken care of instead of returning to college. It almost seemed that I could see them, see their ghosts at play. Then I sat there a while, my coat open, sun on my face. It's surprisingly warmer even a few hours south, once you get out of the mountains.

When I'd started this I'd been excited about writing something this big, this momentous, and it seemed it would help set things right. But it had morphed into more. I'd discovered I'd made a lot of assumptions about Tobin I'd had no business making. And now I wondered what else I'd be finding out.

I got on the road just in time to evade rush hour, eating the apple and carrots I'd brought along and then a rest-stop dinner of Fritos and a Snickers bar. All the basic food groups, plus chocolate.

It was a long drive back. I was having trouble keeping my eyes open, and I ended up pulling over at a rest stop and taking out the sleeping bag I kept behind my seat, wrapping it around me and waking an hour later, cold, and for a moment not knowing where I was.

CHAPTER 26

The house was dark. It was odd to have to fumble for a key and unlock the door instead of just walking in, and odder still not to have Tiger running to meet me. I flicked on my computer long enough to send *I've gotten home* messages to Win and to Jameson.

Maybe I should have tried to force myself to go through my notes before my impressions had dulled, but I couldn't. The best thing I could do was sleep. Sometimes I knew when to quit. Not often, but sometimes.

I woke from a dead sleep to what I thought was the ringing of my phone, but again there was nothing but a dial tone. This time I turned on the light and looked at the caller ID: NUMBER BLOCKED. So I wasn't dreaming. Someone was harassing me, maybe the fired reporter—this I could deal with. I got up and turned on my computer, signed into my phone service's website, and clicked the box to refuse calls with blocked numbers.

But now I was awake, and hungry. This was what I got for not having eaten anything when I'd arrived home. I looked at my clock—half past midnight. I eased down my steep stairs to the kitchen. I'd nearly finished a bowl of granola when I thought I heard something, and set down my spoon and listened. And heard it again.

It was from the front hallway, someone fumbling at the door.

Brent or Patrick weren't likely to be out this late, but Jessamyn might, and could have forgotten her key. I began to walk down the hall toward the front door, and got close enough to see the doorknob turn, and then turn again. The hair on the back of my neck rose. Then I heard a muffled exclamation, and a thump against the door.

I inched closer and peeked around the cloth over the window. Then I reached down and opened the door to Zach, our fifth roommate. Home from his trip visiting his girlfriend.

"Troy," he said. "W-w-what's going on?" For him, coming home to find our front door locked with a curtain over it would be like coming back to an altered universe, a Bizarro World.

I put my finger to my mouth in a *shhh* gesture. He picked up his bag and came in; I reached past him to close and lock the door, and gestured for him to follow me to the kitchen.

"What's going on?" he whispered.

In the chilly kitchen, my voice low, I told him all that had happened. Even condensed, it took a while.

"Where's Tiger?" he asked. Zach was fond of my dog.

"Staying with Win tonight. I got back late from a trip doing interviews."

"But everything's okay now?"

I knew Zach wasn't actually thinking everything was fine; he wasn't as simple as he sometimes pretended to be. He just wanted to know how this was going to affect his day-to-day life and what was expected of him.

"Seems to be," I said. "But it's probably best we keep the door locked for a while. So you'll have to find your key, or I can make you a new one."

He nodded, and went down the hall. I could hear him pausing to pick up his bag and head up the stairs to his room. I rinsed my dishes and went back up to bed, locking my door behind me.

I was surprised to see Jessamyn sitting at the kitchen table when I went down the next morning. It was late for me, early for her.

"You're back," she said around a mouthful of toast smeared

with jam. It looked a lot like my blackberry preserves, but I didn't point that out. Maybe I needed to learn to share.

I nodded. "Hey, Zach got back late last night," I said. "So how's everything? Is work okay?"

"Work's been fine. No one's been hassling me. Brent's been walking me up there, just in case. And Win had me out to the cabin yesterday." She took a bite of toast. "I thought it might be weird to be out there again, but it wasn't. It was good to have someone staying there, not have it dusty and empty, like it was waiting for Tobin."

As it had been. "Have you had any trouble with reporters?"

She shook her head. "No, nothing. Hey, did you know Win has a new car?"

"She changed her rental, right? Or did she pick up her car when she went home?"

"No, she said that's a little sports car and no way could she drive it up here. She turned in her rental and had them drop her at a Subaru place in Albany and just bought one, before she even went home. Like yours, only smaller."

I stared at her. "A Forester?"

"Yeah, that's it. She said she wanted something with four-wheel drive, and she didn't like dealing with a rental, especially when she didn't know how long she'd need it." She laughed at the expression on my face.

"Wow," I said, trying to wrap my head around this. I guess it made sense, if you had enough cash to buy an extra new car on a whim. "So it sounds like she's staying a while."

"Yeah, she said probably until the ice palace is finished. Or at least until the articles are done."

That was a grim thought: staying until the blocks of ice cut from the lake where her brother was found frozen were transformed into a whimsical building. But maybe that would provide some closure. Or my articles would.

And now I was starting to feel the pressure to get to work. I made myself some tea and peanut butter toast with sliced banana, and went back up to my rooms.

I tried the accountant again—no answer. He seemed to have disappeared.

Next I called the three people on the nanny's list and left messages for two. The third was home: a former grade-school teacher, now retired. I stumbled a little over my explanation, thinking she might not know of Tobin's death, but she did. Everyone knew, she said, and she had spoken to Tobin's nanny.

"So you know her?" I asked.

"Oh, yes, she was very involved with activities at the school—she came to the children's events; she made sure they did their homework."

"She came to their events? During the school day, you mean?"

"No, everything. Clarinet recitals, plays, sport events, she almost never missed them. She was more reliable than most parents about attending. She was like a mother, really."

"Their parents?" I asked, letting my voice trail off.

Silence for a moment. "I'm retired, so I can say what I please," she said dryly. "The father wasn't involved at all; you never saw him at school. The mother, sometimes, for daytime events. But evening events, no."

"She didn't like to go out in the evening?"

"She wasn't, well, particularly alert in the evenings." My silence must have told her I wasn't catching on. She cleared her throat and said succinctly, "Mrs. Winslow was fond of cocktails."

"Ah," I said, finally getting it. "But . . . that would mean the nanny was, well, pretty much full time, twenty-four hours a day."

"Yes," she said simply. And if I had wondered why the vital, intelligent woman who had been the Winslows' nanny had never gone back to college, I had my answer.

I asked about Tobin, about her fifth-grade class he'd been in. English, she told me, had been his favorite subject—he loved reading and devoured adventure novels, classics as well as current ones. He'd read beyond his years, she said, and he'd loved the Narnia books. Just as I had.

"I thought he would be a writer," she said. "He wrote some lovely compositions and stories."

"Maybe he would have been," I said. "If . . ."

She finished the sentence. "If his brother hadn't died. Or maybe later, if he'd had more time."

Now I heard the pain in her voice, behind the briskness of a career grade-school teacher.

"Send me a copy of your article, please," she said, and gave me her address. I promised I would.

I sat for a moment after I hung up. I'd never expected to find parallels in Tobin's life to mine, but here they were. Distant parents. Loved books, loved writing. Next I'd find out he'd been a Boy Scout who helped little old ladies across the street. Now I'd have to be careful not to start overlooking less savory parts of Tobin's life because I was falling for the little boy he'd once been.

I'd gotten a message from Dean that he had gotten in touch with Marilyn, who was back in town, and was trying to inveigle her into talking to me. And yes, her last name really was Munro— parents should think hard before naming their children. I heard sounds from downstairs, and then Tiger running down the hallway and bounding up my stairs. A moment later Win poked her head up.

"Hey, how's my dog?" I asked. Which was my way of asking, *How are you doing?*

"Great—she's really good company," she said.

"You're okay staying out there?"

She nodded. "Dean put up a motion-activated outdoor light for me. So your interviews went well?"

As she came up the final few stairs I could see she had something in her hands, a fat album. "I brought this back from home," she said as she handed it to me. "I thought it might help with your articles, and you can use whatever you want."

I opened the bulging album. It was crammed with pictures, her and her brothers' childhood.

"Thanks," I said, surprised. This was a bonanza I hadn't expected—it would help me find the heart of this article, see the child Tobin had been. "Win, is your family going to be able to handle this?"

"They know you're doing it," she said. She looked at a photo on the page I had opened: the three children, lined up on a front-porch step. "That was at our grandfather's."

"You . . ." I started, then said simply, "You had a dog once."

Win sat on my sofa. "Ah, Nanny told you about that. I wondered if she would." She pushed her hair away from her face. "Yes, our parents weren't the sort of people who could tolerate messes. Did she tell you what Tobin did?"

"She said he cried, a lot, that he begged to keep the dog."

"The day after Bunny was taken away he went into their room with a pair of scissors and tried to cut up some of their clothes. Nanny caught him. I don't know whether she stopped him before he damaged much and she could fix them, or if she just got rid of the clothes and never told our parents. But she would have done whatever she had to, to protect him."

She saw my face. She smiled softly. "I think maybe Tobin thought if he tore up things like the dog, they'd send him to where Bunny was, and he could live with her."

I jumped up. "I'm gonna make some tea." If I sat there, I would have started crying.

So we went down and had a pot of Earl Grey, like two friends having a pleasant afternoon tea break.

After Win left, I went through the album, page by page. To me it's a little uncomfortable, almost intrusive, to look at other people's pictures on Facebook or Flickr. And this seemed worse. Someone had selected these photos, painstakingly put them into place. Tobin was a charming little boy, with a sweet grin and full dark hair; his brother was thinner, a little more reserved, but in every picture of the two of them Trey had his arm thrown around his younger brother in a way that seemed genuinely affectionate, not in that just-for-the-camera way. There were no photos of the dog.

I was getting that slightly sick feeling I do before tackling something I'm not sure I can pull off. And I was well aware that the one significant thing I hadn't done was talk to Tobin's parents. I'd written, e-mailed, and left phone messages, all with no response, which was what Win had told me to expect. So I could, with good conscience, put a note at the end of the story: *Tobin's parents declined to comment.*

But the fact was I was afraid to talk to them, afraid to ask these parents about their dead son. Before I could talk myself out of it, I dialed the Winslows' number one more time.

And to my great surprise, this time someone picked up.

"Hello," said a voice. A woman's voice, faint and distant.

"Hello," I said, rattled. I made myself plunge ahead. "I'm Troy Chance, from Lake Placid, and I knew Tobin . . . I'm writing an article about him, about his childhood, and I was wondering . . ."

The voice on the other end of the phone made a sound. It wasn't a cough and it wasn't a gasp, but something between the two, and if I had to describe it I'd say it was the sound of grief. I waited, and then the woman said, in a reedy voice, "Just say . . . just say that we loved Tobin and miss him."

"Mrs. Winslow?" Now I thought I heard a voice in the background, a man's voice.

"Yes," the woman said, a little firmer, still with the thin edge of grief. "Yes, this is Tobin's mother. Please say that we loved Tobin and we miss him."

And as I heard the man's voice again, louder, the connection went dead.

I sat there, phone in my hand. So I had reached Tobin's mother. *Win's mother. Trey's mother.* It seemed I could feel the waves of pain emanating from her, through the phone line.

On impulse, I called back. It rang a long time before someone picked it up. No one spoke. "Hello?" I said. "Hello?" I heard breathing, breathing that to me sounded angry, sounded male, and something told me I had Tobin's father on the phone, standing there holding the phone, saying nothing.

Maybe I was imaging the malevolence coming through to me; maybe I was only imagining this was the father who hadn't been there for his children, who had somehow driven Tobin and Win away after their brother's death. But what I didn't imagine was the receiver being slammed down.

And that was that. For now.

Time to write.

CHAPTER 27

I reread my notes, looked over photos one more time. And then I began to put together the portrait of a rich little boy, a second son: a boy who adored his big brother, who lost his beloved dog, who played pranks, who had stepped in to stop the bullying of another boy.

I'd never written a piece like this. I won't say it consumed me, but it came close.

Around eight thirty I became dimly aware my message light was blinking—I'd hit the Do Not Disturb button on my phone system to send calls to voice mail. I checked my messages; it was Philippe. I stretched, and realized I was ravenous. I ran down to make a PB&J and then ate half of it as I punched the buttons to call him.

"Sorry I missed your call," I told him. "I was writing."

He asked how things were going, and I had to think before I realized he was referring to the media crush. "Oh, good. I think the media sort of gave up, moved on to something else. I'm writing the first article now." I remembered I'd e-mailed about Win being in town and the articles I was writing. I didn't mention the break-in; no need for him to worry. I spoke briefly to Paul and then went back to work.

. . .

I wrote until nearly midnight. The next morning I did more of the same, printing drafts and reviewing them, revising, checking them against my notes, occasionally remembering to eat something. This was hard, very hard. Maybe worse because I had been there, had seen Tobin's body in the block of ice as it had slid past.

Mid-afternoon I e-mailed George that I was close to finishing. He told me he'd stay late if I thought I'd get it in today.

I printed a copy and saved the file on a flash drive, then drove to Baker's house in Saranac Lake. She wasn't a writer, but she was a mother, and I trusted her as much as I trusted Jameson, maybe more. I handed her the printout and drank the tea she made me while her youngest son played in the next room. I hadn't been this fatigued in a very long time. It seemed that the air hummed, the walls of the room shimmered slightly.

She read slowly, deliberately, turning the pages facedown one by one. She looked at me when she finished.

"Holy cow, Troy," she said. "Has anyone else read this?"

I shook my head.

She picked up the pages and neatly stacked them, aligning the edges. "You've never written anything this good."

My head was spinning a little, and I didn't think it was just from fatigue. "I kind of thought so."

"Are you going to show it to Tobin's sister?"

"No."

Baker picked it up again. "You turning it in today?"

I nodded. "Just wanted to get your feedback."

She glanced over the pages, and set them down. "Send it," she said. And I did, plugging my flash drive into her computer and e-mailing it to George, along with the photos.

I was still there half an hour later when my cell phone rang. "Troy." It was George.

"Mmm-hmm," I said.

"Does any of this need fact-checking?"

"Nope. Just proofing. I triple-checked facts." He knew I kept a neat file of sources, notes, transcribed interviews.

"I'm going to lay this out now. Can you come over and check it?"

I told him I'd be over. I gave Baker a little salute on the way out the door. She nodded back. I think she knew this piece was going to change some things in my life, and that it might be time for some changes. Sometimes Baker knew me better than I knew myself.

The front office was dark, but George had left the back door unlocked. I looked over his layout, suggested resizing one of the photos and swapping one for another. Then he had me double-check the cutlines, and saved it.

George didn't tell me this article made Tobin come alive, or it was the best piece I'd ever written. I think he knew I knew it. And maybe he sensed that, in a way, this was my apology to Tobin for never having tried to know him.

"It'll be in tomorrow's paper—page one," was all he said.

By the time I'd left Saranac Lake and turned onto Route 86, a soft snow was falling. I felt a sense of peace as I watched the flakes coming down. In the rearview mirror I caught sight of a car approaching, and it took a moment to realize it wasn't going to slow.

I had nowhere to go but straight ahead. My brain was sending the frantic signal to my foot to press the accelerator when the car zoomed close to my rear bumper, swerved around, and cut in so sharply that I jerked my foot to the brake. And then time jolted into a different dimension as my car went into a glide and then into a swirling, horrible Swan Dance, pirouetting across the road.

There's something oddly liberating when your car stops going the direction you've pointed it, when fate or gravity or centrifugal force takes control and all you can do is ride it out and hope these aren't your last moments on earth. Before I closed my eyes I had time to be thankful Tiger wasn't in the car with me.

Today the stars were aligned in my favor. When the spinning stopped my car was off the road, half in a ditch, but I hadn't hit anything. Something hot and wet had splashed against my legs, and at first I didn't realize it was the coffee that had been in my console, coffee I'd picked up in the newspaper's break room. I reached down and shut off the ignition, and sat, listening to the sound of my breathing.

A tap on the door. I jumped, heart thudding. A man in a dark coat was standing there. He stepped back when I looked up. I flicked the ignition key back on so I could lower the window.

"You okay?" he asked. "I saw you got cut off." We both glanced up the road, but the other car was long gone.

"Yeah, I think I'm fine," I looked around the car, glanced at my coffee-splattered jeans. "My coffee spilled, but that seems to be it."

He walked around the car, looking it over, and came back to the window. I could see his truck pulled off the road, a woman in the passenger seat.

"Don't see any damage," he said. "Think you can drive it out?"

The car was at a crazy angle, but this is what Subarus are made for. I turned the engine on, pressed the accelerator, toggled the clutch. The tires gripped and I thought I was going to make it, and then the wheels started whirring, spinning up slush and digging into the snow. I stopped trying.

The man came back to the window. There was something faintly familiar about him, but I couldn't place him.

"Look, I might be able to get it, by rocking back and forth, but I'm a little shaky," I told him. "Do you mind trying?"

He nodded, and took my place in the car, while I stood off to the side. The snow was still falling steadily, settling on my blue parka. The woman in his truck turned to watch; I saw she had long hair, light in color. He rocked my car a couple of times and gunned the engine at just the right moment, and came roaring neatly out of the ditch. Men either practiced this when no one was looking or had an innate talent for it.

I thanked him and shook his hand, which seemed to make

him uncomfortable. I drove off, and in my rearview mirror I saw him pull out and drive back the way I'd come.

I drove very carefully the rest of the way, with that tingly feeling you have after a near miss. All your senses are heightened and you're absurdly aware of everything: the feel of the steering wheel in your hands, the brightness of the sky, the crunch of your tires on the road. You're very aware of being alive.

At home I made myself tea, then went up and changed out of my coffee-splattered jeans and sat on my sofa, hands around the hot mug, Tiger at my feet. There was a message on my phone, a woman talking fast, and I didn't at first recognize that it was the wife of the Couchsurfing couple I'd stayed with. I had to play the message twice to get it all. She'd mentioned me to someone who had known about the drowning of the first Winslow son, and they'd suggested I talk to a Victor somebody, a policeman who'd been involved somehow with the incident, but they couldn't remember his last name.

It took a bit of Googling to track down one Victor Moreno. It took a little more searching to learn that he was now the assistant chief of police in a small Oregon town. I glanced at the clock: Oregon, three hours earlier. I picked up the phone. He wasn't in, so I left a message with the woman who answered that I'd like to speak to Chief Moreno about a drowning accident back East six years ago involving Bertram Winslow the Third.

I e-mailed Jameson: *Article done. Nearly sideswiped today. Going to sleep.*

I thought about doing laundry, about cleaning my room or trying to cook, and finally realized I simply had to go to bed. I had nearly dropped off when the phone rang.

"Thought I said to call if something happened." Jameson.

"Mmmm. Oh, the car. Yeah, but this didn't seem to be something, not like a break-in. I mean, just a normal bad driver."

He waited.

"It was on the way back from the paper—someone cut me off, passed too close, and I went into a skid. Went into a ditch, but I'm fine; the car's fine."

"You don't know who?"

"No, and he probably never even saw me skid out behind him."

He didn't say anything, so I went on. "I'm sure it was an accident. I mean, it's not like someone would sideswipe me to . . . to not write these articles? Stuff like this happens all the time here. With the snow, you know."

I think Jameson realized I was too tired to converse coherently. "Get some sleep, Troy. Just be careful. And keep me in the loop."

I promised, and fell back asleep.

I slept for eleven hours. When I woke I desperately needed to do something to clear the cobwebs from my brain. I pulled on ski clothes, made cheese toast, loaded Tiger in the car, and drove to the cross-country ski trail behind Ho-Jo's. I skied hard, for me almost recklessly, and skidded out in a mild turn I normally took much slower. No one was around, so I lay in the soft snow and stared up at the sky. Tiger trotted over and licked my face.

Writing this piece had made me feel odd in a way I didn't quite understand. It was like discovering a talent you didn't know you had.

But part of me felt uncomfortably like a voyeur. I could have angled the piece however I liked: with Tobin's father as the male equivalent of Mommie Dearest, or Tobin as a dangerous and disturbed child who tried to slice up his parents' belongings. I'd tried to walk a middle line, but this was hard.

I wondered how Tobin's parents would react. I know that some people feel justified in what they do no matter what, and this father might simply think the article showed him as a no-nonsense parent.

And of course I wondered how Win was going to take it.

CHAPTER 28

It was probably good that I had an interview scheduled this afternoon with Marilyn, the mystery woman who had sent around the newspaper article. I was meeting her at one, before her shift at Price Chopper.

We were meeting at The Cowboy, a noisy place to talk, but it was what she wanted. She'd also insisted that Dean be there, not an optimal way to do an interview. And she didn't want me to use a recorder—maybe she thought if I didn't, I couldn't use what she said.

I got home and showered and ate a quick lunch. The phone rang just as I was starting to head downstairs to leave—Dean was running late, I thought, or Marilyn had changed her mind. But it was Philippe. I told him I'd call him back.

It's just a few miles from my house to The Cowboy, on Saranac Avenue on the way out of town. I sat at the bar to wait, and Dean came in a minute or two later and sat beside me. He ordered a beer and looked at me questioningly. I shook my head. I didn't want alcohol, and I wasn't going to pay three bucks for a soda I didn't particularly want. Or let someone else pay it.

"So did they find out who broke into Win's cabin?" Dean asked.

I shook my head. "No, and there was nothing to follow up on, since nothing really got stolen and no one exactly left a calling card."

"But it was bad, eh?"

"It was pretty well trashed, but we got it cleaned up, and put a new lock in."

He nodded. "I'm sorry I didn't get her call that night—I was in town and didn't hear my cell."

"You ever been broken into, out there?"

"No, it's not hardly worth the trouble, breaking into those cabins. Not like anyone's going to have a lot of expensive stuff, fancy TVs or anything. Sometimes high school kids break in to party or something, but this didn't seem like that, from what Win said."

"So you can't think of anything Tobin would have had worth stealing?"

He shrugged. "Not worth taking a cabin apart, that's for sure."

"You guys were pretty tight?"

"We worked a job or two together, and he'd come over for a beer or a smoke now and then. He was sort of private—I mean, he was friendly, but not the kind of guy you dropped in on. I'd never actually been inside his place. He seemed to like to be alone." He took a sip of his beer. "So I'll bet you'll be glad to get these articles done."

This surprised me. Maybe this was just idle conversation, but maybe Dean was more insightful than I'd given him credit for. Mostly I overestimated people, but once in a while I underestimated them.

"Yes, I'll be glad," I said. "I don't really like poking around, asking questions, not for something like this."

"Like this, talking to Marilyn."

"Yeah," I agreed. "She had to know that sending that article around would stir things up. Have you known her long?"

He shook his head. "No. She's originally from Tupper Lake. She hangs out in the bars here a lot. She sort of liked Tobin, I expect."

"I expect she did," I said, mimicking his tone, and he grinned. "But she sure stirred up a lot of trouble."

"Yeah, I'm guessing it was one of those things, sort of knee-jerk crazy. The news hit everybody hard. Like that guy Stevo, on the street, you know."

I nodded. It was the first time he'd acknowledged the confrontation with Jessamyn on Main Street.

He went on. "But we'd all just thought Tobin had gone out of town and then he would come back, all full of himself. He just didn't seem the type who would die—you know what I mean?"

Somehow I did. Tobin had seemed the type of person who would have managed to walk away from the wrong place at just the right time. Decided to take a stroll before a nightclub caught fire, move from where he was sitting before lightning struck, choose not to take the train that would end up crashing. Maybe Tobin had had a sixth sense, a special talent at surviving, one that had run out one early winter day in the Adirondacks.

Dean finished his beer and looked at his watch. It was ten minutes past when Marilyn had said she'd be here.

"Thanks for setting this up," I said.

"If she shows."

In ten minutes more, she did. She was pretty much what I would have predicted, if I'd had to make a prediction. She probably wasn't yet thirty, but looked like she'd passed it. A slight puffiness to her face, belly straining the fabric of the blouse over her too-snug jeans. A decade ago, right out of high school, she'd likely been cute as a button, but she'd left cute behind some time ago. Too many late hours, too many cigarettes, too much booze. It's a bad combination, and she wasn't wearing it well.

Dean stood up when she came in, and introduced me. She took the stool he vacated, and he sat beside her. She ordered a drink, and the bartender delivered it quickly. They were used to working fast here. She took a sip. It was something dark.

"So," she said, belligerence thick in just that one word. "What do you want to talk to me about?"

Probably better that her animosity was out in the open. "You were a friend of Tobin Winslow's?"

"Yeah, we were good friends." She emphasized the last two words.

I had a pretty good idea that in this case *good friends* meant she hung around the guys in the bar and tried to latch onto Tobin when she could. But I was trying to not be guilty of prejudging. I'd already done enough prejudging for a lifetime.

"You know I'm writing a series of articles for the newspaper on Tobin," I said, so it was clear we weren't just having a chat.

She nodded. I caught Dean's eye over her shoulder. I wasn't sure whether to tread lightly or go for broke. I decided on *go for broke.*

"You don't like Jessamyn, do you?"

She snorted. "That bitch—she thinks she's better than everyone else."

Behind her, Dean tensed. She may have wanted him here to keep her from doing something like this, but I'd lobbed the question so low and fast she hadn't seen it coming. And how we were sitting, in a row, made it almost impossible for Dean to intervene.

"So, did Jessamyn treat you badly?" Meaning, *What did she ever do to you?*

She twisted her lips, in a caricature of derision. "She treated me like I didn't exist, like she owned Tobin Winslow, and she sure didn't."

Behind her, Dean shifted uneasily. I hadn't missed the venom in her tone. "What do you mean, she didn't own him?"

She picked up her drink. "Just that Tobin was a grown man, and he wasn't married. He was free to do what he wanted."

"So you thought Jessamyn, what, kept him on a tight leash?"

"Yeah," she said, "and she thought she was so great."

I leaned in closer. "Is that why you sent that article around to people, to newspapers and radio stations?"

She flushed. "Yeah, well, if she had something to do with Tobin dying, then everybody needed to know."

I paused for a two-count. "Yes, but do you believe Jessamyn had anything to do with what happened to Tobin?"

She set her glass down on the bar surface, harder than necessary. "No," she said, almost sullenly. "I guess not."

"Do you have any idea who might?" I didn't take my eyes off her. A tingly Spidey sense told me there was something here I needed to pay close attention to.

"Who might what?"

"Who might have had anything to do with Tobin's death."

At this Dean moved on his stool. Marilyn looked uncomfortable. "He drowned," she said, seeming confused. "He fell through the ice. It was an accident, right?" She twisted around and looked toward Dean, as if for confirmation.

"No one knows for sure," I said gently. "That's what the police are trying to find out. What do you think?"

Dean was trying not to look startled, at my bluntness, I suppose. But this is the North Country, and people often don't tell you things unless you ask. They might know perfectly well that X is sleeping with Y's wife, but unless Y asks about it, they're going to assume he doesn't want to know.

I was rolling a pen back and forth in my fingers, and it fell to the floor. I leaned over to get it, and on the way back up caught a glance between Marilyn and Dean.

"I don't know," she muttered. I looked at Dean, and he shrugged.

It seemed she knew something she wasn't telling me, but I wasn't going to get much more here. I asked one more question. "Do either of you have any idea what happened to Tobin's truck?"

They shook their heads, and their denials seemed genuine.

"Sometimes Tobin hitched a ride to Saranac Lake if he knew he was going to drink a lot," Dean said. "I don't know if he drove over that night or not. I wasn't there."

I hated it that suddenly I was watching Dean, analyzing what he said and how he said it. He'd been helpful since that first night he'd showed up at Tobin's cabin, and even in the street confrontation he had eased the angry drunk down the street away from us. Now I was wondering if there was something he didn't want me to know. Maybe he was protecting Tobin; maybe he was protecting someone else.

As I was driving home, I thought the whole thing over. Try as I might, I couldn't envision this woman doing this on her own. I couldn't see her with the acumen to pull it off: capturing a screen shot, saving it as a JPG, inserting it in e-mails, looking up media addresses to send it around. Someone had to have helped her. I hoped it wasn't Dean.

At home I started an e-mail to my brother: *Found woman who sent around article—seems to be motivated by spite, but maybe more was involved.*

Then my fingers typed: *It is entirely possible that someone held Tobin under the ice, or knocked him unconscious and dumped him in the lake. I just have no idea who or why.*

But Simon had been adamant that I needed to be seriously considering Jessamyn's involvement, and I didn't want to go into that again. I was used to running things by him, but now I didn't want to. I erased his name from the address line, changed it to Jameson's, and hit Send.

To my surprise, because Jameson almost never e-mailed, a minute later I had a reply: *Just try not to work too hard.*

Jameson knew I had a tendency to fling myself into projects. But I couldn't see any other way to do this. I knew only one way. I remembered something Baker had told me yesterday: *Remember you're writing about Tobin's life, not his death.*

The problem was, it was hard to separate them.

CHAPTER 29

I didn't hear Win arrive, but Zach did. I heard his and Win's voices in the kitchen, and went down. She had a stack of newspapers under her arm—she must have picked them up from the newspaper office, because it wouldn't be on sale on the street until later.

Her cheeks were red with cold. She set down the papers and pulled off her hat and mittens without looking at me. My gut twisted. I was afraid I'd gone too far—afraid I'd written an article too intimate, too intense; afraid it would cost the friendship that had been building between us. No matter that Win had helped set up interviews; no matter that I warned her I might write things she didn't like—that can all go out the window once people see things on the page. But then she spoke.

"This article's amazing, Troy. You didn't make him look perfect, but you captured him, the way he was before the accident, what it was like growing up."

Zach picked up one of the papers. George had put a box on the front page, with the first paragraph from the story and a photo of a young Tobin with his brother and sister, posing on a big wooden play structure.

"Wow," Zach said as he opened the paper. I could see that the article took up more than half a page.

"Has Jessamyn seen it?" Win asked. "Is she in?"

"I think she's here, and no, I don't think she's seen it. I haven't even seen it in print."

She handed me a copy and took another, and headed toward the stairs that led to Jessamyn's room. I carried my copy up to my room. I didn't look at it. Instead I flicked on my e-mail: Alyssa, up in Burlington, had already seen it online and written: *Congrats— well done. This is going to get a lot of attention.*

I wasn't ready for a lot of attention.

My phone rang: George. He wasted no time on a greeting. "Early feedback is good. When can you have the next one?"

A week would be optimal, but I didn't think I could do the research and the writing in the next six days, and I told him so.

"Try for ten days," he said. "If you can't, you can't. Two weeks would be fine. Don't rush it. But if you need help, if someone can do research, do it. I can find money in the budget."

I was used to doing everything alone, and I liked it that way. I didn't always know what I was looking for, or what details I might want to include. But I'd never done articles this involved.

I sent links to the article to Jameson and to Philippe, and, after thinking about it, to my brother as well. And to the nanny and Tobin's grade-school teacher.

Then I called Dean, and thanked him for setting up the meeting with Marilyn.

He sounded apologetic. "I know she wasn't that helpful. She's kind of prickly with people, and she really didn't like Jessamyn." I didn't tell him that Jessamyn didn't even remember meeting the woman.

"Listen, Dean, I need to ask you—do you know who would have helped Marilyn?"

"Helped her?"

"Helped her set up what she did, sending around that newspaper article."

He sounded surprised. "No, I figured she just did it herself. She's the one who gave that printout to my friend."

I thanked him again. It had been foolish, I thought, to have had those vague suspicions about Dean. What I'd seen yesterday must have just been his discomfort at being stuck in an uncomfortable situation.

I heard a knock on the open door at the bottom of my stairwell. I looked over my railing, and waved Win up.

Without saying anything she handed me a brown binder envelope with an elastic cord around it, the one I'd seen once in the back seat of her car. I opened it and saw a sheaf of papers and a stack of postcards. On top was a timeline with dates, names, places: a compilation of where Tobin had been after he'd left home, with addresses and places of work and names of coworkers.

I whistled. "Holy cow, Win."

"Yeah, I've been working on this a while. I found his postcards at home and printed some of his e-mails. I wasn't sure I wanted this much of Tobin out there, but I put it together just in case."

Meaning, I thought, she'd waited to see how I'd handled the first article before turning all this over to me. Ordinarily you'd be suspicious of someone handing you a neat timeline like this. But I could check out everything—and I never would have been able to compile this on my own.

"Thanks," I said and meant it. "This is great. You're doing an awful lot for this, Win."

She shrugged. "It's my brother. I want his story told."

They were going out to Desperados for dinner, she and Jessamyn and Brent and Zach, and then on to Rumors. Part of me wanted to go, but part of me didn't. Maybe it would have seemed a little too much like celebrating this article, which I couldn't handle for several reasons.

I didn't think there was any way to sort this odd mesh of feelings. *Work*, that was the answer. At least for me. At least for now.

So that's what I did. I started going through the material Win had given me. I wrote another carefully worded e-mail to her par-

ents. I left another message for the policeman in Oregon. I made
a list of questions for Win—we were going to meet at her place
in the morning for another interview. I picked up my article and
looked it over. In a perfect world maybe I would have tried to find
more of Tobin's friends, some Win hadn't sent me to, but this was
a feature on a boy growing up, and I thought I'd done a good job
with the resources I had.

But everything was jumbled in my head: the articles to write,
the missing truck, the trashed cabin, Marilyn and her motiva-
tions, the story from the policeman out in Oregon. Questions not
answered, and at the core of it a giant ball of doubt about whether
writing these articles was a good thing or a selfish and intrusive
one. Or both.

On impulse I picked up the phone and called Jameson. Like he
had done last summer in Ottawa, he let me talk. "It's going to be
a story with no ending," I said when I ran down.

"Sometimes that's life, Troy," he said. "Or sometimes you get
an ending you don't want."

Sometimes I wished Jameson could offer platitudes. But then
he wouldn't be Jameson.

Now it was late. If I'd been sensible and turned off my computer
and read a book or watched television like an ordinary person,
that would have been the end to the day. But I was still restless,
and what I did was start checking details of people I'd interviewed
and ones I would interview soon. Next I did some concentrated
Googling on Tobin and Trey, and then I looked up Jessamyn.

I tried her name alone and then combined with "Ohio," where
I thought she'd once mentioned she lived, and got hits for the
writer Jessamyn West, who'd apparently set one of her novels in
Ohio. I tried the name with Jessamyn's year of birth and a few
other combinations.

Had it been earlier in the evening, I likely wouldn't have gotten anywhere. But when it's late and I'm tired, any cutoff valve I

have ceases to exist. Overtired, I just keep going, and I tried some unlikely search combinations and went deeper into results than I would normally. And I found a string of interconnecting bits: a blog entry reflecting on high school days; an excerpt from an old school newspaper; a page from a high school annual with a picture of a freshman with the first name of Jessamyn—one who looked like a young version of the woman living in my house, with unbecomingly short hair, incongruously bleached near-white blond.

It all added up to the story of a girl named Jessamyn Wallace, the right age from the right area, who had fractured her brother's skull with a baseball bat—causing him to miss the rest of his high school football season, which, a decade later, his classmates were still convinced had cost them the state championship.

I pushed back from the computer. In a way, I hated myself. If only I had tried a little harder to fall asleep. If only my brain didn't work this way. If only I weren't quite so good at researching and figuring out how to put bits together. And if only I were someone else, I could ignore it.

But I wasn't.

I wanted to convince myself this wasn't Jessamyn, but I couldn't. It fit too well. The name, the photo, the dates.

I had to ask her about this, and I had no idea how. I don't excel at social skills in normal situations, and this was far from normal. I couldn't explain to Jessamyn that this was just how my mind worked, that this was a part of my personality, how my synapses fired. That when I was on a computer, my brain said, *Oh, let me check out x, y, and z.*

But you always checked out the major characters in anything you were writing. Part of me never quite believed what people told me. Part of me knew that everyone had secrets, especially people who ended up in this remote Adirondack village but weren't athletes or outdoor-lovers.

And I did have an instinct for when things weren't quite right. On some level I'd known something wasn't right with Jessamyn.

I thought of my brother's warning. Of course the police would view this as a reason to suspect Jessamyn in Tobin's death. Maybe my loyalty was blinding me; maybe I was being naïve. But as mercurial as Jessamyn could be—and as damning as it might seem that a young Jessamyn had apparently taken a baseball bat to her brother's head—I could not imagine her hurting Tobin.

At least instinct did tell me that printing out all this and shoving it under Jessamyn's door would not be the best approach. I had to talk to her. But not tonight.

It was very hard to get to sleep.

CHAPTER 30

My phone rang early the next morning.

"This is William Johnstone," said a man, in a deep, slow voice that sounded like someone who had long since passed retirement age. "You were calling about Tobin Winslow. Can you tell me what it is you're wanting to find out?"

My pulse quickened. The lawyer I'd called, the number in Tobin's wallet—I'd been so caught up in other stuff I'd almost forgotten about this. I told him Tobin's body had been found recently, that his sister and I had found this phone number among his things. "We're basically trying to find out whatever we can, to close off his affairs. And to find a will, if there is one."

"So there's a big estate, is there?"

This took me aback. "No, I don't think there is, but his sister would like to close things off."

"I assume you know about attorney-client privilege, young lady."

"Yes, of course. Tobin was a client of yours?"

"I didn't say that. But if a person had kept an appointment they'd made, then that person would have been a client."

Bingo. He was being cagey—he wasn't going to come out and say anything directly. I chose my words carefully. "So if Tobin had an appointment with you . . . would there be a way to find out what this appointment was going to be about?"

"Well, now, that wouldn't be something I could discuss."

I tried again. "Could you tell me the date of the appointment?" He did: the day after the last evening Tobin had been at the bars in Saranac Lake.

"But you can't tell me for what? Or his sister—it might help her to know."

"Is she older or younger?"

This seemed an odd thing to ask. "His sister? She's older, by two years."

"They were close?"

"I think so," I said, puzzled. "They didn't see each other often, but they kept in touch, and yes, I think you could say they were close."

This odd answer to his odd question seemed to be what he wanted. I heard a sound as if he had closed a book. "Well, what I can tell you is that I am the best writer of wills and trusts in this county."

"The best writer of wills in the county," I repeated.

"Yes," he said. "If you were to make an appointment with me, for example, it would most likely be in regards to a trust or a will. It wouldn't be cheap, but you'd get an impeccable document."

In regards to a trust or a will. "Thank you," I said. "I'll tell his sister."

"I'm sorry your friend died," he said.

I almost opened my mouth to say Tobin hadn't been my friend, when I realized that one, you couldn't say things like that and two, maybe Tobin sort of was becoming one. In the past tense.

I was due to head out to Win's, to do that next interview, so I'd tell her about the lawyer when I got there. I checked my inbox: Philippe had read the article and liked it. And my brother had e-mailed.

I almost didn't want to open it—if Simon knew what I had found out about Jessamyn he'd be all over it. I knew I wasn't going to tell him. But his note was short: *Great article, Troy. Sorry I was such a jerk the other day—in the middle of a very bad case.* I wrote back: *Thanks, no worries.* And that was all I said.

Jessamyn wasn't up yet, so I could put off talking to her for now. But as I whistled Tiger into my car I noticed my left front tire was low, so I detoured up to Stewart's for air. I maneuvered my car next to the air hose, uncurled it, and hunkered down in the slush to wedge the hose into position. I hoped it hadn't developed a slow leak when I'd bounced off the road.

Of course it was that moment when, out of the corner of my eye, I saw a truck going past, one that looked like Tobin's.

I dropped the hose and stood and looked after it. But it was gone. I hadn't caught details of a license plate, details of anything. *You're seeing things again*, I told myself. There was too much going on, too much out of my range of experience. I was seeing a truck that didn't exist while trying to figure out what had happened to the truck's owner, while worrying about Jessamyn and things I wished I hadn't turned up. I topped off the tire pressure, and drove on to Win's.

The cabin looked good, the mended cushions back on the sofa, everything seeming brighter than before. Win had started to put Tobin's clothes into boxes. She'd made coffee and set out bakery muffins. I told her about the phone call and the lawyer in Albany, thinking she'd be pleased. But she frowned.

"What?" I asked.

"The problem is, we don't know what it means. Did Tobin want to try to break his trust fund, get more money from it somehow? Had he decided to make a will and didn't get it done?" Her voice almost broke.

"Did you ever . . ." I started to ask, and stopped myself.

"Did I ever what? Wonder if Tobin killed himself?" A single tear gathered and slid down Win's cheek. She seemed unaware of it. "Of course I did."

"I don't think he did," I said at last.

"I don't either, but it's hard not knowing. And this is frustrating. Everything's up in the air and I can't get much of anything done without a will or a death certificate."

"You can't get a death certificate until the tox results are back?"

She shook her head. "No, they can issue temporary ones. But without a court order or some kind of official documentation, the state will only release it to a parent, spouse, or child."

"Your parents won't request one?"

She shook her head.

"How about his mail?" I said. "There might be something in there. You know Tobin's PO box number—you could send in a change of address for him, and have the mail forwarded to you."

"You have to sign those forms," she pointed out.

I've never thought it illegal to sign someone else's name unless you had intent to defraud. But it was a gray area, leaning, I supposed, toward black. I wasn't going to ask about searching Tobin's e-mail account, possibly because I'd gotten myself into so much trouble last summer downloading someone else's e-mails. Best not to go there.

"I don't even know if it's legal to open his mail unless I have legal access to it," Win said, her voice rising. "I don't know what I'm going to do. My lawyer's looking into it, and he may refer me to someone local."

There wasn't much I could say. Life would be easier if everyone could leave directions in plain view about what to do when they died. But no one does that, unless they know they're going to die.

She almost visibly pulled herself together, and went on. "But you came out to interview me. This next article starts with Trey's death, right?"

I nodded.

She took me through it all, a span of a few days during a mellow summer week: her brothers out that afternoon and evening, her out with her friends, the last time she would have a mindless good time for quite a while. The realization the next morning that the boys hadn't come home, calls to their friends and hospitals. The boat found, floating but damaged, not far from shore. The Coast Guard finding Tobin, clinging to a chunk of wood he'd happened across in the water. No sign of Trey; no sign of his body until the next day. And then the funeral, which had been a blur for her.

Afterward, she said, their father started working longer hours, and her mother started drinking more. "All very structured and civilized, of course, but she mostly was in a daze."

"And then Tobin left."

"Tobin left right after the funeral," she said. "He packed a couple of bags and came and told me just before he went—he said he didn't belong there, and never had. He wouldn't tell me where he was going, and maybe he didn't even know. But then he'd call me every few weeks, and later he started sending postcards. Until I finished college and moved away, he never told me just where he was, only where he'd been. I think he was afraid my parents would try to make me tell them where he was—that it would be easier on me if I didn't know."

I made myself ask: "On the boat . . . there were life jackets?"

Win blinked. "I'm sure there were. I remember seeing them. But the boys never wore them. We could all swim like fish. Nanny taught us when we were just toddlers."

"One guy I interviewed said there was only one life jacket . . . that Trey didn't have one."

She frowned. "I don't know. Maybe they only had time to grab the one—or maybe Trey's came off, after."

"But Tobin never told you?"

"No," she said. "He never said anything."

"Did he ever say anything about the accident itself, how it happened, who was piloting the boat?"

"He didn't want to talk about it. I didn't want to think about it. I guess it didn't matter. They were both experienced and they were both always careful on the boat. They worked well together."

"Would he have told your parents anything?"

She shook her head. "Oh, no, definitely not." She sat for a

long moment. When she spoke her voice was firm. "I think Tobin knew our father would have rather Trey survived than him. I think he knew our father blamed him for the accident, blamed him for Trey's death. Tobin wouldn't talk about it, would never say what happened."

We sat in silence for a minute. "What about you—how did you deal with it?" I asked.

"I stayed home the rest of the summer, but I stayed as busy as I could. I got an internship the next summer, and a job right after, and I moved away. I send cards; I meet my mother for lunch sometimes. I don't go there."

She straightened, I think without realizing she was doing it. "I had my work. I had my friends, and I had my grandfather. I had Tobin, at a distance. We were getting closer since he moved here—he'd come and visit for a week or two at a time, go with me to see our grandfather in the nursing home."

"Your grandfather started the insurance company, the one your dad runs, right?"

She nodded. "My father had planned on Trey coming into the business, passing it on to him."

"Not Tobin?"

She shook her head. "Tobin was never interested in working with our father, nor the other way around. Trey was the golden boy, the one who could do no wrong. Tobin heard a lot of 'Why can't you be more like your brother?' But he wasn't bad, just mischievous, and he had no interest in making all A's when he could make B's and C's without lifting a finger."

She got up and refilled our coffee cups. "The last time I saw Tobin was at our grandfather's funeral," she said as she sat down. "And when I didn't hear from him the last few months, I just thought he'd moved on, that he was traveling, and then he'd get in touch when he got wherever he was going."

And now Tobin is gone for good. Neither of us said it, but it seemed that we had, that the walls of the room whispered it, that it echoed around the cabin.

I wasn't close to my parents or sisters, but I had my brother—

miles away, but he was there. I had Baker and my friend Kate, and Philippe and Paul, even Jameson. And I had Tiger.

"Maybe it's time to get a dog," I said. Only after the words came out did I realize how abrupt and trivial it might sound.

But Win knew what I meant. "Maybe it is," she said.

CHAPTER 31

Back at home, Jessamyn's jacket was gone from the pegs in the hallway, which meant she was out. I could postpone talking to her a while longer. I climbed my stairs and sat at my computer.

It was clear by now that Moreno, the Oregon policeman, wasn't going to call me back; I had to drop it or try another tack. On his police department's website I found an e-mail address and sent a note, saying I was writing an article on Tobin Winslow's death that would mention the accident with his brother, and had a few questions. I included a link to my first article.

I'd never felt this edgy about something I was working on. This felt like being caught up in a tidal wave pushing me in directions I hadn't anticipated. Now there was the *tick tick tick* of another deadline approaching, of a story that would be harder to write than the first one, me not knowing if I could pull this off. And not knowing if it all hadn't been a mistake, if I had stirred up things that had better been left unstirred.

Restless, I opened the file with the photos from the day Tobin's body was found, and clicked through them. I looked at the people in the scene: Matt Boudoin, the ice cutters, the policemen, the crowd on shore, the EMTs. Their faces were blank, somber, like at a funeral. This was a small town, and the body was almost certainly going to be someone they knew. One of the faces, and looked vaguely familiar. I zoomed in on him. His face was grim, his expression implacable. I tried to place him but couldn't.

I thought about the fellow Armand, who had told me he still saw Tobin's face whenever he shut his eyes. I should include his and others' reactions in the last article: how Tobin's life and death had affected the people who had known him, who had been there when his body was found, who lived here and would be kayaking or swimming in that lake come summer.

Suddenly I needed to be around someone who hadn't recently had someone close to them die. I called Baker, who said without hesitation that lunch sounded like a great idea and no, I didn't need to bring anything.

"Come on over," she said. "I'll make tuna sandwiches."

She would know many of the people in those photos, so I grabbed my laptop and whistled for Tiger.

Baker had the sandwiches waiting, with fresh-brewed iced tea for me and a Coke for her. Yes, I drink iced tea even in the winter.

I bit into my sandwich.

"People really liked the article," Baker said. "It wasn't what they expected. But they liked it."

I nodded, and picked up the second half of my sandwich. I was hungrier than I'd realized.

"You're working on the next article now?" she asked.

"Yeah. It's going to start with Tobin's brother's death—he died when Tobin was nineteen." I was avoiding saying *drowned*; part of me didn't want to acknowledge it, that two brothers in this family had drowned, in different seasons, different states, half a dozen years apart.

"So it'll be hard to do."

"Yep," I said.

"How's Win holding up?"

"Pretty well. She's estranged from her parents, but she does talk to her mother some."

"And Jessamyn's doing all right?"

"Yeah, she seems to be." I wished I could tell her about Jessamyn, about what I'd found out, but I couldn't.

I asked Baker if she could help ID some people in my photos, and she agreed. I opened my laptop and pulled up a photo of men working on the ice. I jotted down names as she recited them. Then I opened the clearest of the shots that showed people on the shore, standing shoulder to shoulder, and zoomed in on their faces. As she told me names, I wrote them down, left to right. I pointed out the fellow I thought I'd recognized.

"That's the oldest of the Phillips brothers," Baker said. "I don't remember his real name—they call him Crick. There's three boys, I think, and a sister—their parents died in a car crash, and he's raising them."

"Yikes," I said. "That's tough."

"Better now; they're all out of high school and working, except the girl."

We went through the rest of the lineup, and she told me who she thought might be willing to talk.

Baker knew my tendency to work too hard. As I left she thanked me for coming over. She knew that part of the reason for this visit was me trying not to be obsessed with what I was writing about, me trying to think of the other people in my life. The ones who were alive.

On impulse I stopped by the newspaper office on my way out of town and stuck my head in the newsroom. George was talking to a reporter but waved me over.

"We sold a lot of papers with your article," he said. "I guessed we would, and we'd printed extra. You got some, right? I sent a batch over to the *News* for you."

I nodded. It felt good that he'd had that kind of faith in the article—or faith that the story itself would pull in readers. Or both.

"Hey, come back in my office for a minute," he said.

I followed him out of the newsroom. He rummaged on his desk and tossed a handful of papers and envelopes toward me.

"Take them," he said. "They're either for you or about you."

I tucked them under my arm and turned to leave.

"Troy, you're doing good," he said. "This is a good series, and it will help provide closure for some people."

I wasn't sure, at this point, and I didn't think there'd be much peace for anyone until we knew how or why Tobin had died. But there was no turning back. In my car in the parking lot I looked at the things he'd handed me, a collection of e-mails from editors of other papers and a magazine. I read the one from the magazine editor: *If the rest of the articles in this series are this strong, we may be interested in buying them and running it as one long piece.*

Then I opened the last item, a card, addressed to me. From the Winslows' nanny.

Dear Troy: You wrote a moving and lovely story—I cried when I read it. Thank you for capturing Tobin, and for caring about him. Please give my best regards to his sister.

A wave of emotions ran over me. This was more than I could handle: lunch with a good friend, accolades from unknown editors, a heartfelt note from the nanny. Maybe I hadn't cared for adult Tobin, but it turned out I'd cared for the younger one, one I'd never known.

This was partly why I kept people at a distance. I could handle the pain life threw at you—that I had experience with. It was this, the good stuff, the praise, the warm fuzzy stuff that I had a hard time coping with. Sometimes I felt like Spock, from *Star Trek*, puzzled by human emotions. Or like the robot on the 1960s TV show *Lost in Space* that beeped out, "It does not compute." Right now, none of this was computing.

Box away these feelings, I thought. It was the only way I knew to keep going. I sat there a moment longer before pulling out of the parking lot, blinking hard so I didn't cry.

CHAPTER 32

All this had taken my mind off Jessamyn, had let me mentally file away what I had found on the Internet, had allowed me to try to pretend that the person in that high school photo wasn't her. But when I got home, I couldn't pretend any longer. Her jacket was there, hanging on its peg. I climbed the stairs to her room and tapped on the door.

"Can I come in?" I asked. When she answered I went in and closed the door behind me. "I have to talk to you about something." My throat was tight.

She looked at me, a flicker of concern on her face. "Okay," she said cautiously.

There was no chair in her room, so I knelt on my haunches, leaning back against the wall. She was sitting on her mattress on the floor. I took a deep breath and told her that I'd been researching and fact-checking for my articles, had Googled her name, and found a trail of virtual bread crumbs that led me to a story of a girl named Jessamyn Wallace in Ohio who had fractured her brother's skull with a baseball bat, who sounded a whole lot like the person we knew as Jessamyn Field.

She didn't deny it, and she didn't hesitate. "Field was my grandmother's maiden name. Wallace wasn't my real name anyway. That was the guy my mother married." Then she told me all of it. I think she'd been needing to tell it for a long time. Either no one had asked, or hadn't asked the right questions. I sank back and sat, cross-legged, on the floor as she recited it, as if she was telling someone else's story or something that had happened in another lifetime. In a way, I guess, she was.

Her father had left when she was very small, and soon after her mother had moved in with a man. But when Jessamyn was seven, his ten-year-old son had come to live with them. I think I could have told the essence of the rest of it, but she needed to do it. At first, things seemed good, and she loved having a big brother. But when she was nearly ten, it started, little by little. She was afraid to tell her mother what was happening, and, especially at first, she thought she was partly to blame and hesitated to implicate the boy she thought of as her brother. But when she was twelve, bolstered by school announcements and placards that urged her to tell an adult if someone was doing something she didn't like, she did. At least, she tried. Her mother didn't believe her, or pretended not to, and told her to never dare say such things again. Jessamyn went to the hardware store and pocketed two little sliding locks and installed one of them on her bedroom door and the other on the inside of her closet door, for a bolt hole, a line of last defense. And when she was alone in the house with the boy she used to call her brother, she went into her bolt hole and slid the lock shut, dragging a blanket and pillow in with her to sleep. And no one ever asked why she'd installed the lock on her bedroom door, and no one seemed to notice there was a lock on the inside of her closet. One evening when their parents were out the boy caught her unawares because she hadn't noticed he'd loosened the screws in the lock on her door, but the scant moments it took for it to pop loose from the wall were enough for her to yank out the baseball bat she'd stashed under her bed and swing it at his head as hard as she could.

"I thought I'd killed him at first," she said. "And I didn't care. I wanted him to be dead. I wanted him dead for ever touching me, for making me afraid all the time, for making me sorry I ever trusted him." She considered trying to drag him to his room, leaving him on the floor as if he'd fallen out of bed, and pretending she had no idea what happened. But her mother and his father arrived home before she'd had time to decide if that would work.

She knew no one would believe her; her mother hadn't, and that was before she popped the beloved son of the house in the head with a baseball bat. She was the one with poor grades and behavior problems; he was the popular kid on the football team. So she shifted her story before she even spoke. She'd had a bad dream, she told them, letting herself cry, and her brother must have come in her room because she screamed and she had woken and panicked and swung the bat at him, thinking he was part of her nightmare. Everyone swallowed the tale, because they wanted to, and later the policeman at the hospital told her, "Young lady, if you're going to have bad dreams, don't keep a bat in your room." She smiled sweetly at him, thinking she'd like to take a bat upside his head because he wasn't smart enough to consider there could be another reason a young girl might poleax her older stepbrother in her bedroom when neither parent was home. And a few nights later, after dinner with the kid she'd called her brother whose skull now had a hairline fracture, and his father and her mother who'd allowed it all to happen, she'd smiled at all of them, and late that night she filled her backpack and her duffel bag, took the stash of money she'd saved and some food from the fridge, rumpled her bed as if she'd slept in it, and left a note that her father had asked her to come live with him. She'd slipped out, hiked across town to the local Greyhound station, and got on the first bus that went anywhere. She hadn't yet turned fifteen.

She found a waitressing job in the first town she thought was far enough away, spent a week of nights hiding out in the public library after it closed until she had enough cash to rent a room. She got a fake ID in a new name, and moved on every year or so, and didn't relax until the day she turned eighteen.

"That's what Tobin did too," she told me, her face brightening.

"When he left home, he took the first Greyhound bus that went cross-country."

Maybe I was being gullible, but I believed every word of it. It fit. It fit everything: how Jessamyn wouldn't talk about her family. How she was with men, how she went from job to job. How she kept everyone at a distance.

"Did you try to find your father?" I asked.

She shook her head. "If he'd wanted me, he'd have gotten in touch with me long before then. But it was a good story. Even if they bothered to look for him it would take a while, and it would give me time to get away. And time to get old enough that they couldn't make me go back."

"You changed your last name."

"I liked Field—it was my dad's mom's last name before she got married. But I didn't want to lose Jessamyn, although I probably should have. My mother told me she named me after an author."

I gave a short laugh, and she gave me an odd look.

"It's just that I'm named after a character in a book, and so is my brother," I told her. "But not after the author. Which is good, because her name was Ngaio. A New Zealand name: *NY-oh*."

She nodded.

We sat there for a few minutes, me on the floor, her on the edge of her bed. I didn't tell her I was sorry for what happened to her. She didn't want or need pity. What she needed was to know that I could know her story and not treat her any differently.

"Jessamyn, I'll have to tell George that you use a different last name, and some of why," I said.

She shrugged. "I don't care anymore."

"It's just . . ." I started. "Jessamyn, do the state police know any of this?"

"I don't know. I mean, I didn't tell them. They didn't ask if I ever had a different name."

"That's why you were so nervous about talking to them."

She nodded.

"But you did it anyway."

"I had to." Her voice dropped, and she nearly whispered the

rest. "Because I didn't believe in him, Troy. I thought Tobin had left me, and he didn't. So I couldn't run away, even if it meant the other stuff came out."

I felt a sense of pain, so deep it made my throat seize. I was awed by her courage, humbled by what she'd endured, and I wished I could tell her this. I was glad I'd never let myself believe she'd been involved in Tobin's death, glad I hadn't paid attention to my brother's suspicions. We sat there a while, and then I wedged myself up. I was stiff from sitting on the floor.

"You aren't going to tell, are you," Jessamyn said. It wasn't a question. Maybe she was manipulating me, but at the moment I didn't care.

I shook my head. I wasn't sure when I'd made my decision, but I'd made it. "It has nothing to do with my story. And the police could find out. I did. You may want to tell them you used to have another name, because if they find out on their own, it wouldn't look good." She might do it, I knew, blithely call the state police and announce that she used to have a different last name because she'd run away from an abusive home a decade ago. Or she might decide to ignore it all.

I had one more thing I needed to ask. "Jessamyn, did Tobin ever shove or hit you?"

She looked at me, almost in disbelief. "You think I'd get involved with someone who would hurt me? After what I grew up with?"

"But that last week Tobin was here, the week before he disappeared. You had a split lip, Jessamyn. You were clearly hurting."

She stared at me a moment, and then she flushed.

"I got drunk that night," she said. "We were at a party in Paul Smiths and the bathroom was at the bottom of narrow stairs. I tripped and fell, twisting my knee and smacking my face against the door. Tobin got mad at me because I'd drunk too much and hurt myself. But no, he never hurt me." Her voice dropped lower, almost a whisper. "He always treated me like a lady, like I could break. Like I was special. It was one of the things I loved about him."

If she was acting, this was an Academy Award performance. I didn't think she was. "I'm sorry I had to ask," I said.

"I know you had to. The articles."

I nodded and moved toward the door.

"Troy," she said. "I'm glad you're writing these articles. I really am."

But I wasn't sure I was glad. I seemed to have a knack for finding out things, but I didn't have a clue about to handle the emotional fallout.

CHAPTER 33

When you don't know what to do, just get busy. Not the best solution, maybe, but it takes your mind off things.

I called George and told him briefly about Jessamyn changing her last name, and why. He asked a few questions, and I answered, and that was that. Then I laid out the material Win had given me. I printed a map and marked the towns where Tobin had lived, and found contact information for some of the people he'd worked for. On Google Maps I looked down on the places he had lived, the apartments and rented rooms and long-stay motels. I could envision Tobin walking down the street, running errands, on his way to his job of the moment. It was fascinating in a ghostly way— stalking someone's past life, piecing it together, virtually visiting towns I'd never seen.

Then I clicked over to my first article online and read through it again to get a feel for how it had flowed. I noticed comments had been left, and clicked to read them.

Five minutes later I pushed back from my desk. I wished I hadn't seen the comments. I wished the newspaper didn't accept anonymous comments, or at least monitored them. Some were fine. But others weren't. Two came close to saying that Tobin was a stupid drunk who got what he deserved, and one castigated me for writing the piece. Another one said *Love and miss you forever,* which made me uneasy. Neither Win nor Jessamyn seemed the type to leave love notes as an epitaph on a news story.

I printed out the page of comments and took a screen shot. Then I copied the more offensive ones in an e-mail to George, saying, "Possibly time to consider some comment screening?"

And then the phone rang, with an area code I didn't recognize.

"This is Victor Moreno," a man said. When I didn't respond, he said it again. "Victor Moreno, with the police department in Clatskanie, Oregon. You e-mailed me."

I'd been leaving him messages for so long that when I actually heard his voice, it rattled me. "Oh, yes, I did," I stammered.

"And why is it you want to talk to me?" His clipped tone sent me into flustered mode.

"I just—I'm doing this series of articles on Tobin, the brother who died here, and the next one starts with, well, the death of his brother, the boat incident, and someone told me to talk to you."

"*Someone told you to talk to me.*" This was sarcasm, no doubt about it. "Did this someone have a name?"

I had to tell him I had no idea—that it was thirdhand, from a couple I'd stayed with one night near Greenwich, Connecticut.

"And what, you think that because one brother drowned there and another one did in your town, there's a connection?" The sarcasm was biting now.

"No, no," I said. "That's a coincidence, I know, unless, well, unless Tobin . . . no, I mean, I'm sure it's a coincidence." I was blowing this.

He didn't speak for a long moment. "And you got involved in this how?"

I tried to explain, about Tobin and Jessamyn and Win, but it came out more muddled than I'd have liked. He interrupted me.

"The sister will verify this?"

"Sure," I said. "But she's not at home; she's up here now."

"Give me the contact info for your editor at the paper."

I rattled off George's name and number, and Win's as well.

"I'll get back to you," he said abruptly.

More than a little shaken, I went downstairs.

Jessamyn was making a sandwich in the kitchen, and looked up. "What's up?" she asked.

My face must have been showing how I felt. I tried to readjust it. "Ah, just writing this stuff, and researching it. It's tough."

"I bet. I couldn't do it. It's like, well, Tobin's gone but not gone."

"Is it bothering you, the articles, all this stuff?" I realized I hadn't given a lot of thought to how this was affecting her.

"It's a little weird, but it feels like it needs to be done—it's sort of a way to say goodbye. Maybe it'll help Win. She seems pretty down lately."

I took some yogurt out of the fridge. "Well, it's all hard on her, plus it's frustrating trying to track down Tobin's will and stuff."

"What about his lock box? Did she look in there?" Jessamyn asked, unpeeling a banana. I don't think I'd actually ever seen her eat fruit before. Brent was being a good influence.

"A lock box? You mean one of those fireproof boxes?" If there'd been one at Tobin's cabin, it was long gone or so well hidden we hadn't seen it.

"No, like at a bank, a box where you keep things."

"Tobin had a safe deposit box at a bank?" I said slowly.

Jessamyn looked at me as if I were stupid. "Yes, that's what I said. He said he had all his important stuff locked away in a bank, once when I said something about having the key there under the flowerpot."

I looked at her. I don't know why it had never occurred to us to ask Jessamyn things like this. Maybe we'd assumed that Tobin wouldn't have shared these things; maybe we'd just been idiots. "Do you know what bank?"

She shook her head. "I don't think he had a checking account, because I went with him once to the post office to buy a money order for something."

But when I called Win, she wasn't as elated as I'd expected. "I don't think that would help," she said. "Even if we locate the box, without a court order, I couldn't get into it without a key."

And she was right. Back to square one. Before I hung up I told her there was a chance she might hear from a policeman named Moreno. I didn't tell her any details.

What I did next was think about keys. I tried to picture Tobin's key ring, to recall if there had been a small key on it. But no one I knew carried a safe deposit box key around with them—they kept it stashed somewhere in their house. Maybe that's what someone had been looking for in Tobin's cabin, and maybe, just maybe, in the clumsiness of slashing couch cushion linings and emptying kitchen cabinets, they'd overlooked the small places a bank key might be stashed. Unless that key had been fastened to the bottom of a certain coffee maker that was now missing.

I called Win back, and told her what I'd been thinking.

"It's worth looking around the cabin," she said. "You want to come over? Maybe grab us a pizza from Mr. Mike's? I can call and order it. Bring Jessamyn if she's home, but I think she has to work."

I took Tiger for a quick walk, and when I went across the street to pick up the pizza found out Win had already paid for it. It didn't really bother me, but it wouldn't have killed me to spring for a pizza, even a supreme one.

At the cabin, Win and I ate pizza; she had a soda from her small fridge and I had water. To me beverages with taste interfere with the taste of the food—except cookies and milk, of course.

And then we set to searching.

We looked for more than an hour, in every tiny spot we thought someone might put a key: dark corners of cabinets, the toilet tank, along ledges, in the bottom of the container of coffee beans. I emptied the ice-cube trays and peered at each cube. I didn't let myself think of the irony if the key to Tobin's secrets had been frozen into a piece of ice.

Finally we sat back. It had seemed a good idea, but good ideas don't always pan out. It had started getting colder. I opened the stove door to shove a new log in and then stopped, chunk of wood in my hand.

"What's the matter, Troy?" Win asked.

I sat back on my heels and put the log down on the hearth. "Where's maybe the perfect place to hide a small piece of metal?"

She looked where I was looking, into the stove.

"No-o-o-o," she said.

"It's a little crazy. But think about it: you could stash a key under the ashes and no one would know it's there. And there's no risk of losing it if you don't let anyone else clean out your stove."

"It wouldn't melt?"

"I don't think the fire would get hot enough, and the ashes would insulate it."

Win looked at the stove and looked at me. "Well, why not?" she said.

She knelt beside me as I pushed apart the fire, setting pieces of partly burnt log on the hearth, then moving embers and ash into the metal ash bucket. When I got within half an inch or so from the bottom of the stove, I asked Win if she could find a big metal spoon or spatula, and she brought one from the kitchen. Scoop by scoop, I shook ashes into the bucket. Win pulled on her jacket; with the fire out the room was getting chillier by the minute.

I'd just about concluded this had been nothing but a messy exercise—because of course I hadn't been able to avoid spilling some ash—when something dropped into the bucket: something heavier and denser than a piece of wood. I poked through the ashes with the spoon, stirring them up enough to make me cough, and then I had it. Win reached toward it and I shook my head—it could still be hot. She went to the kitchen and filled a bowl with water, and I dropped the contents of the spoon into the bowl. The ashes sizzled slightly as they hit the water, and you could hear something clink on the bottom. I waited a moment and then reached in and pulled it out: a key, a small one. A safe deposit box key.

Win was nearly twitching with excitement.

"You did it," she said. "You found it."

"Yeah, but I almost didn't. If I hadn't been about to put wood in the stove . . ."

Now I was getting cold. Heat seeped out of these cabins pretty fast. I crumpled newspaper, put some twigs on top and lit it, then fed back in the bits of half-burnt wood and a bigger log as the fire began to catch.

Win had pulled out a phone book and was looking up banks in Lake Placid and Saranac Lake. "Tobin must have had a savings account," she said. "He got those quarterly checks from the trust fund, and he'd need somewhere to deposit or cash them."

"So you call the banks and ask if Tobin had a box there, and Bob's your uncle. If it's there, you go in and open it."

"Wouldn't I need to know the box number?"

I thought for a moment. "Not sure. But remember that card Tobin had in his wallet, the one with the lawyer's phone number on one side? The number on the other side could be his box number."

She pulled out her copy and looked at the number, and agreed it was worth a try. If she couldn't locate the box locally, she could try Keene or Tupper Lake, but it would make more sense for Tobin to have a box closer to home. Unless he hadn't wanted anyone seeing him go into the bank.

To celebrate, we finished off the pizza.

CHAPTER 34

Back home, back at my computer, I looked up information on bank safe deposit boxes, and found that getting into Tobin's box might not be as easy as we'd hoped.

I sent Philippe a note, telling him I'd been swamped with work and would call soon, and to give Paul a big hug. And an e-mail had arrived from Jameson. Which said only: *Good article.* I'd wondered why I hadn't heard from him, but I supposed he'd been busy. I e-mailed back *THANK YOU.* In all caps.

The next morning, I was at work early, sorting notes, roughing out the second article, waiting to hear from Win. Finally she called.

"I found part of an old envelope from a bank in Tobin's things and called, and that was it—it's the bank on the far end of Main Street, heading out of town," she said. "I'm going there now. It opens at nine. Should I stop and pick you up?"

"Sure," I said. "But listen, I looked this up. In New York State, unless you've been added as someone who can access a box or are a cosigner, you can't get into it. Not without a will or a court order."

Silence on the other end of the phone.

"Or," I added, "you can just show them the key and Tobin's ID and the article on his death, and hope they let it slide." This was a small town—sometimes you didn't have to jump through the hoops you did in larger places.

Win sighed. "I didn't sign the card, that I know, and I have no idea if Tobin would have listed me on the box. So we'll have to go with option C."

We didn't talk much in the car. When we entered the bank, I could tell Win was nervous only because she held herself more erectly than usual. She told the pleasant woman in the front lobby she was there to get into a safe deposit box, and showed the key. Of course the woman asked, *Is the box in your name?* And Win, with a smile that didn't even hint at how crucial this was, said, "My brother Tobin opened the box, but I believe I'm listed on it," and pulled out her driver's license and a copy of Tobin's.

The next moment would determine a lot—I knew it, and Win knew it. She kept her smile steady as the woman glanced at the driver's licenses and then looked up something on her computer. I think we were both ready for her to say, "I'm so sorry, your name doesn't appear to be on this," followed by a regretful spiel about court orders and wills and death certificates. But the woman just stood up and said, "Yes, your name is on the box. Follow me, please," and we numbly followed her, through the vault doors and into the room with the boxes. The woman unlocked the drawer the box was in, took the box out and set it on the table, and left.

Win looked at me. We were both so tense I think if someone had said boo we'd have leapt a foot into the air. She sat and pulled the box toward her, and opened it with fingers that shook a little.

I imagine odd things are found in safe deposit boxes. I thought of the shoebox I'd kept in my room as a kid and what it had held: a diary, a piece of sassafras, a photo of my dog, a smooth piece of whittled wood, a birthday card, a little man on a parachute you tossed up in the air and watch flutter to the ground. Trash to my mother; treasures to me.

This was Tobin's treasure box. Win pulled the items out, one by one. On top was an old watch on a chain. "Our grandfather's," she said. Then a passport. A lone hundred-dollar bill. A newspaper clipping of the obituary of Bertram Martin Winslow III. A photo of three well-dressed children, a carefully spaced two years apart, wide grins, a puppy at their feet. One of Trey, in a football uniform, helmet in hand. One of an elderly man with his arm around a teenage Tobin, and another of a young girl, head half turned, caught in motion, slightly blurred in an artistic way. Their grandfather, I assumed, and maybe a girlfriend from high school. And one last photo, of Win and Tobin, on a sofa, wrapping their arms around each other, grinning at the camera.

Win stopped at that one and looked at it a long time. "We took that in my place, with a timer, the last time he came to see me."

Next was a thick batch of pages, folded, in a dense envelope. Win lifted it out, opened the envelope, and pulled out the pages. Then she turned it so I could read the top: LAST WILL AND TESTAMENT OF TOBIN WALTER WINSLOW. She skimmed the pages—"It's from two years ago," she said. "Power of attorney and everything to me." She refolded it and put it back in the envelope, eyes glistening.

The last thing in the box was a sheet of paper, folded, filled with neat handwriting and numbers. Win blinked as she looked down at it, and tears ran down her cheeks. She showed me the page, a white lined piece of paper from a pad, filled with information, line after line: a credit card account number, bank account number, post office box number, Win's name, address, and phone number, e-mail account password. At the bottom it said, in scrawled handwriting: *Jess, you are a great sister and I love you always—Tobin.*

It was what you put together for someone who would find your things after you died. *Who in their twenties does this?* Someone whose own brother had died way too young? Or someone who may be considering suicide?

She sat there a moment, then brushed tears from her face. At a glance the box looked empty, but I could see something glinting in the corner. Win reached in and pulled out a key, one with a distinctive shape.

"A post office box key," I said, recognizing it. "They give you two here when you open a box."

Win nodded. She put the passport and obituary and watch back in the box, slid everything else into her bag, closed the box, and stood. After the bank woman came in and locked the box back in its compartment, I followed Win out.

In the sunshine we blinked at the brightness. Win looked toward the coffee shop down the street, and I nodded. Inside, we ordered giant mugs of steaming coffee.

"First things first," she said as we sipped our coffees. "I want to copy all of these—on your scanner if that's all right. Then I'll request the death certificates and take the will to the lawyer in town that my lawyer recommended. Once the body is released I can plan everything. We'll have a service here, after all this is over, not at a church but somewhere informal, with all his friends."

It was clear she was planning this all out as she spoke. I figured if she let herself feel all she was feeling right now, she'd crumple into a small ball. Maybe I wasn't the only one who had trouble processing feelings. Or maybe Win just preferred to fall apart in private.

"I guess you should let the police know about the will," I said. She nodded.

We headed to the post office, and I watched her insert the key into the mailbox that had been Tobin's. It was crammed so full it didn't open at first. She tried again and forced it open, and pulled out everything. I saw one of the yellow cards that tells you there's something that won't fit in your box. When she took it to the counter, the woman handed her a neat stack of mail, tidily rubber-banded. Win put it in her bag without looking.

At the house I ran the legal papers through my scanner for Win, printing copies and saving digital ones as well.

"I'll go call the state police and my lawyer to let them know about the will, and do what needs doing to get a death certificate," she said. "Then I'll sort through the mail and everything this afternoon."

The house was quiet after she left. And then the phone rang, and it was the policeman, Moreno, from Oregon.

CHAPTER 35

"Are you taping this?" he asked.

"No," I said. "Did you want me to?"

"Absolutely not. And this is off the record."

"Okay." I probably sounded as dubious as I felt.

"Write this down: Orville Peterson. He lives in Rye, New York, last I heard. He says he saw the Winslow boat go out that night with three people in it."

"*Three* people," I repeated.

"Three men, according to him."

"But . . ."

"He's an old man; he's eccentric, and he likes a scotch or two every evening. He lived in a boathouse down the beach from the Winslows' summer place—it likely wasn't legal, but the owners were distant relations and let him stay there. No one took him seriously."

"But you believed him."

Silence for a long moment. "Yes, I did. He's eccentric and old, but he's not stupid and he's not senile. But the higher-ups didn't, and the parents didn't. And no one wanted the surviving son grilled. He was too traumatized by the accident, and *of course* there were only two people in the boat. So that was the end of it."

"Did . . . did anyone go missing that night?"

He gave a bark of a laugh. "I like how your mind works, Miss Chance. No, no one was reported missing from the area that evening. That's all I can give you. Find Orville, if he's still alive; talk to him. And find anyone Tobin might have talked to about the accident. And you didn't hear this from me."

"You can't tell me anything else?"

He laughed again. It was a harsh laugh, not pleasant. "What?" he said. "I didn't tell you anything."

"Right," I said. "Of course not."

He hung up. I sat there a while. And then I set to tracking down an old man named Orville Peterson, who may or may not have seen the Winslow boat go out with three people on board a half dozen years ago.

It took some focused computer research and a series of phone calls to find him. He'd moved to a guesthouse of a great-nephew, someone clearly fond of his elderly relative, near the beach. I found the great-nephew at his office, a fellow named Ian, who was ready, willing, and able to talk.

"He can't really live alone, and he wants to be near the water, he has to have his long walks on the beach morning and night. So he's in our little guesthouse; it used to be a playhouse for the kids," he told me. "We take dinner over to him and have someone come in to keep the place up, but he likes feeling he's on his own."

"Could I call him? Do you think he'd talk to me about this?"

I could almost hear the man shaking his head. "He doesn't have a phone. I could get him over to my house, but he hates talking on the phone. You'd be better off trying in person, if you really need to talk to him."

I thanked him, and hung up and called George.

"You think you need to go?" he asked.

"Yes," I said. I didn't try to explain, didn't say that this might be chasing a chimera, but I felt I had to do it.

"All right," he said. "We'll cover your gas again, and a cheap motel. Can you get down there now?"

"Yep," I said.

I called the great-nephew back and got directions. I texted Win to ask her if she could pick up Tiger or if I could drop her off. She answered she'd get Tiger within the hour. I looked up the nearest Motel 6 to where I was going, packed a small bag, left a note on the fridge, and off I went.

I found the man the next morning, just where Great-nephew Ian had told me he would be, walking the shoreline near the guest-house. He peered at me suspiciously, but he'd been told to expect me, and I'd brought the current *U.S. News & World Report* and a bag of crullers his nephew said he would like. He tucked the magazine under his arm and opened the bag.

"Mmm," he said. "Ian just wants me to eat healthy stuff, but sometimes a man needs a good cruller, you know."

I nodded, not telling him that it was Ian who'd suggested I bring them.

"You want to talk about the accident, the Winslow boat accident," he said.

"Yes," I said. "What can you tell me?"

He took me through it: him out walking on the beach that day, toward the private dock where the Winslows kept their boat, seeing the boat, seeing two people board, and as he neared, seeing a third get on, the one he thought must have been the younger son, one with long and floppy dark hair, and watching the boat leave the dock.

"Don't know why they wear their hair like that," he said. "Seems it would make it hard to see." We walked on another minute before he spoke again. "Wasn't a great day for it—looked like it was going to get choppy. But they looked like they knew what they were doing."

"You told the police you saw three people on the boat?"

He nodded, kicking at the sand and dislodging a candy-bar wrapper. He pulled a plastic bag out of his pocket and put the wrapper inside.

"Shameful how much trash people throw on the ground," he

said. "Some days I get nearly half a bag full or more, depending how far I go."

"The boat . . . the police?"

"I heard about the drowning and then saw the report in the paper, the one that said the two boys were out in the boat. I thought maybe it was just a mistake, you know papers get things wrong all the time, but that's what all the papers said. And then I thought about it some more and I called the police and told them. One young fellow came and talked to me, someone with a Mexican name, but he looked more Indian, American Indian, you know, and I told him what I saw and he thanked me, and that was that."

"You didn't hear from anyone else?"

"No." He gave me a sidelong glance. "They don't know who the third person was, so they said it was just two people, right?"

I picked up a bottle cap, and he held his bag out for it. "That's the official version, yes."

"And the other boy, the young one, he died too, you said."

"Yes."

"And he never told anyone who the third person was?" He squinted at me, his wrinkled face showing consternation.

"I don't think he did. But I'm going to ask around."

"Could be they came back after I left, let off the third person, and went back out again," he offered.

"Could be," I said.

I walked all the way down the beach with him and back—it must have been two miles, and he did indeed half fill the trash bag, which I ended up carrying to make it easier for him to drop trash in it without breaking stride. Along the way I asked him if I could take some photos and he agreed, and I snapped some of him from the back, from low, angled across the sand and slanting toward the water.

Back in the car, I called Win. No answer, so I pecked out a text message on my not-smart phone: *Can you think of anyone Tobin might have talked to about the accident?* A few minutes later she texted back: *Not unless it was our grandfather. Or his girlfriend then or his friend Brad.*

Grandfather, dead. Brad—that was the accountant, still mysteriously missing. Former girlfriend—her I could try again, but I hadn't gotten the impression there were any secrets she was going to be willing to share.

Then I looked up the nanny's phone number, and dialed it.

"I'm sorry to bother you," I said when she answered. "But I'm working on the next article on Tobin, the one that starts with the boat accident, and I'm trying to find someone Tobin may have talked to afterward. Anyone he may have trusted, or confided in."

She didn't say anything for a long moment, and I was wondering if I needed to tell her about my talk with Orville, to tell her that someone, a thirdhand someone, had suggested there was more to this than the official version. But then she cleared her throat.

"Is it important?" she asked.

"Yes, I think so," I said. My voice nearly cracked. I was nearly crying and had no idea why. There was something here I was close to, something I had very nearly missed, would have missed but for that phone call from the Couchsurfing couple.

"Talk to David Zimmer," she said. "He knew both boys." She spelled the name for me and told me the name of the company she thought he worked at. I didn't ask more.

I drove to a Panera's, which I knew had wi-fi, bought a soup and a half sandwich, and pulled out my laptop and logged on. And I tracked down David Zimmer, at the company the nanny had mentioned, and called him at work. I fumbled through the mail system, and after a few rings his voice mail told me he was out of the office for the day. I spoke slowly, choosing my words carefully, because I didn't know if this man knew that Tobin was dead. I told his voice mail who I was, that I knew Tobin, that I worked for a small paper in the Adirondacks, that I was writing an article about Tobin and wondered if I could interview him. I left my e-mail address and my phone numbers, and clicked off. Then I ate my soup and my sandwich, and sent a congenial e-mail to Tobin's college girlfriend, on the off chance he had talked to her about the boat accident that had left his brother dead.

And then I drove home, my brain churning hard.

CHAPTER 36

I got a return e-mail from Tobin's old girlfriend, who knew nothing. I left Zimmer a second message, and a third, and a fourth, and began to wonder if I wasn't going to get anywhere and if I should drop it. I reminded myself I wasn't investigating a drowning from years ago—but I *was* writing about Tobin's life, and that did include his brother's death.

Win called late that afternoon to tell me she'd ordered the temporary death certificates and started going through her brother's mail. Among them, she said, were two letters from her, and on this her voice broke.

"I'm sorry he didn't get them, Win."

She changed the subject. "How is it going? The article."

"Okay," I said. I didn't tell her about a mysterious policeman and an old man I'd walked the beach with, and someone named David Zimmer I couldn't get to call me back. I needed to keep journalistic separation where I could, and the fact was I never liked talking about things I was working on.

I took Tiger out for a brief walk. When I got back, there were no messages, but I checked incoming calls. I had missed one call—from the number I had for David Zimmer

I called back. "Troy Chance calling for David Zimmer," I said, when a man answered. A pause. I added, "From Lake Placid. I left a message before."

"You left a lot of messages." His voice was dry: neither angry nor friendly. "Just why is it you're calling me?"

"I'm writing an article on Tobin Winslow, and someone suggested I talk to you, and said you knew him and his brother, Trey."

Another pause. "And who are you writing for?"

I told him. "I'm doing a series . . ." I said, then paused. "Have you . . . I didn't know if you knew, but Tobin died here, and his body was recently found."

"Yes," he said. "I knew."

"The paper's doing a series on Tobin, including his life before he moved up here. I've talked to their sister a lot."

"Jessica Winslow?"

"Yes, Win. I mean, she goes by Win now, at least here."

"So she gave you my name."

"No, actually it was the Winslows' nanny."

"The nanny?" He seemed surprised.

"Yes, I interviewed her for the article. And when I asked if there was anyone Tobin might have talked to about the accident, she gave me your name."

"Why do you need to talk to me, me specifically? Why do you even need to discuss the accident?" he asked.

He was sounding annoyed. I sensed he was near that moment where he would hang up—that this was when I had to risk telling him more. I took a deep breath. "This next article starts with the accident, the boat wreck, when Trey died. And I've been led to believe, from someone who saw them that night, that there was someone else on board."

An intake of breath, and a pause, a long one. I could hear him breathing. Maybe it had been a mistake to tell him this.

"Send me the link to the first article, and I'll call you back," he said briefly, decisively. So I did.

Thirty minutes later my phone rang.

"That's a hell of an article, Miss Chance," David Zimmer said. His voice was different, deeper. Less terse.

"Troy. My name is Troy."

"You're in Lake Placid? Do you have a car?"

"Yes."

"There's a diner at Exit 22 from the Northway in Lake George, about eighty miles from you. Can you meet me there in two hours?"

I blinked. "Well, yes, but we could just talk on the phone."

"No, I'd rather meet." He told me what he would be driving—a two-year-old gray Saab—and I told him I had a blue Subaru wagon. We exchanged cell phone numbers. I hung up the phone and stared at it. And then went to get ready for a road trip.

Before I left, I wrote a note: *Just in case I'm going off to meet a homicidal maniac, here's who I'm going to meet—I'll be home or call before dark.* I added name, phone numbers, car make, destination, and taped it to the fridge.

That would give the roommates a laugh, but I was covering my bases. I e-mailed Jameson. And took Tiger with me. Just in case.

I was glad the roads were clear—I was jittery, not knowing what I was heading into. But Win's nanny would have, I thought, warned me if there was any reason to beware of this man. When I arrived he was already there. He stepped out of his car when I pulled up, and followed me into the restaurant. He was slight, with light brown hair, sharply dressed, but didn't carry himself with that sense of entitlement that many attractive, well-dressed people do.

"You're a good writer," he said. "You work for a very small paper."

There seemed to be an implied question in that, so I answered what he hadn't asked. "I freelance for them, and some magazines."

"You knew Tobin?"

"Yes, but not well. He dated one of my roommates, and I met his sister when she came up recently. She's staying in Lake Placid a while."

We nodded yes to the waitress when she came by with a coffeepot, and waited while she filled our mugs.

"And you know the Winslows' nanny?" he asked.

Just to interview her, I told him, but I'd liked her. Then I looked at him and asked the question I probably wouldn't have had the nerve to ask on the phone. "Were you on the boat?"

"On the boat?"

"Were you on the boat that night? Were you the third person?"

He set down his coffee cup. He laughed oddly, a laugh that was painful to hear. "Oh, no. I wasn't on the boat. We wouldn't be sitting here if I had been the third person on that boat."

"But you know about it? You were friends with Tobin and Trey?" He looked at me, full on, and I caught my breath. His face was filled with grief, deep and awful. His eyes held more hurt than I'd ever seen, like falling down an endless dark hole. He coughed, a sharp bark of a cough, the sound you make when you're choking back pain, and I realized this man was still grieving for Trey Winslow, who had died six years ago.

"I knew Tobin, but it was Tobin's brother I knew well," he said simply. He saw it dawning on me, saw in my face that I was starting to understand that the person who had died that night was more than a friend to him.

He took a sip of coffee and grimaced. "This stuff is awful. Look, my friend has a condo here he lets me use, with a machine that will make a much better brew than this. Then we can talk privately, if you're comfortable with that."

Sometimes in life you decide to take chances, and this was one of those times. I got in my car and followed him, and parked where he indicated. As I was getting out he nodded at Tiger in my back seat. "Bring your dog up if you like." So I did. I don't know if he was considering Tiger's comfort or mine.

The condo was spotless, with a bright kitchen and a long, tiled countertop with padded stools. I sat on one while he started the fancy espresso machine. It made rumbling brewing noises, and then he filled two cups, and added steamed milk from the spigot on the side. He sat down across from me and started talking.

"I didn't call him Trey," he said. "He'd been Trey all his life—what is that, really, bastardized Italian for *third*? He didn't want to be a third anything—he wanted to be himself. I called him Martin, his middle name." He sipped his coffee; I sipped mine. He was right, it was infinitely better than the stuff in the restaurant. It took him a moment to start again.

"I'd known Martin for four years, and we'd been together for two. He hadn't told his family. They had his whole life planned out, where he would go to college, when he would come into the family business, who he was going to marry, how many children he would have. And he wanted to make them happy. If he could have done it, he would have. He'd ended things with the girl, but his family acted like it was just a temporary tiff, that they'd get back together. He'd decided he couldn't go through the rest of it, he couldn't work in the family business, live in the same town, see his father every day and his mother every Sunday for dinner, living a lie, pretending the whole time. We were going to move to Colorado."

He smiled sadly. "He had just told his father he was going to leave." He sat silent for a moment, and I wondered if this was all he was going to tell me. But he went on. "They were all in the boat, you know."

I looked at him, not sure what he meant, or who.

"All three of them were in the boat: Tobin, Martin, their father."

He watched me take this in. Their father had been the third man.

I hadn't even begun working this out in my head when he started talking again. Usually it had been just Tobin and Martin on the boat, he said, sometimes a friend or two, but most often just the two brothers. It was something they loved to do together, spending hours out on the water. That day their father insisted on going—he had paid for the boat, he said, and he was going to take the wheel. He'd been drinking, and he drank more while they were out on the water. "He started driving like a madman," David said, "and they couldn't get the controls from him. And when he whipped the boat around, Tobin went over. Martin grabbed life jackets and jumped in after him."

He stopped, and sipped his coffee. He said nothing for a long, long moment.

"And then?" I prompted. He had, I thought, imagined this scene so many times that by now it was like a movie he had seen, over and over.

"And then, nothing. Martin found Tobin; they put the jackets on; they found something in the water, a log or broken mast or something, and hung on to it. And their father never came back."

I stared at him.

"He crashed the boat—they found it the next day—but somehow got himself to shore and home." David got up and refilled his coffee cup. "Did you know life jackets can go bad?" he said, conversationally. "They can. They can leak, they can get waterlogged. If you don't store them properly, the material inside can harden, and then they just don't work anymore. Who checks life jackets regularly? Almost no one."

"The life jackets were bad?" I whispered.

He turned his eyes to me, those dark, sad eyes that made me wish I were an artist so I could capture them in a painting, or that I knew the secret to making that sadness go away. "Only one."

"Martin's." I whispered the word.

"No, Tobin's, actually. It was pulling him down. Martin wrestled him out of it; took his off and made him put it on. He knew what he was doing. He was the older brother; he wanted Tobin to live. He knew they couldn't hang on to that chunk of wood all night in that cold water; he knew what would happen if no one rescued them. He chose to die so Tobin could live. That was Martin; that's what Martin would do."

We sat there a while.

"Their father—did he hit his head in the crash, pass out?"

He shrugged. "I don't know. Tobin didn't know. Maybe their father was so drunk he didn't notice the boys had gone overboard. Maybe he crashed the boat and didn't remember what happened."

"So he just went home—like nothing happened? And never said anything?"

He took a drink of coffee before speaking. "Apparently not. Everyone assumed it was just the boys on the boat as usual; people thought Tobin asking about his father was delirious rambling. He was pretty hypothermic by the time they found him, and hysterical about Martin. And once he realized his father wasn't going to admit he was on the boat, Tobin let people assume what they would."

"How . . ."

"Tobin came to see me as soon as he got out of the hospital and told me all of it, every moment he could remember. He told me he kept his hand twisted around Martin's shirt to try to help hold him up, that Martin was hanging on to that piece of wood they'd found, but Tobin kept dozing off in the night, and the last time, when he woke, his brother was gone. He told me he thought about taking off the life jacket, throwing it away, letting the water take him. But he knew that wasn't what his brother would have wanted, that it would have negated what Martin had done to save him. Tobin didn't cry when he told me, just sat and told me every detail, every single thing Martin said to him and what they said to each other, and then he hugged me. And then, the next day, he left. He got on a bus and never came back."

"I think I'm going to throw up," I whispered. David directed me to a bathroom off the kitchen, and I was sick, quickly and thoroughly, into an immaculate off-white toilet. Then I sat on the bathroom floor and I cried, for Win, for Trey-who-had-been-Martin, for Tobin. I cried for the bad thoughts I'd had about Tobin without having any idea of who he was and what he had endured, and I cried for David, who had done his mourning in private. Then I washed my face in the sink and blotted it dry on a beautiful white towel.

When I came out of the bathroom I was shaking a little. "You need to eat," David said decisively, and made me a sandwich without asking. He put it in front of me, cut neatly in half, with a glass of milk, and I ate it and I drank the milk. The sandwich was ham and cheddar on wheat, and it was very good, and the milk made my stomach feel that just maybe the food would stay there peacefully.

"So their father never told anyone he was with them, or that he crashed the boat," I said again.

"Apparently not."

"He just went home."

"Yes."

"Someone must have noticed his clothes were wet."

He shrugged. "Maybe Mrs. Winslow did. Maybe he dropped them in the laundry room and the maid took care of it. Maids don't talk about the dirty laundry they find."

"*He let people think Tobin was responsible for his brother's death!*" I was nearly screaming.

David sipped his coffee. He was calm, but he'd had six years of living with this. "I've always wondered if he managed to convince himself that he never went out on the boat, that the boys took the boat out. Just blocked it all out."

"Tobin didn't tell anyone?"

He shrugged. "Other than me? Other than asking about his father when they picked him up? I doubt it. His sister was paralyzed with grief; how could he tell her? She was closer to her father than her brothers—was Tobin going to tell her their father was a drunk, a liar, a coward, responsible for her brother's death? He couldn't do it. But he wanted me to know what Martin had done, how he had died. He knew what Martin and I meant to each other." He saw the way I was looking at him. He brushed a hand over his eyes. "You don't get over it," he said. "Some people you love while they're there, and some people you love forever, whether they're there or not. Me, I figure I was lucky to have that sort of love once."

When my cell phone rang, I jumped. I pulled it out of my pocket and glanced at the caller ID—Win.

"Tobin's sister," I told David, in a near panic. It almost seemed that if I answered my phone, Win would know where I was, know I was with this man, know what awful thing Tobin had said happened that night their brother drowned. But I felt compelled to stop it ringing, to not leave Win on the other end reaching no one, so I thumbed the Answer button, and answered as brightly and cheerfully as I could.

"Troy, Jessamyn told me about the strange note you left. Is everything all right?"

"It's fine, all good."

"You don't sound all right," she said. "What happened?"

"Win, I can't tell you over the phone, but I'm fine. I'll come out to see you tomorrow and we can talk then."

"Tell me," she said, and her voice was steel. "Tell me, or I'll call the police and tell them you need help."

I looked at David. This was not something to be said over the phone. "Win, I'm fine. Really."

The voice from the phone was loud enough that David could hear it, and to make it clear I hadn't convinced her. David nodded at me. "Tell her," he said.

I took a deep breath. "Win, this is something very difficult that I just found out. But I met a man who knew your brothers, who was close to Trey, and he says . . . he says Tobin came to him after the accident and told him it was your father who took the boat out that night, the night they went overboard."

Silence. "And he left them there?" she asked, just as I had.

I started to explain, to tell her that someone had seen the three of them, but my voice broke. David took the phone from my hand, possibly the most considerate thing anyone had done for me in a long time. He told Win who he was, and then he told her the story of that night, just as he'd told me.

When he was finished, he answered some questions, and handed the phone back to me.

"Can you use this?" Win asked. Her voice was cold and hard.

"The old man wouldn't be considered a reliable witness, Win.

And this is just one person, saying what Tobin told him, and nothing to back it up. There's no proof."

She was quiet for a moment. "Maybe someone else saw him go meet the boys, saw him in the boat alone. Or saw him come home that night."

"Win, if this comes out, your father could be held liable in your brother's death, for leaving them out there, for not reporting it."

She made a sound like a snort. "No one will charge him with anything. He knows too many people."

"Look, we can talk about it when I get home. We have to think this through. Promise me you won't call your parents, you won't talk to them, you won't tell anyone, not tonight. Not until you've thought about it and we've talked about all the ramifications."

We talked on until she promised, and she seemed to mean it. When I hung up I was drained. It must have showed.

"I don't think you should drive home tonight," David said, turning from the window. "It's snowing, and you're tired. There's an extra bedroom here; I'm leaving very early in the morning and you can just lock up behind yourself."

"But I have my dog."

He shrugged. "She won't rip up the furniture, right? She doesn't look like a furniture ripper to me." We both looked at Tiger, lying there watching us. She'd never ripped up anything, not even as a puppy.

"No, she won't, but she'll probably sleep in the bed with me."

He smiled, and I saw what an attractive man he was. "Dog hairs come off in the wash."

I called the house and got Zach. I told him I wouldn't be home until morning and asked him to toss the note from the fridge. He gave me a lot of hassle about having to convince him I hadn't been kidnapped, and I told him I'd have *him* kidnapped if he didn't do what I wanted. David pulled two of what I would best describe as designer meals out of the freezer, not like any frozen dinners I'd ever had. He asked me if I had a recorder and had me get it out and turn it on, and repeated the story he'd told me earlier, in calm and measured tones, then told me more about Tobin and about the man he called Martin. Maybe he needed to talk. Like Win, like Jessamyn. Like the old man who had seen three men go out on a boat, six years ago.

"You never told anyone," I said.

He shook his head. "It was Tobin's secret. He wanted to keep it that way."

"But now . . ."

"Now you found a witness. Now you're writing about all this. And now Tobin is gone." He smiled wryly, sadly. "Maybe this secret's been kept long enough."

Before he went off to bed he told me, "Don't ever stop writing."

I promised I wouldn't.

CHAPTER 37

I called Win on the way home and stopped at her cabin. I hated that she'd ended up hearing about her father over the phone, but probably it was better with David explaining it to her. That she had believed it instantly told me more about her father than I wanted to know. And she wanted me to run it as fact in the article.

"We can't," I told her again. "It's thirdhand; it can't be verified. The paper would be sued for every penny it has. Even if I mention it as a possible scenario, we're on thin ice." It was a horrible metaphor, and I realized it the moment the words were out of my mouth.

"But couldn't you just present it as one person's account of what Tobin said, and quote the old man? Newspapers do that all the time."

"Yes, but your father could still sue the paper and even if he didn't win, the cost of a lawsuit would ruin the paper." I think that's what's called a Pyrrhic victory—you win the battle, but your losses are so great you lose the war.

"What if we have backup, more facts? More things supporting Tobin's story. When they first rescued Tobin . . . he would have asked them where our father was, what happened to the boat."

"It would still just be hearsay. Was it someone out on a boat who found Tobin or the Coast Guard?"

"I think someone passing by reported that they thought they'd seen someone, and the Coast Guard found and rescued him. I guess they have an official record, official notes."

I started to say that she shouldn't get involved in this, but she *was* involved. This wasn't something she was going to drop.

"Would a maid remember the day Trey died?" I asked. "Would she remember finding wet clothes, that night or the next morning?"

Win's lips pursed. "She might. I remember one of the maids didn't stay on long after Tobin left. I think she was gone by the time I went back to college that fall. The other one has retired, but I can find her."

"Win, you really have to think about this—think if you want to get involved, if you want this stirred up."

She looked at me as if I'd said something really stupid. "My brother died. My other brother took the blame when our father was responsible. It's not a question of stirring it up. It's a question of how."

George needed to know about this, and it would be better told in person. I called to see if we could come in—we could. Win followed me to my house, where we dropped Tiger off, and then we drove on to Saranac Lake in my car.

"I knew there was something," Win said, as she stared out the window at the snow-covered landscape. "Tobin wouldn't tell me. He stayed for the funeral and then left and never went back."

In George's office we laid it out for him, succinctly, as if reciting a movie plot. The maids needed to be located and questioned; the Coast Guard interviewed and copies of reports obtained; more questions asked of the police—and Tobin's father interviewed, or comments from his lawyer if he wouldn't talk.

George was weighing the costs of letting Win help, but it was clear that without her we wouldn't get this done. I didn't have the resources to find two former Winslow family maids who were,

Win admitted, almost certainly illegals and not eager to talk to a reporter. And whose native language was Spanish, which I didn't speak, and Win did.

"So you think they'll talk to you?" George said to Win.

She nodded.

"Get it recorded," he said. "Be sure you have permission on the recording or video itself. If you get a written statement, have it notarized. And, Miss Winslow," he said as she started to rise. "Realize there's no going back here. You have only one set of parents."

"And I had only two brothers," she said. Which pretty much put an end to that discussion.

What have we started? But we hadn't started it, I thought as we drove back to Lake Placid. It had started half a dozen years ago, on a boat. No, it had started a lot earlier. It had started with parents who were distant and disapproving, a father who wanted to destroy a child's puppy because it chewed on something, a mother who drank so much she couldn't attend her children's events. Maybe what we were doing was finishing it.

We wouldn't tell Jessamyn about this, we decided, but I'd warn her before this article came out.

There was a message on my phone from Philippe when I got home: *Troy, call me when you get in, no matter how late.* I realized I hadn't checked messages since I'd left to go meet David the day before. I picked up the phone and called Philippe at the office.

"I'm so sorry," I said. "I went out of town unexpectedly and didn't think to check messages."

"That's okay," he said. "I was just a little worried. I haven't heard from you for days."

Had it been days? "Gosh, I'm sorry. I lost track of time. I've been working on this series like crazy. I have to turn in the next article soon, and there's some new developments."

There was a pause. I knew he wanted to ask if I'd bitten off more than I could chew. I didn't want to explain what we'd found out, didn't want to tell him about finding out Tobin's father's involvement in the first son's death, that I'd soon be writing what might be the most powerful and potentially libelous article of my career. I told him to give Paul a big hug and kiss from me, and that I'd try to stay in touch more.

And then I spent the next several hours researching, tracking down reports on the boat incident, from the police, from the Coast Guard; calling and e-mailing people. I dashed off an e-mail to Jameson, short and precise, catching him up.

There'd been no reporters at the door for quite a while, so when I heard the knock I assumed it was Zach, who kept forgetting his house key. So I opened it without looking. But it wasn't Zach.

The man on the doorstep didn't appear to be local, but neither did his clothes suggest he was an out-of-area reporter. He was tall and slight, and seemed nervous. He brightened when I opened the door, but when he looked at me more closely confusion passed over his face.

"Yes?" I said bluntly, ready to be rude if I needed to.

"Are . . . are you Jessamyn?"

"No, I'm not. What did you need?"

He pulled off his cap and a mass of black hair escaped, and I saw that his eyes were green. "Is it possible to speak to her?" he asked.

Something caught in my throat, and it took a moment to answer. I don't know how I knew it, and I don't know why I spoke before he told me his name. "You're Jessamyn's father," I said.

He nodded.

"I think you'd better wait here," I told him, and went upstairs to find Jessamyn.

PART THREE

A LOADED ICE SHEET WILL CREEP, OR DEFORM,
WITHOUT ANY ADDITIONAL LOAD.

CHAPTER 38

I tapped on Jessamyn's door. I'd made more trips over to this side of the house in the last month than I had the entire time she'd been living here. She called out for me to come in.

"Jessamyn, there's a man at the door . . ." She looked at me blankly. I tried again. "Jessamyn, your father is here."

Blank stare.

I said again: *"Your father is at the door.* Your father—your real father."

It took a moment, and then she managed to form words, moving her mouth as if her lips belonged to someone else. "It can't be."

"Maybe not, but there's a man on the front porch who looks a lot like you, who says he's your father."

She looked around the room wildly, as if looking for answers or somewhere to hide. But this room was so small it didn't even have a closet. "What do I do?"

"What do you do? We go let him in, I guess, and I don't know, make him tea, and then ask him how he found you and where he's been the last twenty years. But I don't think we should leave him standing out there."

For a minute I think she considered it, thought about asking me to tell him to go away. And maybe that would have been the smart thing to do. But then she got up, her face pale, and followed me downstairs. She stood back as I opened the door and then she stared at the man who said he was her father. He stared back at her.

"Jessamyn," he said, and he said the name like it was music, like it was a song he hadn't sung for a long time.

She let out a noise that was more of a squeak than anything, and he took a half step toward her and she took a half step toward him and then they both moved forward and he grabbed her up in his arms, lifting her off the ground like she was a little girl.

"Daddy," she said. "Daddy," and she was crying, there in the open doorway, mindless of the cold.

I stepped back, and fisted tears from my eyes, and went to the kitchen and put a kettle of water on the stove, and got out mugs and tea bags, the good kind, the fancy ones you set out when a long-lost father appears. I waited a minute more and then went back to the open door.

"Hey, you guys, come on in," I said, and they unlocked their grip and looked at me as if I were the stranger. "Come on in," I repeated. "I'm making tea." They came in then, and I shut the door behind them, closing out the cold. They followed me to the kitchen, where they sat on opposite sides of the table, staring at each other. All you could hear was the hiss of the flame on the gas stove, the creak of the kettle heating up and, faintly, the sounds of their breathing, in unison, as if to a metronome.

Seeing them together, you couldn't doubt they were father and daughter, from the shape of their faces, their coloring, even the way they moved.

"I remembered you," Jessamyn said to the man, this near-stranger who sat across from her. "I didn't think I did. I couldn't see your face in my head anymore, but I did remember you, I just didn't know it."

His face twisted. "God, Jessamyn, I've been looking for you for a long time."

"I didn't know . . . I didn't know you wanted to find me."

This was too much for me, and it was a scene I had no right to be a part of. I stood up and muttered something about taking Tiger out. I pointed to the kettle. Jessamyn nodded, and I grabbed my coat and called to my dog and went out for a long walk, long enough, I thought, for them to find out at least the basics of how they had lost each other and found each other again.

They were still sitting there when I got back. Jessamyn looked younger, brighter. She happily introduced me to her father. His name was Daniel Harris, she told me, and he'd been looking for her since her mother moved and changed their last name and cut off contact—the CliffsNotes version of the last two decades. I never would have thought I'd use the word "beam" to describe an expression on Jessamyn's face, but that's what she was doing, beaming, beaming like a kid on Christmas Day who had found an impossible gift under the tree, a dreamed-about pony.

He was good-looking and trim, looking younger than he certainly was despite the lines in his face, with black hair like Jessamyn's, his thick and unruly. His clothing looked comfortable, not new, but well made. I hoped this man was worthy of being her father. Jessamyn had been let down so many times that she'd built the framework of her life around it, and I didn't know if she could handle another letdown. Not one of this magnitude.

"He lives in Boston," she told me, as if she'd known him forever instead of mostly just the last half hour. "He's an architect."

I shook his hand, and his grip was firm. I told him I was glad to meet him.

"Jessamyn tells me you've been a good friend to her," he said.

This took me aback. Had I been a good friend? I'd given her a place to stay when she was looking for a room. I'd whisked her out of town when the newspaper article brought reporters to our door, but in a way I'd been the cause of that in the first place. And I'd discovered her unhappy past and pretty well forced her to tell me about it—probably the single best thing I'd done for her, and I'd done that by accident. I'm not sure how all that stacked up in

the giant scheme of things, if good results canceled out the dubi-
ousness of the actions that got you there.

What I had done, I supposed, was believe in her.

They had finished their tea, their empty mugs sitting before
them. I turned the kettle back on; I needed a hot drink.

"He found me just like Win did," Jessamyn said. "By asking
around town."

I was wondering how he knew to look for her here in the first
place. My face must have asked the question.

"I've always done searches for her name, and kept Google
Alerts running," Daniel said. "One with just the first name, and
one with other spellings. Then that article in the paper popped up,
the one that disappeared. The last name was close to my mother's
maiden name, so I called a PI in Plattsburgh to check it out. He
came down here but wasn't able to see her or get a photo of her,
but at least found out the right spelling of her name. Then I decided to come up. I knew if I saw her, I'd know."

I thought of that moment at the door when the eagerness on
his face had turned to confusion, when he could tell I was the
wrong woman, that I wasn't his daughter. I remembered the business cards that had been stuffed in our door. I picked up the stack
on the end of a pantry shelf, flipped through them, and showed
him the PI one.

"That's him," he said.

Plenty of parents abscond with their children, whisking them
away and starting a new life. Sometimes with good reason, sometimes not. I'd have done it myself with Paul last summer if I'd
thought he was in danger, if I thought his father wasn't to be
trusted. I wondered if Jessamyn's father had any idea what had
happened to his daughter during the lost years, knew why she'd
hit the road, where she'd been since she'd run away. I had a feeling
these two would be talking long into the night.

I caught Jessamyn's eye and inclined my head toward the
downstairs bedroom and raised an eyebrow. She made her face
into a question mark and I nodded. This was me saying, *Your fa-*

ther can stay in the downstairs room if you want and her asking,
Are you sure? and me responding, *Yep, it's fine.*

Now I was an extraneous character, someone who had wandered onstage. Time to exit. I poured the boiling water over the
tea bag in my mug and headed toward my stairs. As I went up
I heard Jessamyn say to her father, "Listen, we have an empty
room downstairs and you can stay there if you want. Troy says
it's fine."

In my room I sipped my tea and ate a granola bar I had stashed
away. I glanced over at my computer. But I didn't go look up Daniel Harris, architect, Boston. I had no doubt he was her father—
you couldn't look at him and not know he was related to her—but
I didn't want to find out anything I'd have to debate whether
to tell her. At least not now. Let her have her Christmas-pony
evening.

But I had to tell this to someone; this was too big, too emotional a turnstile to keep to myself. I turned on my computer, and
wrote Jameson:

*Turns out Tobin's father was responsible for the other son's
death and let Tobin take the blame.*

Today Jessamyn's long-lost father showed up.

One wild ride.

I tried to think how to tell Win this news. I didn't know when
she was returning from Connecticut, or how long Daniel would
be staying, and I didn't want her showing up and meeting Jessamyn's apparent Prince Charming of a father without warning, not
so soon after Win had found out what her own father had done.

I ended up texting her: *Hope all is well. Big surprise—Jessamyn's
father she hasn't seen since she was 3 is here. Seems nice.*

When Zach and Brent and Patrick arrived, from their jobs and
their ski outings, I told them Jessamyn's father was here and staying in the downstairs room. They showed mild surprise, but no
one asked questions. I imagined they were privately thinking that
female roommates were a lot of bother. Male roommates might
have buddies who crashed on the sofa or in the spare room, but

none of them had long-lost parents or sisters of boyfriends arriving to stay. At least, not so far.

Jessamyn tapped on my door and told me she and her father were going out to dinner, and asked if I wanted to come. I thanked her and said no. This was their evening. Later I heard them come back, and I could hear the buzz of their voices in the kitchen beneath me.

It gave me an odd feeling, an empty feeling. I'd never talked to my own father as much as they'd talked today. And I couldn't for the life of me imagine him searching for me for two decades, had I gone missing.

CHAPTER 39

Me being me, first thing in the morning I did check out one Daniel Harris, architect, Boston. No arrests, no criminal records, no donations to extremists, nothing dubious. And the bio and photo of him at his architectural firm matched, so he seemed to be just who he said.

I clattered down my stairs and found Jessamyn and her father in the kitchen. There were steaming cups of tea on the table and she was at the stove stirring something. I imagined Daniel had offered to take her out, but she must have wanted to make her father breakfast. For the first time ever. I wondered if I should excuse myself so she could have this event, this first, to herself.

"Hey, guys," I said, ready to wave and walk past.

"Hey, Troy," Jessamyn said from the stove. "Look, I made a lot of oatmeal here if you want some." She frowned at it. I went over and looked.

"It's sort of runny," she said under her breath.

She must have followed the instructions on the box, which call for more water than you need. "Just turn up the heat and keep stirring," I told her. "It'll cook down. You can shake in some wheat bran or something if you need to."

I went over and pulled raisins and brown sugar from my

shelf, and got milk from the fridge. Daniel smiled at me. I couldn't imagine where he'd thought he might find his daughter, if he'd ever let himself envision it—but other than finding her in a high-powered job or Phi Beta Kappa at a university somewhere, this wasn't bad. She had a job; she was living with friends. She was his daughter, and she was making him breakfast. This was, I thought, possibly the best day of his life.

"Hey, Troy, tell my dad about the pie I made in Ottawa," Jessamyn said, turning to him. "Dad, I made an apple pie from scratch, with a top and everything."

"It was good," I allowed. "Really good. We finished it that night."

Daniel smiled.

"Troy has friends in Ottawa; we went up there for a few days. It was a really cool neighborhood and her friends are great, with this really nice housekeeper, Elise, and we went downtown and saw the skaters on the canal and everything." Jessamyn went on to tell him every detail of everything we'd done in Ottawa, down to the walk around the block and the drive to Paul's school.

Finally she declared the oatmeal ready, and dished it out. Patrick came in, dressed in ski clothes, and she introduced him and pointed toward the oatmeal. Patrick said hello, thanked her, grabbed a bowl, filled it, and disappeared. He never passed up free food.

"Your roommates?" Daniel asked, and Jessamyn gave him the rundown. I wondered if she'd told him about Tobin's sister being in town; I figured she had.

For the second time since I'd known her, Jessamyn took the day off work. From the kitchen we could hear her on the phone in the hallway announcing to her boss that her father was in town and she wanted to spend time with him.

Across the kitchen table, I caught Daniel's eye.

"She's had a tough time," he said. Not a question.

I nodded. "Yeah, she has. But now she has you." The message was loud and clear: *Don't let her down.*

He nodded. I think he knew exactly what I meant. Somehow I trusted him, as I'd trusted David Zimmer. Maybe suffering brings a person's essence closer to the surface.

On impulse, I said, "You've had a tough time too. You lost your daughter, for a long time."

Something glinted in his eyes. He blinked. "Yes, I did. But I just kept looking. She had to be somewhere."

Jessamyn came back from her phone call. She wanted to take her father for a walk through town, and show him where she worked, and maybe to Pete's for lunch. Of course she wanted to show him off—half the fun of getting a Christmas pony would be showing it to people. Daniel didn't seem to mind. I figured when Jessamyn went to visit him in Boston, he'd be doing the same thing with her. The thought made something twist in my chest.

This was like a puzzle whose pieces fit together in a way they probably shouldn't have. Daniel had found his daughter from the sidebar that never should have been in the paper, which had sent us fleeing town, so the PI he sent hadn't found us—but he'd ended up here anyway.

I gave up on trying to figure out cause and effect in this. Maybe it was karma, the universe striving to right itself. Maybe life was just random and I was nuts for trying to figure out any of it.

Now I had work to do. I'd spoken to the Coast Guard and gotten the reports faxed, and had left messages at the police department. When I heard from Win what she'd found out from the maids, I'd start trying to interview her father. I spent the next few hours roughing out the new article, what I could write of it now.

As I worked I could hear normal house noises of people going out and in, and then a *rat-a-tat-tat* on my stairwell door. Only Zach did this little knock to get my attention, I think because the distinctive knock let me know it was him, erasing a little pressure and lessening the chance of his stuttering.

"Troy! Hey, Troy, come down here a minute."

Now what? I went down.

"Come outside." Zach was wearing a coat on top of his ski suit.

I rolled my eyes at Zach for being mysterious. But I pulled on my parka and my boots without lacing them, and followed him out. He walked me around to the far side of my car, and pointed. The tires on the street side were flat. Not just spongy or soft—pancake flat. Completely, impossible-to-drive-on flat.

"Cripes, one was a little low the other day, but not like this," I said. I squatted by the wheel well of one tire and then the other, but couldn't see any damage. But then Zach pointed the same moment I saw it—the little caps over the tire valves were missing.

"Someone let the air out," I said, and he nodded.

Some drunk on his way home must have decided it would be fun to give someone two flat tires. It takes only moments to unscrew that little cap and push down the spring in the middle. Way better than having two damaged tires, but still a pain. It did cross my mind to wonder if this could be connected to the break-in at Win's—but this was a prank, a petty one.

"You have a floor pump, right?" Zach asked.

I nodded.

"I have to go meet some guys at Mount Van Hoevenberg," he said, gesturing to his car, rumbling away. I waved him off and went inside and dug out my old floor pump, one with a Schrader valve that would work on a car tire.

It takes a long time to pump up a car tire by hand—it holds a lot less pressure than a bicycle tire, but a lot more volume. I wasn't trying to get them to full pressure, just enough to get up to Stewart's to use the air hose. I had the first one up to twenty pounds and had decided that would do when Jessamyn and her father returned from their jaunt through town.

"Flat tires," I said, unnecessarily. "Someone . . . let the . . . air out."

I was panting—tire pumping is intensely aerobic. I'm surprised they don't have little pumping machines in gyms. Actually I'm surprised no one has figured out how to harness all that energy being expended in gyms, on treadmills and bicycles, stair

machines and those strange elliptical contraptions, all going nowhere. You ought to be able to hook them up and use the power to
generate electricity.

Daniel took the pump from me, attached it to the second tire,
and started pumping. He was in pretty good shape. By the time he
was breathing hard, it was done.

"Thanks," I told him, and opened the car door and tossed the
pump in. "I'm going to go get more air."

At Stewart's it took only seconds to blast the tires to full pressure. Back at the house, I rummaged in my toolbox for extra valve
caps and went out and screwed them on. They kept out dust and
crud, and I suppose slowed down someone who might be inclined
to let the air out of your tires.

Now I was hungry—somehow I'd forgotten to eat lunch—and
cross.

CHAPTER 40

Win called soon after—she was nearly back to Lake Placid. She'd gotten my text about Jessamyn's father.

"Her dad showed up?" she asked. "I didn't know she kept up with her father."

"She didn't; she hasn't seen him for twenty years. Apparently after a bad divorce her mom disappeared with Jessamyn."

"Well, good, if he's a good guy, I mean."

"I think he is." I didn't want to say more, to a woman who'd pretty much just lost the father she might have thought she had.

"Listen, Troy, I got what we need."

"You talked to the maid?"

"Yes, and more. I'll tell you when I get there—I'll be there soon."

"Okay," I said. I was eager to know what she'd found out, if there was enough to go to her father with. But it could wait until she got here.

"Is Jessamyn's father staying? I'd like to meet him."

"He stayed here last night; I'd guess he's staying tonight as well. She'll definitely want you to meet him; she'd probably drag him out there to meet you if you didn't come in—she's pretty excited . . ." My voice trailed off.

Win knew what I was thinking. "Troy, it's okay. I haven't

been close to my father since Trey died. And he wasn't that great a father before that."

I was in my office when Win arrived. She looked exhausted. She opened a bag and set a stack of papers and a DVD on the corner of my desk.

"I filmed the interview with the maids, in English and in Spanish; they're on the DVD."

I picked up the papers. On top was a notarized statement, typed, in English, from the maid who had found a soggy set of Mr. Winslow's clothes in the hamper of the downstairs bathroom the day after Trey Winslow had drowned. And there was more, notarized statements from two nurses on duty in the hospital where Tobin had been.

"What's this?" I asked, surprised.

Win shrugged. "I thought it wouldn't hurt to talk to them. And the last ones are being faxed straight to the newspaper, from the lawyer's office."

"The last ones?"

"Notarized statements from my mother and father."

My jaw dropped. *"Your mother and father,"* I repeated. "Win, you didn't."

"Yes, I had to do it, Troy. I had to face them." Her voice broke. She sat on my sofa. "I went to them and I laid it all out, all the statements. At first my father denied all of it, said he'd never been out that night. And then my mother looked at him, just looked at him, and said, 'Bert, why would Gloria have said she found your wet clothes?' and he broke—not all the way, but he broke. And he said, yes, he'd taken the boat out, with the boys, but he didn't remember anything else. That's all he would admit to."

Win smiled then, a mirthless smile that was more of a grimace. "My mother said it. I didn't think she would, but she said it. She said, *'And you let Tobin take the blame for this all this time.'* And she got up and went upstairs."

I couldn't speak. I was astounded Win had done this, confronted her father. This wasn't what we'd agreed on—she'd jumped ranks, so to speak. Suddenly I remembered her saying what seemed long ago: *Maybe it's time to air the linen.* Maybe she'd suspected something all along, had a notion of her father's involvement, realized the nanny may have known something. Maybe I'd been the tool here, following the path Win had laid out, interviewing the people she'd aimed me at, using the photos and tidy timeline she provided. For a moment I felt ill, as if I'd been a dupe this whole time.

But this was her father, and they were her brothers. She was deeply fatigued; I was exhausted. I had an article to write. We could sort the personal side of this out later.

I took a deep breath. "Will your mother be all right?" I asked.

"I think so. In a way it answers a lot of questions for her, why Tobin left. She blamed Tobin too, you know, even though she never said anything, and he knew it. Trey was everyone's favorite. She'll have some guilt to deal with, and anger. A lot of anger."

She stood up. "You may want to call the paper, to see if the faxes have arrived. Once you have those, and once George has the newspaper's lawyer look them over, I imagine you'll be good to go."

I looked at her. "Win, I haven't decided yet what I'll use in the article."

She blinked in surprise and started to speak, and I held my hand up. "Just write down the maid's name and contact information for me," I said, and pushed my pad of paper toward her.

"It's all there, all in the tape, in the transcript." Her tone was taut.

"Win, please. Just write it down for me." My voice caught. Now she was starting to see that all wasn't right with me. She didn't argue. She took the pad and wrote down the information.

"I'm going to the cabin to crash," she said, suddenly toneless.

I nodded. "Eat," I said. "Eat, sleep, and a hot bath. Maybe not in that order."

She smiled wanly and left.

I sat and thought, and thought hard. I didn't know what of this I could use in the article. It had been one thing to have Win interview the maid, but interviewing her parents was something else altogether. It would be sensationalism to run an interview done by a daughter of a man admitting something like this, unless that was the focus of the article. And this was about Tobin, not about Win, not even about Trey or his death.

I called George. I told him I wasn't comfortable with using the material Win had gotten from her parents, and maybe not from the maid, either.

George listened and then said, "Okay. The stuff that was faxed here we'll turn over to the newspaper's lawyer. I'll walk it over myself. It can just sit there."

Not for the first time, I was grateful George was George. He wasn't going to push me; he would trust me to make a sound decision.

He paused a moment. "Troy, is your friend okay with this? No matter what, there's going to be a huge response when this comes out. It's going to stir up a lot."

"I think she will be," I said. "I hope she will."

I made phone calls, talking and listening and typing notes on my computer. And then I stayed up writing long into the night.

CHAPTER 41

The article opened with the two brothers in the water, the elder forcing the life jacket onto the younger. It told of the father piloting the boat, crashing, managing to swim to shore and drag himself to the house and pull off his wet clothes, of the maid who put his drenched clothes in the wash; about Tobin being found midmorning, semiconscious, and rushed to the hospital; about his brother's body being found the next day.

And that while no one ever, ever said that Tobin had been responsible for the accident, the rumor had taken on the weight of fact.

David, I said, was a friend of the brothers Tobin had confided in after the drowning; David had told me he neither wanted nor needed to have his relationship spelled out, and very much doubted that Martin would have. At my request Tobin's father's lawyer had faxed me a brief statement from Mr. Winslow, stating that he now believed he had been on the boat with his sons but he remembered nothing of the night of the accident. And that was that.

I wrote about Tobin's bus trip across America as if I'd been on that bus with the nineteen-year-old mourning his brother, hating his father, numb that his mother hadn't bothered to ask who had piloted the boat. I wrote of his years of odd jobs: the gas station, the construction work, the job on a ranch in Wyoming; a couple of DUIs, a drunk and disorderly that earned him a few nights in jail. I interspersed quotes from people he'd worked with, factoids about the towns he'd lived in, bits of the e-mails he'd sent to his sister, and scanned images of the postcards, cheerful images of places he'd been. I wrote of his exchanges with the man who owned the cabin in Lake Placid, and how Tobin made the decision to move there. *It's time to come back East and be closer to my sister and grandfather,* Tobin had written. *I've been gone long enough.*

And that's where I ended it, with that e-mail.

Writing it was the hardest thing I'd ever done.

I edited and proofed, and edited and proofed, and did it a third and a fourth time. I e-mailed it to Baker and asked her to review it, and she did, promptly. Then I sent it off to George, with JPGs of the photos. This one George would fact-check, and run by a lawyer before publishing. I'd have at least a day before it would hit the newspaper and the blowback would start.

As soon as I hit Send, I realized I was hungry, seriously hungry. I went down to raid the refrigerator for anything edible. I hadn't heard from or seen Win. I was dimly aware that Zach had taken Tiger for a walk. Or two.

As I started up my stairs, my phone rang. George.

"Good, really good, Troy. This will come out tomorrow or the next day. Listen, I'm expecting a lot of response. You may want to batten down the hatches. You and that sister of Tobin's are going to be hearing from news media all over New York and Connecticut. I've doubled the press run and expect we'll sell out."

I told him I'd contact Win. I'd warn Jessamyn as well, but I thought Win would be bearing the brunt of this one.

Win didn't answer her phone; I left a message.

I e-mailed Philippe: *Finished second article—whew. Big stuff.* He'd sent me an e-mail with a link to Snapfish photos of Paul and his puppy I'd just glanced at, so I pulled that up and spent some time going through the photos. It seemed that Paul had grown

even in the days since I'd seen him—kids changed way too fast.
I'd have to take some photos to send him, maybe the next time I
visited Baker and her kids. I wanted to call Jameson; I didn't want
to try to e-mail all this, but I was too tired.

Then I went downstairs to check that the door was locked. We'd
become lax about locking it since the media crush had died down.

CHAPTER 42

In the morning I went for a ski, and by the time I got back and showered, the article was online. I sent the link to Philippe and to Jameson and my brother, to Win and David Zimmer, to the nanny. I'd mail some actual newsprint copies as well.

I sorted my notes, listed people I needed to talk to for the last article, sent a few e-mails. Mostly, I was keeping busy until the paper would be out.

When I figured it was time, I bundled up and walked down the street to our local sister weekly, the *Lake Placid News*, and picked up the stack George had sent over for me. I glanced at the front page. There was a photo Tobin had sent his sister from Wyoming, grinning, leaning back up against a fence, a horse in the background. I turned to the article, there in the front hallway of the *News*, and without intending to, started reading. It had been painful to write and it was painful to read: two sons on a boat with their father, one coming home alive, one coming home dead. It was a different approach to a difficult subject, and I hadn't been sure I'd pulled it off until I saw it on the newsprint in front of me. I finished reading, blinked back a tear and drew a deep long, shuddering breath, and folded up the paper. The only person in the office, a woman across the room at a cluttered desk, was watching me.

"It's a great article, Troy," she said. I think she was one of the ad women—I didn't know her name. I thanked her, tucked the papers under my arm, and left.

That evening, Jessamyn's father wanted to take everyone out for dinner—he'd be heading back to Boston tomorrow—but we convinced him to order pizzas from Mr. Mike's across the street instead. With the newspaper article out today, it wouldn't be the best time to be celebrating in public, especially not with Win, who was coming to join us. She arrived just as the guys got back with the pizzas, and she was her usual gracious and charming self. Jessamyn was beaming once again, proud to show her father that the sister of her dead boyfriend was a lovely and accomplished woman.

I thought about pulling Win aside, about telling her why I couldn't use her interview with her parents. But she caught my eye across the room, and I knew I didn't need to. I understood that she'd had to confront her father—whether she'd had some suspicions of him all along didn't matter. She'd done what she had to do, and I'd done what I had to do. This might be a blip in our relationship, but only that. We'd been navigating a tricky road from the start.

This, I realized suddenly, was friendship. You didn't always agree, and you both might do things the other person wished you didn't, but it didn't mean things came to a grinding halt. It didn't mean you stopped being friends. You got over it, and you moved on. Maybe most people worked this out earlier in life, but this was a revelation for me. In my family, there had been no room for error. At least not for me.

After we ate, Patrick excused himself, but Brent and Zach hung out for a Pictionary match and then we emptied out all the ice cream in the fridge. It was after ten when I turned to Win.

"Hey, if you don't feel like driving out to the cabin, you can have my sofa for the night. I've slept on it, and it's not bad."

The light snow coming down was nothing for a Subaru. But it didn't seem like a night Win should be alone, and she agreed she didn't feel like driving.

I asked her if she had a copy of the newspaper. She shook her head, and I handed her one. I gave her a T-shirt and sweats to sleep in, and made up a bed for her on the sofa. She curled up there, unfolded the paper, and began to read. Like me, she'd seen it online earlier, and like me, I don't think the full impact hit her until she saw it on paper. I left her there, but left my door open in case she wanted to talk.

When she did speak, her voice was low. "I think they knew, Troy."

"What?" I got up and went to my doorway. She was sitting up on the sofa.

"I think the police knew. I think they knew all along that my father was the one piloting the boat," she said, her voice small.

"Maybe they did," I said.

"They didn't push it, because of who my dad was. They just let everyone think Tobin did it."

"And Tobin let them think it," I said gently. "That was his choice then. But now people know."

There wasn't much more I could say. Sometimes letting the truth out lets people heal, and sometimes it makes things worse. And you couldn't really know which, until you did it, and sometimes only later.

CHAPTER 43

The next morning, a buzzing awakened me. I thought at first it was my cell phone, but realized it was coming from my outer room, and remembered Win was out there. A moment later I heard the beep that signified a call going to voice mail, and then the faint sound of phone buttons being pushed, as I drifted back into a doze.

When I did get up, Win was already gone.

I felt like I'd been run over by a dump truck. I was exhausted, achy, mildly headachy, and ravenous.

The house was quiet, no one downstairs. I cooked oatmeal and eggs, and drank several glasses of water and then tea, hot and strong. I took a long shower and then and only then did I turn on my computer.

E-mail messages rolled onto the screen. I rubbed my eyes and started sorting them.

Some were messages forwarded from the newspaper, but some were from friends.

Baker wrote: *Looks great, Troy.* Simon wrote: *Hey, Troy, you sure you don't want to go back to writing engagements and weddings?* Alyssa sent one word: *Congrats.* David Zimmer wrote: *You did good, girl.* Nothing from Philippe. Or Jameson.

There was a collection of phone messages I hadn't listened to last night. I turned to the phone and hit the Play button.

George—sounding almost giddy.

Six from other reporters, asking about the story.

And one from Paul. *Crap*. He'd be in school and I wouldn't be able to talk to him until tonight. For now I'd send an e-mail that he'd see when he got home.

Jessamyn's father was packed up to leave. I shook his hand and told him goodbye and took Tiger for a walk so Jessamyn could say goodbye in private. It was oddly reassuring to walk the streets of this small town and nod at the people I knew.

When I got back, Jessamyn was pulling the sheets off the bed her father had used. It surprised me she'd thought of this, but this wasn't the Jessamyn I'd met last year. This was Jessamyn-with-a-father, Jessamyn no longer hiding from her past. I wasn't foolish enough to think that people reinvented themselves overnight or that she didn't have plenty left to work out. But she had a father now; she wasn't alone. Now she knew her father hadn't abandoned her, had never intended to lose her.

She was going to go visit her dad the weekend after next, she told me as she stuffed the sheets in our little washer and turned on the water, and he'd already bought her a train ticket. He'd taken her shopping that morning—he wanted to get her a better winter coat, he'd said that's what a father would do—and she'd let him. He wanted to buy her more things, she said, but she only let him get her the coat, and a sweater they'd seen in a window.

She pulled at the hem of the sweater to show it to me. It was lavender, a striking contrast with her black hair.

"It makes him happy to get things for you, Jessamyn," I said. "I mean, he hasn't been able to."

"I know, but if he gets me too much stuff, he might think that's why I like him." She scrunched up her face. "And I like him, I really do."

It wasn't every day a long-lost father appears, and I could tell she needed to talk. So I stifled that little voice in my head that was urging me to get back to work. I made tea and sat down, and Jessamyn let the story spill out. When she was young, her mother had told her that her father had left, that he had a new family, that he didn't want to have anything to do with them and didn't send any money. It was true that he hadn't sent money after the first six months, but that was because he hadn't had anywhere to send it. His ex-wife had moved, left no forwarding address, moved his daughter out of his life. One day he was a father with a child, and the next day he wasn't.

"Do you know why . . . why your mother did that?" I asked.

"I think just to be mean." She pushed her hair back from her forehead, behind her ear. "My mother held grudges. If she didn't like someone, that was it. My dad must have pissed her off somehow and that was that."

She laughed. "I bet when I left my note it scared their socks off, where I'd said I'd gotten in touch with my father. They didn't dare do a thing, because my mother would be charged with parental kidnapping, all that. That worked even better than I planned."

She stirred sugar in her tea and sipped it. "I just wish . . . I just wish I *had* found my dad then, that I had gone to look for him." Her voice broke and she put her head down on her arms, like she had the day she'd found out Tobin had died.

We sat there a bit. I thought of things I could say, to tell her that, at fourteen, after a decade of being told her father didn't want her, of course she wasn't going to go try to find him. At fourteen, even if she had been able to find him, she might not have been able to cope if he'd sent her back to her mother. But I didn't think it would help. She needed to grieve, for the years she'd lost and the life she might have had.

After a bit she sat up, finished her tea, went to wash her face, and then left for work. She wanted to cram in as many shifts as possible, she said, to make up for the ones she'd missed the last few days and the ones she'd miss when she went down to visit her father. She'd never been to Boston. A whole new world was about to open up for her.

CHAPTER 44

Upstairs, I went back to work. It felt like a clock was ticking, with too many unanswered questions: the truck, Marilyn, why Tobin had wandered out on the ice, if anyone else had been involved. For this article, I decided, I'd ask Win if I could use that recent photo of her with her brother, maybe even the one of him with their grandfather. I pulled up the photo of people standing at the edge of the lake, the day Tobin's body had been found, and the list of names I'd gotten from Baker. I was going out to the bars in Saranac Lake again tonight with Dean, to get some quotes for my last article, and might see some of these guys. Again I saw the fellow who looked vaguely familiar, so I pulled the photo up and zoomed in on the face. This was the man named Phillips, I remembered, the one with a funny nickname—Crick. I studied it a moment, wondering if he just had one of those faces that seem familiar, and then I had it: this was the fellow who'd stopped to help me after my car had spun out, the one who'd driven it out of the ditch for me.

I was thinking about trying again to follow up with Marilyn, to see if I could get more out of her, when the phone rang. I glanced at the caller ID, which showed an 897 prefix, Saranac Lake or nearby. I answered. It was Ray Brook—the state police investigator.

For a moment I thought maybe the tox results on Tobin had come back—but the police wouldn't be calling me to report; they'd call Win. The man was asking me a question, and it took a moment or two to mentally switch gears and hear what he was saying: *Did I have any idea who could have left the threatening note on Miss Winslow's car?*

Maybe I should have said, *What threatening note?* Because I sure didn't know what he meant. But I went for short and simple: "No."

"Have you received any threatening notes?"

"No. There were some comments online on the first article I wrote on Tobin, and probably there will be on this new one too."

A pause. I felt stupid.

"That's it?" he asked.

"Well, some hang-ups at night, but they were blocked numbers that I could set my phone system to reject."

Another pause.

"And well, the other day I had two flat tires on my car, not slashed or anything, just the air let out. But I live on Main Street, it could be anyone passing by."

Then in a too-patient tone, the one that lets you know the person thinks you're an idiot, he asked, "Do you have any idea who might be doing these things?"

I shrugged. "A friend of Tobin's. Someone who doesn't like Win being here. The reporter who got fired. I don't know."

Pause.

"What reporter?"

Oh, yikes, I didn't mean him to take me seriously. "I don't really think he had anything to do with it, I don't think he's still around—but the reporter, Dirk somebody, who did that first article, the one that was deleted. He got fired that day. He's not from here; I imagine he moved away already."

"Then why did you mention him?"

Because I'm thinking on my feet and because I always manage to say the wrong thing to the police. "Just popped in my head." No way was I going to mention that I'd thought I'd seen Tobin's truck a time or two. This man already thought I was a flake.

Some more back and forth, and I managed to get off the phone. Then I called Win.

"Miss Winslow," I said, "is there anything you neglected to tell me?"

"What?"

"I'm sorry, did I interrupt you? Just wondering if there's something you neglected to tell me—*before the police called me about it.*"

"Oh, he called you already," she said. "I'm sorry. Troy, I wasn't sure I was going to tell anyone—I found it on my car this morning, outside your house. I just crammed it in the side pocket, but then I started thinking about it. Dean stopped by to split some firewood for me and I showed it to him, and he thought I should tell the police. Just in case."

"What exactly was it?"

"It's stupid, like out of the movies, a warning note. Oh, heck, I'm coming back into town to take it to the police; I'll stop by first to show it to you."

Twenty minutes later, Win handed me a sealed clear plastic bag. On the cardboard inside were letters in black marker: WE KNOW WHAT YOU HAVE AND WE WANT IT BACK. I laughed, without meaning to. Win looked startled.

"I'm sorry," I said. "But this looks like a prank, like that story you hear about the kid who called people at random, saying, 'I know what you did,' and it turns out they all had some terrible secret they thought the caller was referring to."

"So you think it's a prank."

"I'm not saying that—it's just that this is so dramatic and so vague. Why doesn't it say 'We know you have some stolen diamonds and you'd better return them' or 'We know you have those nude photos and we want them back'?"

Now Win laughed.

"You know," I told her, "I want to call my friend. He's a policeman, and he's good at thinking these things through."

I didn't like to call Jameson at work, but he'd told me to call if anything happened, and this seemed to qualify. As soon as Win left, I picked up the phone. He answered on the second ring, and I told him about the note. His reaction was much the same as mine: someone sadly unsophisticated, or a coincidental prank.

"You've asked Tobin's friends about it?" he asked.

"Win asked Dean, who lived near Tobin. He's the one who told her she ought to tell the police."

"Is she staying alone out there?"

"Mmm, off and on. Sometimes Tiger stays out there with her."

"Don't have a good feeling about this, Troy. There are too many odd little incidents. Can you get her to stay at your house for a while?"

"I can try."

"Oh, and Troy—good article." He cleared his throat. "Just be careful."

I promised, and called Win and told her voice mail that my policeman friend suggested that she stay in town here for a few days, and that her suite downstairs was ready for her.

CHAPTER 45

Dean was coming by at six for our outing, so I went to shower and put on decent jeans. It was early, but on a weeknight people would be in the bars early. I'd talked him into letting me buy him dinner at Casa del Sol in Saranac Lake first—it wasn't expensive, and he had helped me out. And I felt slightly guilty over having had those tendrils of doubt about him.

We'd just placed our order when I felt my phone vibrate in my jeans pocket. I pulled it out—Win. I nodded at Dean in apology, mouthed "Win," and put it to my ear. I repeated my invitation to stay at the house. She didn't want to, but I got her to agree to pick up Tiger and keep her overnight. "I'll be out all evening anyway," I told her. "You'll be doing me a favor. Tiger gets lonely."

I didn't fool her, but she promised.

I clicked off. Dean had been politely pretending he didn't hear every word.

"I'm not comfortable with Win out there alone, especially after that note left on her car, and with you not there," I told him.

"But she's taking your dog."

"Yes," I said, and he nodded.

"Has anything else happened?"

"Oh, I don't know. Probably it was random, but someone let the air out of two of my tires."

He raised his eyebrows, and I explained.

"Just pushed in the valves, or pulled them out?" he asked.

"Pushed them in. Why?"

"Then it's spur of the moment, not planned. If someone planned it and was serious, they'd pull out the valve core with needle-nose pliers."

I gave him a look, and he grinned.

"Hey, I'm not saying I've ever done it, but that's what someone would do if they really wanted to mess with you."

Our food came—I do love Mexican food. We had a slight tussle over the bill when it arrived, and I compromised by letting Dean leave the tip. Men seem to like to tip, which I always find awkward. You're basically telling someone how much you approve of them by how much you leave. And I've never understood how restaurants get away with not paying staff a decent wage.

At the bar in Saranac Lake, the guys seemed pleased to see me. They'd seen my articles and liked them. This time I asked more specific questions, and asked a few of his friends if they had any idea why someone would have broken into Tobin's cabin. One admitted that Tobin might have had a little weed, but certainly not enough to tear up a cabin for.

I saw Armand, the fellow who had told me he couldn't stop seeing Tobin's face, and something in the way he greeted me told me that he wanted to talk. We found a relatively quiet corner, and it took him a couple of beers to get going. And then he told me, his voice low, that he had heard there had been a scuffle over the pool table the night Tobin disappeared—that someone thought Tobin had butted in when it wasn't his turn or had gotten mad over something, and some shoving had occurred. Nothing serious, and Tobin had bought the guy a beer, and then beaten him at pool. But Tobin may have bumped his head against the wall.

" 'May have bumped his head,' " I repeated. Chowder had told me Tobin had complained of a headache. "But you didn't see it? You don't know who it was who may have shoved him?"

He shook his head, but a moment later pulled my reporter's pad toward him and scribbled down some names. "These guys will know," he said. It looked like code, names that weren't really names, but Baker, I knew, could help me figure out who they were.

I looked at him, wondering if he knew how significant this might be. "No one told the police?"

He shook his head. This was the Adirondacker code of silence: what went down in the bar stayed in the bar. He looked at me, his eyes half-lidded from the beers he'd been downing. He must have seen the question in my face.

His voice was hoarse. "I need to stop seeing Tobin's face."

I sat with him for a while longer, not saying anything, and then I excused myself and went off to the bathroom.

So now I had something. I didn't know what, but it was something. I needed to find out who these guys were and get them to talk to me. It could be that the altercation wasn't as peaceful as it had seemed, that the man or one of his friends had followed Tobin out of the bar that night. Sure, I could turn over the info to the police, but if that state police guy came knocking on doors, no one would remember anything and no one would have seen anything.

When I came out, a man passed, someone familiar looking, and I realized he was the fellow I'd noticed in the photo, the one who had driven my car out of the ditch. He didn't recognize me at first, but then he did, and nodded at me.

But all at once, which happens in crowded places for me, it became too much: too many people, too noisy, too hot, too dark. I needed air. I made my way to the door. As I went out, pulling on my coat, a girl, bundled up, passed me on her way inside. I stood there a few minutes, gulping in cold air to clear my head, then walking around so I wouldn't get too cold.

As I turned to go back in, the girl I'd seen minutes before came out, followed by the drive-me-out-of-the-ditch guy. *Crick.* That was his name.

"Hey," I said. "Thanks for getting my car out of that ditch the other day."

"Oh, yeah, right," he said, glancing at the girl and then at me, in that uncomfortable way men sometimes have around women if they think one might get the wrong idea. When I'd been the sports editor, coaches' wives had been uneasy until they realized I was interested in the sports their husbands coached, not their husbands. I turned a smile toward the girl, and she glanced in my direction. Her face was muffled in a scarf, but even so I could tell she was striking-looking, far more than most women around here. She was, I thought, the girl I'd seen in the truck with him. He tugged her arm, and they trudged off. By now I was good and cold. I went back in and asked for some coffee for the drive home, then went to see if Dean was ready to go.

We'd driven over in my car, because Dean had said his had been temperamental lately. Which turned out to be a good thing, because when we reached my house, his car was as dead as a door-nail. The engine turned over once, with a sluggish *ker-thunk*, and then nothing.

Dean muttered a word I couldn't quite make out, and then said, "Excuse me." And opened his hood and peered in.

I figured he couldn't see a whole lot by moonlight, but I didn't feel like digging out my flashlight and standing there holding it while he investigated the innards of his car and I froze my ass off. "We could jump it, I guess," I said. "But look, it's really cold. What if I just run you home and then you can take care of it to-morrow? Probably Win could bring you into town."

He glanced at me, and for a moment I wondered if he thought this was me making a pass instead of me being tired and cold and not wanting to dig out jumper cables and go through the shenani-gans of maneuvering cars and attaching cables when it was almost certainly less than ten degrees. My eyelashes were freezing, and that's a good indicator.

"Sure," he said.

His turnoff from the highway was the same road that led to Tobin's, and he directed me to the side road to his cabin. A thin trail of smoke was coming from his chimney—he'd done a good job of banking his fire when he'd left. He'd be coming home to a warm cabin.

"Can I ask you something?" I said, turning to him. He nodded. I probably should have asked him long before, but up until now I hadn't been sure he'd give me a straight answer. "Do you have any idea if anyone might have wanted to hurt Tobin?"

His eyes widened slightly. He shook his head. "I don't think so, but look, you want to come in for a minute? I've got to go to the john."

He led the way inside and excused himself. When he came back he pulled off his hat, opened the damper on the woodstove and opened it, stuck a log in, and stirred it with a poker. Then he sat back, beside the stove, the fire making his skin seem to glow, lighting the line of his jaw. He was, I thought, better-looking than his younger brother, who had seemed to rely a lot on his ready grin and easy manner.

"I thought about it, Troy," he said. "After his body was found. Of course I did. I was probably his best friend here. I mean, maybe some guys were a little jealous of him—Tobin didn't have kids, he didn't have expenses, he didn't seem to have to work a whole lot. He, well, women liked him."

"He was good-looking," I said helpfully.

"Yeah, and he sort of had that air about him, that anytime he wanted he could pick up and leave here, move on to something better, and that really pulls in some women."

I knew what he meant. Attractive people sometimes didn't realize how much of their day-to-day life was shaped by people reacting to their looks. "Did he, er . . ."

Dean grinned. "He could have. I think pretty much any woman in the bar would have gone home with him, but as far as I saw, he never seemed interested. He was nice to them and all, but women like Marilyn weren't his type, and I think he did have a thing for Jessamyn."

He pushed the poker in the stove to adjust the logs. "But Tobin getting someone pissed off enough to knock him off? I don't think so."

"What about accidentally?"

He blinked at this. "Like he died in a fight and they dumped him? Or someone was out with him on the ice and he fell in and they left him? Didn't tell anyone? That would eat someone up, I'd think, to leave someone to die." He winced. "That's what Tobin's father did, right?"

So he'd read my last article. I nodded.

He shook his head. "I don't know anyone who would do that." His tone was decisive.

Me, I knew people who might not risk their lives, but they'd at least run for help, even if they knew it would be too late. But they'd go through the motions so they could tell themselves they did all they could. Few people are coldhearted or desperate enough to just walk away.

Dean closed the woodstove door. I realized it was time to leave—if I loitered, he truly might get the wrong idea. As he stood I said something about needing to get back home, and he walked me to the door.

It seemed stupid to shake his hand, so I made the quick decision to go for the brief hug. I did like him; he had been helpful, and he was making an effort to help out.

But in the split second before I ended the hug, I saw over his shoulder, on his countertop, a coffee maker that looked a whole lot like Tobin's.

CHAPTER 46

Maybe at another moment—not so late, not so cold, not on my way out the door—I could have said casually, *Say, Dean, that looks an awful lot like Tobin's coffee maker.* Then he could have said something like *Yes, I saw his and liked it so much I got one just like it.*

But maybe not.

As I started my car, I mentally shook myself. No one would steal a coffee maker from a dead friend's cabin a short walk away and set it out on their countertop. But then again, who could recognize it? Me, Win, and Jessamyn. Only three people he'd have to keep out of his cabin to avoid seeing it, and me he'd invited in without hesitation. But he'd had quite a few beers and maybe wasn't thinking clearly.

Sometimes I hated my logical brain.

Surely, I thought, he'd just seen Tobin's coffee maker, admired it, then gone and bought one. It likely was pricey, but you can find bargains.

But what if he did break into Tobin's cabin? What if he saw me see the coffee maker? What if? . . .

It was late. I wasn't thinking straight. Win was staying in Tobin's cabin, but I wasn't going to show up on her doorstep bab-

bling about a coffee maker. But I was uneasy. I pulled over and
texted her: *Are you awake?* The answer came quickly: *Yes.*

So I punched the button to call her and said I'd just driven
Dean home because his car broke down, but now realized I was
too tired to drive back to Placid and wondered if I could sleep
on her sofa. She might have thought I'd orchestrated this so she
wouldn't be out there alone, but wasn't going to say no. So I
drove over and carried my sleeping bag in with me, greeted my
exuberant dog, and curled up on the tiny sofa. And fell asleep
immediately.

In the morning, a coffee maker that seemed to resemble
Tobin's seemed like nothing. I'd only caught a glimpse of it, and
wasn't all that sure what Tobin's had looked like.

Win told me the police had logged her report about the note
on her car, but didn't seem all that concerned. I don't know which
one of us suggested it first—searching the cabin again. Sure, we'd
been through it once, but that was looking for something tiny, a
safe deposit box key. Maybe we'd missed something. Something
bigger.

We looked around. No attic, no heating vents. We tapped
on walls and checked under sinks and in cabinets, as if we were
Nancy Drew looking for secret cupboards. Then we did what the
first searcher must not have done—went over the floorboards on
our hands and knees.

And found what maybe in the back of my mind I remembered
from washing that floor by hand: one floorboard that was a bit
lower than the others. When you looked closely you could see it
was set with small screws, not nailed down. I got some tools from
my car and spun out the screws. They came out easily, as if they'd
been loosened not too long ago. I slid a flat screwdriver under the
edge of the board and levered it up. It was dark beneath, but by the
diode light on my keychain we could see a wad of crumpled newspaper. Win pulled it away. Underneath was a package, wrapped
in what looked like butcher paper. We looked at each other, and
she reached in and took it out, and pulled away the paper. What

was left was two packages, tightly bagged, air sucked out of them, something that had once been green and growing but was now dry and grayish and densely packed. Win opened one bag, pulled out the bag inside, poked a hole in it, and pulled out a pinch of something and smelled it. It wasn't oregano.

She sat back on her heels.

"So that's all this was," she said. "Weed. Marijuana. What a letdown—all this for a couple of bags of weed."

I looked at it. I'd seen people smoke the stuff and smelled its distinctive aroma, but I'd never seen it up close, and certainly not this quantity. It looked innocuous, a collection of dusty crushed leaves. "Is that a lot?" I asked. "I mean, is that worth a lot of money?"

"It's not an insignificant amount. Even I can tell this is more than a few thousand dollars, especially if it's high grade."

"Worth trashing a cabin for."

"I suppose. Especially if it's not your cabin."

We looked at each other again. If Tobin had been dealing dope and people knew it, surely they would have searched his cabin weeks ago, long before Win arrived on the scene.

"Do you think it was Tobin's?" I asked. "Or maybe someone left it here later, after Tobin was gone—used the cabin as a place to store it."

"I don't know," she said. "I know he smoked, but I wouldn't have thought he was selling, especially not on this scale. He would have been more likely to have given it away than to have sold it to people."

"No one I talked to seemed to think he was dealing."

"And he had the trust fund income every quarter. But really, with the break-in and the note on my car, I figured we'd find bags of money from a bank robbery or horrible blackmail videos, or worse." She let out a dry laugh.

"Now what?"

We sat and looked at it. We could call the Lake Placid police and tell them we'd found a stash of marijuana. That would be reported and talked over; Tobin's past would be rewritten as drug-dealing ne'er-do-well. Which didn't seem right, particularly since we didn't know if this was his. But at least whoever knew the weed was there would stop hassling Win.

Or Win could keep it, or give it away, but this was a lot, and I imagine being caught with it would carry more penalties than a slap on the wrist. Or we could, well, just go drop it somewhere. Before we could think about it more, Win opened the door to the woodstove, picked up the bags, and tossed them in, in one swift motion.

I watched the plastic begin to pucker and smolder, and then made a face. "Win, you shouldn't burn plastic."

She started laughing and couldn't stop. I guess she'd expected me to say, *Win, you can't burn that,* but I wasn't going to tell her what to do. It wasn't mine; this wasn't my cabin; Tobin wasn't my brother. And there didn't seem to be any happy option. I didn't want it; she didn't want it. She wasn't going to try to find out the rightful owner of a large quantity of an illegal substance. If we turned it over to the police, it would be logged in and sit around gathering dust until it got "lost" or destroyed. She was just cutting out several steps in between.

But with this much in the stove, I imagine anyone within a mile or two radius would be smelling it.

I opened the door of the woodstove and used the poker to break up the mass. The plastic bags had mostly melted, and the tightly packed marijuana was smoldering. Fire needs air, so I moved the clumps apart until they were burning merrily, and closed up the stove.

It was aromatic to say the least, in a not-unpleasant way. I pictured birds and squirrels in the tree above the cabin getting stoned from the air wafting out of the chimney. I breathed deeply. I'd never smoked the stuff, never wanted to. I don't see the sense in going out of your way to do something that's against the law, especially with a substance that you have no idea where it was grown or handled or how it will affect your body chemistry. So this was as close as I was ever going to get.

CHAPTER 47

This was when I mentioned that when I'd dropped Dean off at his cabin last night, I'd seen a coffee maker on his countertop that looked a whole lot like Tobin's.

Maybe I was under the influence of those fumes I was breathing, because this was not the best timing—Win was in no mood to sit on information like that, or to react calmly. She pulled out her cell phone and called Dean before I could protest. She spoke into her phone, and when she closed it up turned to me. "He's at Strack's; his brother gave him a ride to take his car in and they're working on it now. Do you think we can get into his place?"

I stared at her. "You want to just go in?"

"Why not?" she asked. "If it's not Tobin's coffee maker, end of story. We don't have to bother him."

I thought of the night before, seeing Dean opening his door without a key. "I don't think he locks his door."

We walked over to his cabin, me following her. My gut was churning. I kept trying to think how to talk Win out of this, but maybe this was the easiest way to resolve it. When we walked up onto the porch, it felt like a step toward something there was no turning back from. But I took that step, and I watched as Win knocked crisply on the door. No answer, and she put her hand on the knob.

Now I did speak. "Win, Win. Are you sure? You don't want to wait and ask him?" I wished I'd never seen that coffee maker; wished I'd been able to convince myself it just happened to resemble Tobin's. Like the truck I thought I'd seen.

At that moment you would have thought Win was a prosecuting attorney. She looked at me, looked through me, and then turned back to the door. She opened it and stepped inside. I followed, and stopped just inside the doorway.

Dean's cabin was much like Tobin's, not quite as tidy. But you couldn't miss seeing the coffee maker on the kitchen countertop. Win went over to it, pulled it toward her, opened it, inspected it. She set it down.

"It's Tobin's," she said definitively.

"You're sure? You only used it that once, right?"

"Absolutely. It had a scratch on the top and that little dent on that one side."

We stared at each other. "It doesn't make sense to steal a coffee maker from the next cabin," I said weakly.

"Yes, but it's Tobin's," she said, in the steely tone I'd heard from her before. She pulled her phone back out.

"Win, wait. Don't call the police. Ask Dean. Ask him where he got it. Maybe the thieves threw it out; maybe he found it."

"Troy, what, are you sweet on this guy?"

"I just think we need to give him a chance. He's really been helpful. I don't . . ." My voice trailed off.

She snapped her phone shut. "Fine, you call him and deal with this."

I didn't think this was fair, but it had been me who had mentioned the coffee maker, me who had come over there with her. By any reckoning, that made me pretty culpable. I pulled out my phone and went out on the porch. It didn't feel right calling Dean from his house. Not that his porch was much better.

"Troy," he said when he answered. "What's up?"

"Listen, do you think your car will be fixed soon?"

"Yeah, he's just finished and he's writing up the bill. Why? Do you need a ride somewhere?"

"No, I'm out . . . I came out to Win's. Listen, Dean, when I was at your place last night, I noticed . . . well, something's come up that we want to ask you about."

"What?"

I could hear voices in the background and banging sounds, presumably from the garage area. "We'd rather talk to you in person. Can we come meet you?"

"You're out at Win's, right?"

"Um, yeah," I said. I didn't tell him I was standing on his front porch.

"I'll just come there."

"No," I said rapidly. "We'll meet you at your place." And I hung up.

Win was back on the front porch by then.

"He's on his way back here," I told her.

"And you want to ask him about it when he gets here?"

"Yeah," I said. "Yeah, I do." Maybe Dean had been behind the tossing of Win's cabin, but I wasn't going to assume it because of a coffee maker on his countertop. If Dean hadn't done anything, he didn't need to get hauled into the Lake Placid police station for questioning. This town had a fast and merciless grapevine. Next thing you know, rumors would start that Dean was involved with Tobin's death.

I sat there, on the front porch, until Dean drove up. It was cold, but I didn't want to move. Win leaned up against the porch post.

Dean got out of his car and looked at us, puzzled, but didn't say anything. He went into his cabin, and gestured us to follow him in. He opened the door on his woodstove, poked it and added wood, and then turned to us, his face seeming open and guileless. And puzzled.

I gestured toward his kitchen. "Could you tell us where you got your coffee maker, Dean?"

"My coffee maker? Why?"

I started to speak, but Win interrupted.

"Where did you get the coffee maker?" she asked, abruptly.

A touch of anger flickered across his face, but it was gone in an instant. "What's all this about?" He looked from her to me and back again.

"Where did you get it?" she repeated.

He paused half a beat, and then decided to answer. "From my brother, why?"

"Eddie?" I said. Eddie, the high school quarterback, the local football star, Eddie with the easy manner and fast grin. Eddie, who should have been off playing football at least at a junior college somewhere. Eddie, who I'd seen in the Saranac Lake bars both times I'd been in them lately.

"Where did your brother get it?" That steely tone again.

The way Dean looked at Win, I don't think he was caring much for her right then, but he kept his cool. Barely, but he kept it. "*What the . . .* he got it in a garage sale, over in Saranac Lake, for my mom, but he said she didn't like it, so he gave it to me."

Win walked over to the coffee maker and turned to Dean. "This is Tobin's coffee maker."

He looked at her blankly. "What?"

"This is Tobin's, and it was taken from his cabin."

He looked at me as if to say *What the heck?* I remembered him saying that Tobin had been a private guy, that he'd never been at Tobin's cabin. I remembered I'd never told him the coffee maker had been stolen.

Win spoke again, not as harshly. "That was the one thing taken in the break-in, Dean. Tobin's coffee maker."

He shook his head, as if trying to clear cobwebs from his brain. "You're sure it's his?"

She pointed to the top. "Scratch on the top; dent on the side. It's his."

Dean looked at me. "Then I'll call Eddie and find out where

that garage sale was, where he bought it, and that'll be the person who broke in."

He pulled out his cell phone, flipped it open, and then stopped. Maybe it was the expressions on our faces—Win looking skeptical, me looking sad. Then he started working it out: Who has a garage sale in the middle of winter? Right after a break-in where this particular coffee maker was stolen? I watched his face as he argued it out with himself.

He closed his phone and put his head in his hands, and when he looked up, he looked older. "Eddie," he said, and his tone was bleak. "What has he done?"

He sat for a long minute, and then picked up his phone and called his brother.

While we waited, Win made coffee, which seemed to give her comfort. I think we were all hoping that Eddie would have some explanation we could all live with. That one of his buddies had tossed the cabin, taken the coffee maker, and given it to Eddie, not knowing his brother lived just a long stone's throw away. That Eddie saw it stashed in someone's garage and offered to buy it. Stranger things have happened.

But when Eddie showed up, it took only a moment for those hopes to dissolve. He stepped inside and took one look around, saw me and saw Win, looked confused—then saw the mugs of coffee, saw the coffee maker in the middle of the counter, and he knew. He opened his mouth, as if to say something jovial, to try to talk his way out of this, but stopped. He closed the door and leaned back against it.

"I'm sorry, Dean," he said. "But I was really desperate."

Dean's jaw worked, but he didn't say anything, and Eddie started talking.

He'd been dealing weed, just for friends, getting it from suppliers in Plattsburgh. But then he'd decided he wanted to earn more, wanted a better car, wanted to buy stuff for his girl, and he started selling more, and working with dealers from Montreal. "There's a big market here," he said. "Not just the locals and the kids working in the hotels, but the tourists—they want to kick back while they're on vacation, and they'll pay big bucks for good weed. There's a whole network set up for them, and I wanted to break into that. I took a pretty big delivery, and I got to take it with just a down payment. I didn't want to store it at my mom's house, so I asked Tobin to keep it. He'd done it for me before, just not as much, in exchange for keeping him stocked. He said he had a really safe place. But then he disappeared. I thought he'd taken it and left town, so I didn't even think about searching his place." He looked from one of us to the other. "I mean, his truck was gone, he was gone, I figured the weed was gone. I was pretty mad. The guys didn't expect payment right away, and I kept trying to pull it together, but I couldn't do it, not even close. I just kept telling them it was taking me a while to sell it. Then when Tobin was found I figured the weed could still be here; I saw his sister out that night, and I had a copy of the key, so I went in and searched. I'm sorry I left a mess, but I really needed to find it. I went out of town for a while, but now they're really putting pressure on me. These guys mean business." His voice was high pitched.

"You took Tobin's coffee maker," Win said. Her voice was ice.

He blinked. "Yeah, I thought it was cool. I thought my mom would like it."

I thought of Eddie his last year of high school: the star quarterback, good-looking and popular, cheered whenever he'd walked onto the field. Probably he'd sailed through school. Probably he'd had any girl he'd wanted. And then high school was over, and he hadn't gotten any college scholarships, couldn't afford to pay tuition somewhere and play walk-on, and had gone to work at a gas station. He'd been used to being a star, having things go his way. And then they hadn't.

Dean put his head in his hands.

"What? That's the only thing I took," Eddie protested.

"You were going to give our mother a stolen coffee maker.

From my dead friend. Whose cabin you trashed." Dean's tone was flat.

Eddie looked down at the floor. He started to speak, and Win interrupted.

"How much do you owe?"

"What?"

She repeated it, enunciating every word. "How much do you owe?"

He winced. "Four grand," he said. "I paid them a thousand. I don't know what I'm gonna do. I saved a couple of hundred more, but that's it. I was gonna use it to leave town."

Win opened her purse. Dean looked up. Maybe he thought she had a gun stashed in there and was going to pull it out and shoot his brother, and at that moment I don't know that he would have stopped her. But it was a pen she pulled out, then a checkbook. She uncapped the pen and she opened the checkbook.

"Is your name Edward or Edmund?" she asked.

"What? It's Edward."

"Your last name is Whitaker, right, W-H-I-T-A-K-E-R?"

He nodded, confused. Win wrote quickly, concisely, decisively. She tore out a check and handed it to him.

He looked at it, and looked up at her, more confused. "Four thousand dollars."

She nodded. "The product was in Tobin's possession. I burned it; it's gone. I'm responsible for its destruction, so I'm paying for it."

Eddie blinked.

"I assume you're the one who left the note on my car."

He flushed, and nodded. I wanted to ask if he was the one who had done the hang-up calls or let the air out of my tires, but I'd find out later, or I wouldn't. Right now I didn't care.

"You can cash the check anytime; I assure you it's good," she said.

"Thanks," he said, hardly believing this was happening, that she hadn't called the police, that she was bailing him out. "I'm really sorry about the mess . . ." His voice trailed off when he saw the look on her face.

Dean stood. "Eddie, get out."

"Dean, I just wanted to get ahead, to—"

"Eddie, you trashed my friend's cabin; you stole from his sister. How do you think Mom would feel if you got sent away? If you got your arm broken by some dealer you stiffed, or worse? You took that risk, just for money, just for stuff. You . . . I can't believe it." He slammed his fist on the table. "If you wanted a new car, you work for it. Or you ask me for a loan. You don't risk everything. You don't deal drugs. You don't steal." He spat out the last words and glared at his brother a long moment before turning his back, facing the wall.

Eddie stood, his face white. He was smart enough not to say anything. He left, closing the door quietly behind him.

Dean was shaking with rage. After a moment he turned and faced Win.

"I am very sorry for what my brother did," he said. "I know I can't make this right, but I can pay you back, bit by bit."

Her face was drawn, but the tension was gone. "It isn't your debt to pay, Dean, and I wouldn't accept it from you. Either your brother realizes that it is his debt, and takes care of it, or he doesn't. I'll inherit more than that from Tobin, so you can think of it as Tobin's payment, for his role in this, for storing it for Eddie in the first place."

She reached out, and it took Dean a moment to realize she was reaching to shake his hand. He shook it, and didn't speak.

Win drained the leftover coffee, unplugged the coffee maker, and picked it up. Dean knew not to offer to help.

I walked with her back to Tobin's cabin and watched her put the coffee maker in place, moving the new cheap one aside. Then I watched her fill her suitcase. She didn't tell me she didn't want to be at the cabin tonight or that she didn't want to drive. She just got into my passenger seat, and I drove to the house in Lake Placid and she went into the guest bedroom, all without speaking.

CHAPTER 48

How do you apologize to a man for having helped crush his vision of who he thought his brother was? I'd been the one who told Win about the coffee maker and I'd let her walk into Dean's cabin and pick it up. Maybe I should have asked Dean privately about it. But I'd hoped we'd find out it hadn't been Tobin's, and Win and I could laugh about my silliness, and that would have been that.

I e-mailed it all to Jameson, letting it spill out on the page. It would be easier, I thought, to be a policeman, to have a set of rules that governed what you did. Of course there were times when you made difficult decisions, walked fine lines. Jameson had walked them last summer, when he'd treated me like a suspect when I think he'd known at heart I wasn't involved. But as a policeman I imagine you get used to seeing people doing things you wouldn't have thought they would.

I sent Dean a text message: *Sorry, very sorry.* There wasn't much else to say. He didn't answer. I'd try to talk to him later. But I'd be on my own for the rest of my poking around. Dean wouldn't be escorting me to any more interviews, taking me around to bars to talk to people.

The break-in, at least, was solved. I could weave it into my article without saying who did it, but I'd more likely end up leaving it out. You're always making decisions about what fits in articles and what doesn't.

Win moved back to the cabin after just one night at the house; she was one tough woman.

I sought out several of the guys on the list Armand had given me, and after I got two of them to agree that Tobin's sister deserved to know what had happened with her brother on the last day of his life, they talked. Separately they told essentially the same story: sharp words, a shove, a stumble, Tobin banging his head against the wall. Neither of them wanted to tell me the name of the person who had done the shoving, because both insisted it had been over on the spot, that the other fellow left the bar hours after Tobin, and by then had been so drunk he could barely stand upright.

Now what? If there had been an iota of a possibility that this fellow had followed Tobin, I'd have to tell the police. But what if the shove, the bump on the head, had affected Tobin, had something to do with his late-night ramble across the lake and through the ice? Would the person who had happened to shove him in a minor scuffle over a pool table need to have that hanging over him forever? What good would that serve? Maybe this needed to be forgotten, to be filed away, another Adirondack secret.

It was too much for me at the moment. For now, I just wrote. I started to weave what I had into an article, and I worked well past noon. By then I was beyond hungry, and realized my food supplies were pretty much down to peanut butter and jelly. I ate an apple past its prime and a sandwich on bread that would have been considered stale a week ago, then headed up to Price Chopper. I did remember that Marilyn worked there, but I don't know that I expected to see her. But there she was, gathering carts to push through the slushy parking lot into the store, as if I'd planned it.

"Can I talk to you for a sec?" I asked.

She gave me a dour look but didn't say no.

"Did you expect what happened, when you sent that article around?"

I think my question surprised her. She almost looked chagrined. "No," she said. "I didn't know it would blow up like that. I was just mad, mad at Jessamyn, sort of mad at Tobin, for dying." She tugged her hat down around her ears. "Look, I knew I never would have a chance with Tobin. But I liked him. And I didn't like Jessamyn."

I hadn't expected this much frankness. So I pushed on. "Someone helped you send around that article, didn't they?"

She looked down. "Yes," she said. "A guy I knew."

I waited. She reached for another cart and shoved it into the two she had already gathered. "It was that guy, Dirk—the one who wrote the article for the paper."

The kid reporter. The one whose name I barely remembered. The one who'd started all this.

"You were friends with him?" I asked.

"I knew him from around—he knew I was pissed off about Jessamyn. So he gave me the thing, the photo of the article, and showed me how to put it in e-mails to send around."

So the kid had solicited this woman to send his scurrilous article around. I'd bet he barely knew her, but figured she was malleable enough to talk into it.

"But you don't actually know anything about how Tobin died?"

She shook her head. "No. I just heard a rumor that someone was mad at him for putting the moves on their girlfriend."

"Jessamyn?" I asked.

"No, not Jessamyn—someone else. I don't know who. And I don't even know if it was true. You know how people are."

Yes, I did. She couldn't remember where or from whom she might or might not have heard the rumor.

My brain worked this over as I headed into the store. It was possible there was no rumor, that Marilyn just wanted to give me a sop, a bit of information even if it was false. I did my shopping, put my canvas bags in the car, then started to swing into my seat.

This time when I saw the truck that looked like Tobin's, I wasn't exhausted from having worked all morning at the paper. This time, I wasn't kneeling beside my car filling a tire with air. This time, I closed my car door, turned the key in the ignition, and pulled out and followed.

To me, the back of a pickup pretty much looks like the back of a pickup, aside from color. But something made me think this truck was Tobin's—maybe the pattern of the scratches in the paint had settled in my memory, or part of the license plate numbers. And I couldn't keep letting this imagined—or not imagined— truck taunt me.

It turned down Route 73. All I could see inside it was the silhouette of a man driving. The truck passed the road to Tobin's cabin, and kept going, toward Keene Valley. I checked my gas gauge: three-quarters of a tank. I seldom let it get below half full in the winter, because you never knew when you might get stuck somewhere.

I couldn't read all of the plate through the snow and slush on it, but I could make out all but two digits, and I jotted it down on a scrap of paper. I called Win. No answer. I called the house. It rang a long time, and Brent answered.

"Does Jessamyn happen to be there?" I asked.

"No, she went up to work."

I was fast approaching an area where my cell service would likely go out. "Brent, is there any chance . . . you wouldn't happen to remember what kind of truck Tobin had, would you?"

"Sure, it was a 2005 Dodge Ram," he said, without hesitation. "Why?"

"Because, well, I'm following a truck that looks a lot like it."

Silence. "Does the plate start with FGY?" he asked.

I glanced at my slip of paper, and something inside me went cold. "Yes. Yes, it does." I didn't ask why he remembered Tobin's license plate number. I wasn't sure I wanted to know.

"Where are you?" Brent asked.

I told him: Highway 73, nearly to Keene.

"I'll call the police for you, Troy."

"Call the state police," I said, and told him who to ask for. "And if you can't get him, call the Saranac Lake police, I guess." I hung up and kept driving.

The state police in Ray Brook were miles away, but maybe there was a trooper out and about close to me. We were fast approaching the turnoff to I-87. To my relief, the truck pulled into Stewart's in Keene. I watched the driver get out and go inside— a good-sized guy, in what looked like workmen's clothes. I called Brent again.

"Did you get through?" I asked.

He had. He'd told the investigator I was following Tobin's truck down Highway 73 and had left my cell phone number. I told him we were at Stewart's, and he said he'd relay the information.

I sat there, shivering, until I saw the man come out of the store, a cup of coffee in his hand. I looked around—no police in sight. My phone wouldn't work much past here, and the signal wasn't great now. Before I could think it through, I got out of my car and moved toward the truck, and spoke just as the man was reaching for the door.

"Excuse me," I said.

He turned and looked at me. He was unshaven, with a not-unfriendly face.

"That looks like Tobin Winslow's truck," I said. My teeth were almost chattering, not just from the cold.

He blinked. "Yeah, I bought it from him."

I cleared my throat, keeping my distance. "Er, but it's still titled in his name."

He didn't ask how I knew this. He took a sip of his coffee, eyeing me, maybe wondering if I was a disgruntled spouse tracking down assets. "Yeah, I haven't gotten around to transferring it. I was waiting to save up a little more, to pay the registration and tax and stuff. Tobin said he didn't mind and he'd leave the insurance on it till March if I needed. Why, is he complaining?"

I looked at him. He was frowning, in a slightly annoyed way. "You haven't been around much lately, have you?" I asked him.

Now he was confused. "No, I've been on a job in Rouses Point, up near the border, why?"

"Tobin's dead," I said.

Maybe I shouldn't have told him, or not so bluntly. He seemed shocked. He leaned back against the side of the truck. "Dead?" he repeated.

I nodded. "His body was just found a few weeks ago. The police have been wondering where his truck was."

He didn't move quickly, which is maybe why what he did next didn't alarm me. He set his coffee down on the hood, opened his passenger door and the glove box, pulled out a piece of paper, and held it out to me. I looked at it. It was a title, signed over, dated the day Tobin was last seen. A thin chill ran down my spine.

"You paid Tobin in cash, didn't you?" I asked.

He nodded. So there had been a wad of cash, and this was where Tobin had gotten it. He'd sold his truck. The question was why, and where the money had gone.

I stayed with him until the state police arrived. They could sort it out. I was pretty sure it would turn out to be exactly what this guy had told me. And then they could figure out if it would be legal to transfer a title signed before the owner died, or not.

I called Win and told her, and stopped at her cabin on my way back. She looked as if she'd been crying. Maybe she'd been pinning her hopes on this truck, that finding it would supply some answers about Tobin's death. We'd found Tobin's safe deposit box, solved the mystery of the break-in, found out about their brother's death. But we seemed no closer to finding out why Tobin had died or how it had happened.

"At least we know Tobin didn't drive his truck onto the lake, that it's not under the ice," I said.

She smiled wanly. "Yes, that's some consolation. It's just frustrating—everything we find out seems to raise more questions. Like, why on earth would Tobin have sold his truck?"

"Maybe he was about to buy something else. Or he wanted money for the lawyer? The one he was going to see in Albany."

"Maybe. There wasn't much in his savings account, and his next trust fund payment wasn't due for another month or so. But how would he have gotten to Albany without his truck?"

"He could have been going to take the train."

"So he sells his truck to pay the lawyer to make a new will? Or try to break the trust or borrow against it? Why couldn't he just wait until his next check?"

We thought on it a while, but we couldn't work it out. Trying to figure out what dead people intended could drive you mad, especially when many people didn't really know what they wanted even when they were alive.

I told her goodbye and headed home. I was tired. Body tired, bone tired, soul tired. I called Philippe. He wasn't in. I tried his cell phone, and it went to voice mail. I couldn't call Jameson, not when I was this low. Not now. I felt hollow and alone. This was wearing me down.

I needed for it all to be over.

CHAPTER 49

The next morning my phone rang early, just after I had taken Tiger out.

It was Win. "My mother called this morning. She's left my father—or, more accurately, he left. He moved into an apartment in the city. And she wants to see me."

"Okay," I said, unsure if this was good or bad.

"And she wants to meet David."

Not what I expected.

"She read the last article?" I asked.

"Yes, she found it online. And I mentioned David when I met with them, just not by name."

I told her to come over. When she arrived we talked it out over omelets and toast and jam, whether she was comfortable meeting with her mother and why her mother might want to see David.

Win rolled her eyes in indecision. "I want to hear what she has to say. But to be honest, I'm not completely sure I'm up for it. And I have no idea why she wants to see David—she didn't say, and I don't want to ask."

"Did she know about David . . . before, I mean?"

Win shook her head. "Looking back, I think whatever she knew, whatever she admitted to, she thought was a phase Trey would grow out of, that Trey would settle down and marry and have kids like he was expected to. And maybe he would have. Maybe he wouldn't have been strong enough to stand up to them. Maybe he knew that Tobin was the one who could and would. But Trey never imagined Tobin would be blamed for his death. Neither of them could have imagined that."

She thought for a moment. "I met David a few times, just a college friend of Trey's, I thought. I liked him. I don't think I ever thought it was more than that, just one of Trey's friends who seemed really nice."

She finally decided she should go, and that David should be asked. And that it would be better if I relayed the message to him. I debated whether to e-mail or call—not something you'd find the answer to from Amy Vanderbilt. Finally I called, and had the luck to reach him quickly. He listened to me, and then I put Win on the phone.

A half hour later, Win and I were in her car, heading to Greenwich. I wasn't sure at what point it had become apparent this wasn't something she wanted to do alone. Win was nervous about seeing her mother, and about seeing David, and she wasn't the type of woman who got nervous. My work could wait a day. I wasn't looking forward to writing a story with no resolution, and I wasn't at all sure what I was going to do about the whole shoving incident. Which I hadn't told anyone about.

We met David at a McDonald's not far from his office. The good thing about McDonald's is that there's one everywhere, and those big golden arches are easy to find. I introduced him to Win in the parking lot, and she gave him a hug. It wasn't the best place for meeting, but we hadn't had much time to plan this.

I got into his Saab; we'd follow Win to her mother's house. It seemed polite to keep David company, and Win had told me she could use the alone time.

David and I drove in silence at first, a not uncomfortable one.

"Do you know Jessica's—Win's mother?" he asked.

"No, not at all. I spoke to her once, very briefly. I left them messages, of course, when I was writing those first two articles, but they never got back to me."

He smiled a little. I looked at him questioningly.

"It's not really anything," he said, "I was just thinking—Tobin's the only one of the three who kept his name. People close to Trey called him Martin, and Jessica goes by Win now."

But Tobin's the one who left, I thought, so maybe he didn't need to change his name. And Tobin was a cool name. Jessamyn also had clung to her unique first name, which had let her father find her. Another thing she and Tobin had in common.

David turned to look at me. "That was brilliant how you did that second article, how you set it up, how you put it together."

I felt my face get warm. "Ah, yeah, well, it wasn't an easy article to write—and it was tricky doing it from bits and pieces."

"You did it well," he said. "You made it work. It's a powerful piece."

We drove several more miles before he spoke again. "Do the Winslows expect legal ramifications?"

"I don't know," I said. "If the police send someone to talk to Mr. Winslow, I think he'll just say he passed out after the boys went overboard and doesn't remember going home, didn't remember being in the boat until just now—that it all just came back to him. Or that he still doesn't remember, but that the things that have come up have convinced him. Something like that."

He glanced at me. "Sure you haven't met him?"

"No, why?"

"You've got him pegged. Or did Tobin or Win talk about him?"

I shook my head. "No, Tobin never talked about family. Win did, a little. But sometimes you can tell what someone is like by the space they leave."

He looked at me.

I tried to explain. "Not a space so much as how their presence affected people. How he affected Win and Tobin, and how it affected them when they left home." I shook my head. "I'm not making sense."

"No, no, you are. I get it."

"And the nanny," I said. "The nanny sort of told me stuff." Or didn't tell me, but it amounted to the same thing.

We were in a fancy neighborhood now, the homes stately and on large lots, some with driveways so long the houses were barely visible. David slid the Saab neatly around a corner. "You don't have any idea why Mrs. Winslow wants to see Win or me?"

"No," I said. "And I don't think Win does either. It was a surprise to her."

"So her mother asked to see you, too?"

"Me? No, I'm here for moral support. I may end up just waiting in the car."

But I didn't.

The house made Philippe's home in Ottawa look like a summer cottage. It was enormous, elegant without quite being ostentatious, as if a designer had been instructed to come as close as possible to the edge without going over it. The furniture and décor were exquisite. The woman who let us in was wearing a neat black dress that wasn't a uniform, but left no doubt she was a servant. We were led into a pristine room, sunnier and deliberately more casual than a living room. There a woman was awaiting us, seated in a tall, slimly stuffed chair.

Win, beside me, seemed composed, but I could feel anxiety radiating from her. David was calmer, but this wasn't his family, and he'd known these secrets for a long time. And he could walk out and leave this all behind. Part of Win was still here, might always be here, in the rooms she'd grown up in with her brothers.

The woman was slight: medium height, slim. Not a gray hair in evidence, hair immaculately coiffed. Her clothing was simple, but the simple that meant impressive price tags, not simple like "came from Target." She nodded at the woman who'd showed us in, which presumably meant *Leave us now* or *We are ready for tea.* Apparently very rich people communicated with their underlings through nods.

We sat down, neatly, primly, on the edges of our seats. Win

introduced us, first me and then David, and Mrs. Winslow nodded at us in turn. She asked politely about our drive and asked David where he lived and worked. Then the tea arrived. It was good tea, with an enticing aroma, served in a lovely pot, with little cookies and tiny crustless sandwich thingies. We hadn't had lunch, and I wondered how many of these little sandwich thingies I could eat without seeming rude.

We sipped our tea, and having tea and cookies did seem to help us relax.

Mrs. Winslow set her teacup down tidily. For a moment it seemed that the next words out of her mouth would be *We are gathered here together,* but of course they weren't. She surprised me by speaking to me first.

"I read your articles, Miss Chance. You did a fine job of telling about Tobin's life after he left here. I thank you for that. It was lovely reading where he had been, and the comments from his friends."

I nodded, and murmured a thank-you. She didn't mention that I did a fine job of telling the story of her first son's death, but I hadn't expected her to. It didn't seem she hated it, and she apparently wasn't suing me, and that's about the best you could hope for in this situation.

Then she looked at David, a long look, and then at Win, as if she were memorizing this moment before she spoke. And when she did, it was to the room, not directly to either of them.

"I was never aware that my husband was in the boat that evening. He was out, but he was often out, at his club and elsewhere. I never asked where he went." Her tone was brittle. I pictured a bombastic man, doing what he pleased, in charge at work, in charge at home, trampling people along the way.

"If I had known . . ." She stopped, and then started again, articulating carefully. "If I had known that my husband, that their father had been with them, had taken them out, left them . . ." Her voice choked, and I didn't think this was deliberate. My throat tightened in turn. I didn't dare look at Win or David.

"If I had known, I would have turned him in to the police myself." She said it flatly, emotionlessly. The air resonated, her words almost echoing.

David was the one who moved, almost before the words were out of her mouth. He went to her side, took her hand.

"I am sure you would have, Mrs. Winslow. But of course you had no way of knowing." Whether he believed this or not, I don't know, and I suppose it didn't matter. Of course she wanted to think she would have turned in her husband. Whether she would have or not was another thing, but this was the mother of a man David had loved, still loved, and this was what he needed to say to her, and what she needed to hear.

She grasped his hand and when he moved to hug her, she wrapped her thin arms loosely around him, her hands on his back looking incongruously old. I looked away, not wanting to intrude, not wanting to witness something so emotional. She held tight for a long moment, and then David moved back to his chair.

Win sat, not moving. She might have been seething, seeing this all turned so graceful, something that had been raw and ugly and awful; having her father's act acknowledged in such a genteel way. She had lived out the nightmare of one brother drowning and the other being blamed, and she'd had that awful confrontation with her parents.

But while this might not be the apology or acknowledgment Win needed from her mother, it was a lot for a proud woman who had lost two sons and now, in a way, her husband. The act of saying it, of calling us there, was significant. And there was no doubt she was suffering. When Win did move, it was all of a flurry, and then she and her mother were wrapped up in each other, two sets of shoulders shaking.

I met David's eye and without saying a word we got up and wandered off. He'd been here before, he said, to Winslow parties, and knew the way to the kitchen. There was a plate of extra sandwiches on the countertop; he pulled off the cover and took one, and I did the same. We leaned up against the counter and ate.

"Good sandwiches," he said.

"Yep."

"Whew," he added lightly, after a moment. "Guess that's all I was really here for."

"You did good," I told him, and then we were hugging, tightly. We separated, with pats on the back, then smiled at each other and took another sandwich section each.

"Think we should go back in now?" I asked when we'd finished our little sandwiches.

"We'll wait another few minutes or so." So we did. By the time we reentered, Win and her mother had separated, red-eyed, acting as if it wasn't obvious they had been crying. The woman in the black dress appeared as if responding to an invisible button, and replaced the pot of tea with a fresh one. Mrs. Winslow turned toward David.

"David, we have some books of Trey's here, in his old room. If you'd like to have some of them, we could go up and take a look."

This startled him. Emotion ran across his face, and then it was gone, and he said smoothly, "That would be lovely, Mrs. Winslow," and off they went.

Win looked at me. "Thanks for coming," she said.

"Wouldn't have missed it for the world." I grinned at her, and after a moment she grinned back. "Have some more sandwiches," I told her. "They're really good."

David and Mrs. Winslow were gone at least twenty minutes, and when they came back he had a handful of books under his arm. I don't know if he wanted them or just took them because she wanted him to. Either way, I was glad he did. He told us he'd better be getting home, and Mrs. Winslow went to the door to see him out.

I turned to Win. "Want me to go for a walk or something so you can visit with your mother some more?"

She shook her head. "I think that's enough for one day. We'll stay a little longer, if it's okay with you, and then head home. I know you have work to do."

When her mother came back, we chatted a bit, and told her we needed to drive back. She made the offer for us to stay there, but I think she knew we weren't going to. She hugged Win tightly at the door and shook my hand. Then she leaned in toward me and said, close to my ear, "I wish I'd let him keep the dog."

It rattled me, painfully. She was astute, to have picked out the thing that had hurt me particularly about Tobin's life, the scene that had embedded itself in me. This could have been emotional grandstanding, but her body radiated hurt. I wanted to say, *I wish you had too,* but I didn't. I couldn't. I'd follow David's lead, take the graceful route. I said softly, "You would have if you could have." I didn't know if this was true, but I wasn't going to deny her the comfort she wanted. If she was emotionally manipulating me it would be deplorable, but more deplorable for me to assume that was the case. There had been too many assumptions. Too much death, too much pain.

Win and I didn't talk much on the ride back to Lake Placid. Sometimes you need to let your feelings sort themselves out. And sometimes you don't need to talk. I took out my laptop and tried to work, but I was tired, my brain overfull and my emotional reserves drained, so I gave up and packed my computer away.

It was late and dark by the time we reached my house. Win said she needed to go on to her cabin. She needed to be alone. And so did I.

CHAPTER 50

I e-mailed Jameson. I didn't quite tell him that I'd followed the truck all the way to Keene and in essence confronted the driver, but I don't think it would have surprised him. The police told Win that the fellow's story checked out—he'd withdrawn cash from his bank the day before Tobin's disappearance, and had been in Rouses Point much of the time since.

The first time I thought I'd seen the truck had been my imagination, as neither the man nor his truck had been anywhere near here, and the second time was unlikely. So I'd been haunted by a truck that hadn't been there, but the one time I'd been in a situation where I could follow the truck I thought was Tobin's, it was. Go figure.

The final toxicology results on Tobin showed no drugs. Alcohol, yes, but not seriously drunk. I hadn't tried to contact the man involved in the shoving incident in the bar, and neither had I told the police about it. I'd decided it would cause more pain, needless pain, and raise more questions than it answered. I'd hint at it in the story, but not in detail. I was tired of finding out things, of turning over rocks and seeing what lay beneath.

I wrote the bulk of the last piece, and told George I'd finish it after Tobin's memorial. Win was having Tobin cremated and would take his ashes to Connecticut, but she wanted to have an informal service for him, just a few of us, out on the ice in Saranac Lake, near where he was found, and then a gathering at the bar for everyone afterward. She asked David Zimmer, and he came up. Her mother didn't; I didn't know if that was Win's decision or her mother's.

There were eight of us out on the ice: Win and Jessamyn, David and me, Patrick, Brent, and Zach, and Dean. The ice palace was nearly finished. Win and Jessamyn held hands. David held my arm, Dean on my other side. Word had gotten out and there were a couple dozen people on the shore: the men who had helped get the body out from the ice, Tobin's friends from the bars, people he'd worked with, Matt Boudoin, George. They stood silently. The ice creaked as we stood there, seeming almost to moan.

Win spoke, her voice melodic in the cold air, carrying across the ice. "My brother Tobin loved living here," she said. "I will miss my brother forever, with all my heart, but I am glad he had his time here and I am glad he had friends here. And I thank everyone who cared about him."

Jessamyn was crying. She spoke some words, but the wind whipped most of them away. I think she said something about loving Tobin, and I know she said goodbye. Dean said something, and then I did, just three words: *Thank you, Tobin,* and maybe only Win heard me, and maybe only she knew what I meant. And then Win sang. I hadn't known she was going to, but she sang "Amazing Grace" in a clear and beautiful voice that floated out across the ice, and by the end I doubt there was a dry eye anywhere within the range of her voice. As she sang I looked over at the walls of the ice palace, reaching toward the heavens.

We turned and walked back toward the shoreline, and I was grateful for David's arm steadying me. The people on the shore had started moving, mingling, some turning to walk toward the bar. I noticed one girl standing apart, eyes red, face pale. I thought I recognized her, and then I did: she was the girl I'd seen briefly in the Saranac Lake bar with the man who'd gotten my car out of the ditch, the girl who had been in the pickup truck that had stopped to help me back onto the road. She saw me looking at her, saw me recognize her, and smiled, a heartbreakingly sad smile.

Something made me turn to David and tell him I needed to go speak to her, and he nodded and went on. I walked toward the girl, my boots crunching on the ice. She turned her head toward me, and waited.

She was beautiful, thin, and blond, an ethereal beauty, with a face that could have been in a painting by one of the masters. The man I'd seen her with before must have been her brother—you could see faint traces of him in her features, but in her they were refined, delicate, almost breathtaking.

"You were a friend of Tobin's," I said, and after she nodded I added, "I'm Troy."

"Cadey," she said. "Cadey Phillips. You met my brother Wade, sort of. The one they call Crick."

She shifted on her feet and her hand moved toward her middle, just the suggestion of a movement, but it led my eyes there as if she had an arrow pointing toward her abdomen. And I saw, through the billowiness of her long coat, a slight mound of a rounded belly.

She opened her mouth to speak, but tears came into her eyes. She turned away slightly, and at that moment I realized who this was. She was the girl whose photo I'd seen in Tobin's safe deposit box.

And things fell into place for me, with a giant clanging roar that seemed it should shatter the ice beneath my feet.

I thought, counted. "Four months, plus?" I asked.

She nodded.

"Tobin's?" I asked, and she nodded again, and her tears began to fall steadily. For a moment I couldn't breathe.

We started walking, the two of us. Someone saw us, a man who was a younger version of the brother I'd met, and moved toward us, but she waved him away and he retreated. As we walked she told me the story, almost whispering at times.

She lived in Saranac Lake, she said, and was still in high school. Her parents had died five years back in a car crash and she lived with her three older brothers, Wade and the one we'd just seen and one in between. She'd met Tobin when she'd been hitchhiking over to Lake Placid to a friend's house; she'd told him she was eighteen, a student at North Country Community College. She had thought he was gorgeous and charming and funny in a way unlike the other men and boys she knew.

"I know it was wrong to lie," she said, "but I liked him and I didn't want him to know I wasn't even seventeen."

She'd seen him twice more and they'd been together only the once, the last time, at a friend's house, but then somehow he'd found out her age, had looked at her driver's license, and told her he couldn't see her anymore, even though she'd cried and told him age didn't matter. Then she'd missed her period and missed another and hadn't been going to tell him, but he'd run into her and asked how she was, and then she had.

"Did you know about his girlfriend, about Jessamyn?" I asked.

She nodded, crying more. "I just liked him so much," she said. "I know that was wrong."

"He gave you money," I said, thinking of the wad of cash, the money from the sale of the truck.

"I didn't want to take it, but he said it was important, it was important that I saw a doctor right away, that I had prenatal care, vitamins and things, that I had a warm coat and took care of myself, and he gave me money that night, that last night I saw him. And he said he was going to make sure the baby was taken care of."

"Do you know what he meant by that, 'taken care of'?"

She shook her head. "I think he meant money, that he was going to set up a fund or something."

We walked on. My brain was whirling.

"What happened to Tobin that night?" I asked at last. My mouth was dry. She stopped and turned her face toward me, those exquisite features filled with pain beyond her years.

"You need to talk to my brother," she said.

. . .

We turned back. We could see some stragglers crossing the street, heading home or toward the bar, but the boy she'd waved off was leaning against a signpost. Her youngest brother, Jake, she told me. He looked at us as we approached, weariness and strain etched on his face.

"Tell her," Cadey said. "Tell her all of it." She moved off toward the others, and we watched her go.

The boy turned toward me. He wasn't beautiful like his sister, but he was good-looking, and something about him said he'd had to grow up too fast. I guessed he wasn't yet twenty. He stared out across the ice and started talking. He seemed to know who I was.

"We were pretty upset when we found out Cadey was pregnant," he said. "Especially Wade. He's the oldest, the legal guardian, the one who kept us all together when Mom and Dad died. Cadey didn't tell us, but she was getting sick in the mornings, and he guessed. She wanted to have the baby, whatever it took. She wouldn't tell us who the father was. We thought it was Jimmy, the kid she hangs out with in school, but she said it wasn't. Wade asked around, he found out that Tobin had given her a ride once, and then he went to Cadey and acted like he knew who it was and she gave Tobin up without realizing it."

He kicked at the snow under his boots. "I think Wade was angrier because it was him, an out-of-towner, you know, someone not from here. Someone older, someone he thought was using her. Wade went looking for him and found him outside the bar that night, and we followed him. Wade wanted to have it out with him, show him he couldn't come here and treat our sister that way."

"You were there?"

He nodded. "Me and my brothers. We followed Tobin, across the street and then out onto the ice a ways. He was just standing there, looking out across the ice. We said stuff, we threatened him, we called him names. He didn't say anything. He just sort of smiled at us and turned his back and walked away. Wade was furious, he wanted to go after him and fight him, beat him up, but we pulled him back. Told him it wasn't worth it, it was too late, it was too cold. We'd deal with it later." He looked at me and his face twisted. "I wished we'd let him, if he'd beaten him up Tobin would be alive, but Wade was really mad and we were afraid he'd lose control, break his jaw or something, maybe get arrested, and then Cadey would go to foster care and we wouldn't be together."

I walked a few paces away from him, out onto the ice, staring across the lake.

"And then what?" My voice was emotionless. All my feelings had drained out of me, as if through my feet and through the ice and into the water below, into the lake where Tobin Winslow had died, died the day before he'd planned to visit a lawyer to have his will changed to provide for a child not yet born.

"And then nothing," he said. It was almost precisely what David Zimmer had said to me had happened when Tobin and his brother had been left by their father. *Then nothing.*

"What do you mean?" My voice was sharp.

"We saw Tobin walk out a ways, and then we left. We figured he'd wait until he saw we were gone and then he'd come back. No one thought he'd go out too far, that he'd go into the ice, that he'd fall through, that he'd drown. We only found out later he'd banged his head in the bar that night, that maybe he wasn't feeling good from it, that maybe he was woozy. We didn't know, we didn't know. We didn't."

I turned and he was crying. I don't know if he needed absolution or if I was the one to give it to him, but I moved toward him and wrapped my arms around him, this nearly grown man who was crying like he was six years old.

"I know you didn't," I said. "I know you didn't."

"What are you going to do?" he asked, stepping back, scrubbing the tears from his face, gulping for air.

"I don't know."

· · ·

And I didn't.

What I did was get him calmed down and walk him back to the bar, check on Cadey, exchange a few words with Win and David and Jessamyn, chat with George, and then plead tiredness and tell them I was heading home. I walked to my car, my feet heavy and cold. I turned on the ignition and my seat heater and sat there and shook in my cold, dark car.

I could picture it: the moonlight on the ice lighting the scene to a blue dimness. I could envision them, moving toward Tobin, standing there, a wall of disapproval. I could see him deciding to walk away, that he didn't want an altercation. That he didn't want to try to explain that he'd had no idea she was a minor, that he was going to do the right thing by the child, do whatever was right for Cadey. I could see him, turning his back on the cold eyes of the men staring at him and walking across the ice, a long last walk by moonlight, the ice crunching beneath his feet.

So he'd gone too far, walked until the ice grew thin, and in the darkness got confused which way was back to shore. Or maybe, just maybe—and this was my worst fear—he had decided to keep walking, decided he was tired of living. Didn't want to deal with the child, with Cadey, with Jessamyn. Maybe he just gave up on that cold winter day and walked on until he sank beneath the ice.

I picked up my cell phone and called Philippe. He was out, Elise told me, at a play. I called his cell, but it went straight to voice mail. I hung up and cried a while, and then I called Jameson. I couldn't get any words out at first, just noises.

"English, please," he said, and I made a sound that was half laugh and half crying. "Are you safe, Troy?" he asked.

I managed to say yes.

"Are you home?"

"No, I'm in my car, in Saranac Lake."

"You're not injured."

"No," I whispered.

"Can it wait three or so hours?"

"Yes," I said. He told me he was going to drive down, that this didn't sound like something I should tell him over the phone, that maybe I needed to talk this out in person. I cried more, and again managed to say yes.

"Are you okay to drive to your house?"

I nodded, and then remembered I needed to speak, and told him yes, I could drive, I was stone-cold sober, and he told me he'd call me when he got close, to go home and get something to eat and drink, and hug my dog and get some rest if I could. I told him I would, and hung up, and wiped the tears from my face and then the thin layer of icy condensation that had formed on the inside of the windshield. And I drove home, slowly, carefully.

Jameson made it in just over three hours. I'd had chamomile tea and crackers and cheese; I'd taken a very hot shower and put on my sweats and curled up in bed with my dog. But I hadn't slept. After he called that he was close, I went down and waited in the living room until I saw the lights of his car, then opened the door for him. His face was tense, tired, but something in him relaxed when he saw me. He came in and then I was in his arms, holding tight under his open coat, my face against his chest. He held me, tightly, and then pulled back.

"You're okay?" he asked.

I nodded. "Do you need something to eat, to drink?" I asked.

He shook his head. "Just tell me what you need to tell me, Troy."

He followed me up to my room, pulling a chair over to sit across from me as I curled up under the covers, and I told him. I told him Tobin hadn't been a great person, but hadn't been the awful person I'd thought he was. And I told him everything that had happened, about Cadey and the rest, and about the brothers, following him, watching him start the walk across the lake to his death.

"What do I do?" I asked him. "They didn't kill him. I don't think they laid a hand on him. I think they were just there, standing there."

"But they didn't go after him."

"No," I said.

"They let him walk off, across the ice they must have known would break."

"Her brother said they never thought he'd keep going, that they thought he would stop and come back when they left. But Tobin had hit his head in the bar, in that scuffle over the pool table. Maybe he passed out. Maybe he stopped and got confused and walked the wrong way. Or maybe . . . maybe he did it on purpose."

I cried then, hard and wrenchingly, and he reached out and held my hand as he had in the Burlington hospital last summer, and I clung hard, as I had then. "His family, would it help his family to know, to know that the people in this town may have helped cause his death?" I said, when I could speak, "What good would it do? And the baby, I don't think he wanted them to know about the baby. And Jessamyn, this would all hurt her so much."

He didn't tell me what to do. I didn't expect him to.

He sat there and let me talk and then moved over and sat on the bed beside me so I could lean up against him. He stayed there until I was nearly asleep, and in the morning I found him on my sofa, his shirt hanging neatly from my desk chair and shoes and belt on the floor, with one of my pillows and a blanket from my closet. I didn't remember getting the blanket out. Maybe I hadn't.

We went to breakfast at Ho-Jo's, and it felt good to be with him. Afterward we took Tiger for a walk. I thanked him, and we exchanged one of our overstuffed-sofa parka hugs, and he headed back to Ottawa, and I went upstairs to make some phone calls.

I called Cadey's brothers. I told Wade who I was, and told him he needed to call the state police and tell them about seeing Tobin on the ice that night. We talked a long time. He told me Cadey and Jimmy were getting married, that they'd stay in the house while they finished high school, and all the brothers would help with the baby. And he told me the name of the fellow Tobin had had the scuffle with in the bar, someone who had been in school with Cadey's youngest brothers, someone who'd maybe had a crush on her. And somehow it didn't surprise me to find out it was the young Saranac Lake policeman, the one whose name I'd somehow never gotten, who had come to our house to question Jessamyn the morning after Tobin's body had been found.

Then I looked up that man's number, and called him too, and told him politely but definitively that he needed to call the state police, and call them now, and tell them about Tobin falling against the wall in their pool table scuffle that night.

Both he and Wade could tell the police it was Tobin's memorial service that made them realize they needed to speak up, to clear the air, so his sister and family could have some peace. I didn't need to come into it. I called George, and told him I would need one more day to finish writing.

For this article I'd done a first-person sidebar about seeing Tobin's body being taken from the ice, about the rumors that ran through town and the ugliness that had ensued, about getting to know Tobin's sister and becoming friends with her. The main article covered his life here, and I'd interspersed bits from his friends here, their favorite stories about Tobin.

Now I wrote an ending to the main piece, from the imagined perspective of someone who had been there. I wrote of the shove in the bar that night, the bump on the head, but didn't name names. I wrote of Tobin walking out on the ice with his head aching, perhaps sinking to his knees and then lying down on the ice to rest and sliding under. I didn't say that maybe, just maybe, Tobin thought of the night his brother had drowned to save him, to give him a life, and that maybe Tobin had just walked on until the ice cracked under him. Neither did I mention that he had been with a sixteen-year-old girl with an ethereal beauty that had entranced him, that she was most likely carrying a child that was his, who would be brought up bearing another man's name.

Nothing in the story was a lie, but neither was it the whole truth. These truths didn't belong to me; they weren't mine to share. Even if some people suspected that Cadey's child wasn't Jimmy's, even if they put the pieces together, no one would say a word. This town would close ranks. Cadey and Jimmy would be one more set of local teens who married young with a baby on the way.

After I finished the piece and turned it in, I called Win. She came in to meet me, and we had a long talk as we walked around the lake, and I told her about a baby, one being born to a local girl who had briefly loved her brother, a baby that would be born in late spring or early summer. And the two of us agreed not to tell Jessamyn any of this, or anyone else.

It took George a day to review the story and have lawyers vet it. He ran it with a photo I'd taken of the hole left in the ice after Tobin's body had been removed. I thought it wonderfully appropriate, and hauntingly beautiful. It made me think of one of the postcards Tobin had sent his sister soon after he'd moved here, a snow-covered Adirondack scene. *I think I'm going to like it here,* he'd written. *It's a cold and lonely place—but it suits me.*

CHAPTER 51

Jessamyn went off to live with her father in Boston. She got a part-time job, because she likes to be earning money, which made Daniel proud. And she got her GED and started community college classes, which also made him proud. Brent sometimes goes down to see her. This is a lot of new for Jessamyn: new father, new home, new boyfriend. I imagine it's going to take some getting used to. But she seems to be taking to it. It's the life she was supposed to have, coming later but not too late, and in an odd way brought to her by Tobin, from the article on him that mentioned her name and brought her father to her door. In death, Tobin brought her what she'd perhaps hoped he could give her in life: somewhere she belonged, someone to belong to.

If there's an afterlife, I imagine Tobin's smiling at that. He's also probably smiling at me becoming friends with his sister.

Win ended up buying the cabin, and made plans to return in the summer. And she got a dog, an eight-month-old Australian shepherd mix from the animal shelter in Westport. She took him home with her in her new dog-friendly car, and started a new life, with a rescued dog that adored her and a mother she could see once in a while, at least, and somewhat at peace with what had happened to her two brothers. She was, she said, considering law school, which didn't surprise me. She would be one heck of a lawyer.

I sold a version of the articles to, of all places, *Rolling Stone*, for an absurd amount of money. They had no problem with how involved I was with the piece—it was one of the things that sold them on it. That clipping would open an insane number of doors for me professionally. There were a lot of articles I could write involving this region, a lot of stories to tell. I had mixed feelings about it—all this had taken a lot out of me—but Baker told me, emphatically, that this sort of writing was what I was meant to do. And maybe she was right.

Dean pretty much forgave me, although I think my role in revealing what his brother had done still made him uncomfortable. Eddie cashed the check from Win and paid the drug debt, and ended up enlisting in the Army—partly to please his brother; partly, I think, because he knew he wouldn't change if he stayed here. Every two weeks, Win gets a check for fifty dollars from Eddie. We didn't know if he would keep it up, and we didn't discuss it. But it helped Dean to know about it, and Win would never tell him if the checks stopped coming.

I told most of the story to my brother, not all of it, and he told me what he could of the tough case he'd been working on. I heard back from the accountant in Greenwich I'd never interviewed, the childhood friend, who had flown to England after his brother was seriously injured in a small plane crash. I found out through an efficient grapevine—Marilyn, in fact—that it was the fired reporter, the kid Dirk, who'd made the hang-up calls to me. I guessed he was the one who'd let the air out of my tires, or had gotten someone to do it. Now he'd gotten a job in Massachusetts, so I figured that was the end of his vengefulness. I hoped he'd learn to be a better reporter.

The near miss that sent my car into a ditch? Most likely just a careless driver. The Saranac Lake policeman who'd shoved Tobin, the one who'd been captivated by Cadey when he'd been in high school with her brothers, left the force and went to work in his brother-in-law's plumbing business. Win let the Lake Placid police know she'd found out who had trashed the cabin, the person had made restitution, and she didn't want to press charges. Case closed.

Paul and Philippe came down for a long weekend—I turned my rooms over to them and stayed in Jessamyn's old room. I hadn't rented it out yet. I was doing okay financially, with the sale of the articles, so wasn't in any hurry. Paul wanted to see the ice palace, so we went over to Saranac Lake, and I stayed on the shore as he and his father walked through it, and then we went to visit Baker and her husband and their three boys.

Philippe took me aside when Paul was playing with Baker's kids. "I need to talk to you," he said, his voice odd, and we bundled up and went outside.

This wasn't good. I knew it wasn't good. It never is when someone says they need to talk to you. They're either going to tell you they're moving away or they have a life-threatening ailment or something else that's going to shake up your life, and not in a pleasant way. So off we went for a walk, me trying not to show how rattled I was.

To give him credit, he went pretty much straight to the point. "You know I care deeply about you," he said. "You know you are very important to my and Paul's life."

"Yes," I said, and it seemed that the breath was leaving my body. This was not the sort of preamble that led up to suggesting moving in together, to pulling out a ring, to making a proposal. It was the kind of speech that led up to what he said next.

"We live a long way apart, Troy. I've . . . I need to tell you that I've started seeing someone."

I like to think of myself as the type of person who would be stoic when hearing something like this, all brave and stiff-upper-lip and all, but I couldn't pull it off. Tears started to fall and then I was sobbing, and he was holding me. My world had just upended, turned inside out, and I had never seen it coming.

"I'm sorry," I said between sobs. "I'm sorry I was so busy, I'm sorry I didn't come up more. I'm sorry I wasn't ready. I'm sorry, I'm sorry."

"No, no, no," he said. "It's all right, it wasn't that. I didn't plan it, I didn't plan on meeting someone, it just happened."

But who plans on something like that? No one. It happens. And it happens because there's a space for it to happen, an opening, a gap. If I'd been in Ottawa, if I'd been able to make a commitment, take a risk—never mind that we'd agreed that the time wasn't right, that neither of us was ready—it wouldn't have happened.

Or maybe it would have. Maybe it would have been far worse. And maybe if Philippe had been perfect for me and I'd been perfect for him, maybe I never would have left, or he would have waited a while longer, waited until the time was right for both of us. Maybe I'd just been a coward, afraid to take a step toward a new life when I should have.

"Of course you're still welcome to visit," he said, but then I cried harder, thinking of the house I loved, the meals I'd shared with them, the times I'd driven Paul to school and hung out with Elise, who would now be cooking meals for some other woman. Some other woman would be sitting at the table with Paul, driving him to school, checking his homework. I felt such a sharp pain in my chest it seemed my heart had to have stopped beating, but I could feel it, hear it, a steady, slow *lub-dub*; it had betrayed me by keeping on beating when it should have stopped, should have frozen in my chest.

I had thought it all would be waiting for me, Philippe and Paul and the house in Ottawa, waiting for me to be ready, but it wasn't. My retreat, my mecca, my safe haven, gone. The place that had felt like home, gone. The gates clanged shut before I'd known they were even starting to move. Maybe before I'd even realized they'd been open. *I thought I had more time.* Until Philippe winced, I didn't know I'd said the words aloud.

"I'll need to see Paul," I said thickly. "I can't lose Paul."

And now he was crying too. "You'll never lose Paul," he said. "He needs you. I'll bring him down to see you; he can visit on holidays."

We walked until I could control myself, and we rubbed our faces with snow so they would just look red with cold, and we went back and pretended to be cheerful, and then Philippe and the child I loved beyond reason went off to Canada, and I went home, home to my dog. And laid in my lonely bed and wished hard I hadn't taken the high road, the sensible path. Wished I had stayed up in Canada last summer, that I had gone for it, rushed it, risked it. At least I would have had that time and I'd have those memories, and I wouldn't be wondering *What if*. But I'd been careful, and I'd been cautious, partly to safeguard Paul, and maybe myself as well, and now the decision had been made for me.

I didn't tell Baker for a few days. When I did, she said, "Troy, it's not over until it's over—he's just seeing this person, not marrying her." And I suppose she was right, but it seemed that the tiny window Philippe and I might have had had closed, sometime when we weren't looking. Maybe it had never really been open and we'd only come together because of Paul; maybe it had slammed shut after the death of Philippe's wife. Maybe I'd let it slide shut bit by bit while I was busy writing articles that had altered life for other families, brought Jessamyn a father, lost one for Win; estranged Dean and his brother, brought David Zimmer some peace.

I couldn't judge this at all. All I knew is that I was alone, and it hurt.

Of course, I had to wonder if I'd done the right thing about Tobin, about Cadey, about the baby. I'd exposed one set of family secrets and let a new one remain hidden—that Tobin had apparently left a child, not yet born, one that his parents would never know about. This was a weighty decision, and we'd likely never know if it was the right one.

But I think it was.

Tobin's baby would grow up here, in the Adirondacks. The

child would grow up hiking and fishing, skiing and ice-skating and snowshoeing with uncles and mother and the man he or she would call father. The child wouldn't know Tobin's parents, wouldn't be pressured to go to a prestigious school or take a prestigious job. Win would quietly start a trust fund, moving some of Tobin's share of her own trust fund into it, one that would help pay for college or first-home-buying or other expenses. The one thing Cadey agreed to accept was a family health plan, covering her and Jimmy and the unborn child and whatever children they might have. So this child would have health care, and some financial help when needed, and would likely never know the family history on the birth father's side.

And no one would ask for a DNA test to show who was or wasn't the father. It was better no one knew for sure, and the fact that Tobin had wanted to provide for Cadey's child was enough for Win. And with Jimmy's name on the birth certificate and without a DNA test, presumably Tobin's parents would never get wind of a small child growing up in the Adirondacks their son may have fathered.

I don't think Tobin killed himself. I think his death was an accident, a confluence of events, the day his luck ran out. Maybe in a way he'd welcomed it. Maybe when he'd slipped under the ice he hadn't fought the water, hadn't struggled to keep the lake from claiming him. Maybe he was tired and until that moment when the ice cracked hadn't known just how tired—tired of carrying the weight of his brother's death and his father's perfidy and his own transgressions and a thousand other things. We'd never know. Everyone could envision whatever version they could live with.

The ice palace had begun to sag. I was looking forward to its melting away, to the last remnant of ice leaving, so that the space where Tobin's body had been found would be only a distant memory, would be only a spot in a clear blue lake under a bright shining sun, and it would no longer hurt me to look at it.

ACKNOWLEDGMENTS

Thanks to:

Sandy Ebner, Cynthia Christian, Quinn Cummings, Teresa Rhyne, Debbie Patrick, Robert Smolka, Mike Modrak, Ben Malisow, Howard Frank Mosher, and David Freed for reading, cheerleading, or both; Wayne Mackey, former New York state trooper, for background info; Anthony R. Mascia, MD, for medical information; Reed Farrel Coleman, for being a great CP.

Amy and Topher King (and the small Kinglets), for everything; my cousins, for their love and support; Joe Mascia, for being a particularly astute reader.

All the great booksellers and librarians out there—you know who you are.

And the wonderful readers who fell in love with Troy and her friends, and let me know about it.

ABOUT THE AUTHOR

SARA J. HENRY, like her protagonist, was a newspaper sports editor in the Adirondacks for several years, and lived in Lake Placid and Saranac Lake. She freelanced for various magazines and was a magazine editor, health and fitness writer, book editor, and copy editor before turning to fiction. She also spent a very short time as a soil scientist, and later loved working as a bicycle mechanic.

Her first novel, *Learning to Swim*, won the Anthony Award and Agatha Award for best first novel and the Mary Higgins Clark Award, and was nominated for the Macavity and Barry Awards. She was a featured author at Booktopia Vermont.

A native of Oak Ridge, Tennessee, Sara graduated from the University of Tennessee, attended the University of Florida, and received a master's in journalism from Carleton University in Ottawa, Ontario. She now calls southern Vermont home, but frequently visits Nashville, where she wrote her first novel, and the Adirondacks, which somehow still feels like home.

Her website is www.SaraJHenry.com, and she loves to hear from readers.

1. The novel opens with the discovery of a body—someone Troy knew but didn't particularly like. Her first reaction is to notify her roommate Jessamyn. Would you have done anything differently?

2. The Saranac Lake community seems tightly knit, capable of keeping secrets and cutting off outsiders. Troy thinks she's in a better position to find answers than the state police. Do you agree? Should she have involved the police more?

3. Other than the newspaper assignment, what do you think compels Troy to keep digging? How do her professional responsibilities affect her personal relationships, and vice versa?

4. Troy's brother, Simon, says that her loyalty is her blind spot. Did you find this to be true? Which friendships are most important to her? Is she too quick to trust some people, such as Win, Dean, or David?

5. Troy, Win, and Jessamyn bond through a traumatic experience. Do you think they would have become friends under different circumstances? What assumptions do they make about one another, and about other women?

6. Jessamyn never talks about her past. Have you ever known someone who you thought might have had a difficult background, as Troy thinks Jessamyn did? Did you encourage them to talk about it? Should Troy have tried to get Jessamyn to talk earlier?

7. How do you feel Troy evolved or grew during the course of this novel? If you've read the first novel in this series, *Learning to Swim*, how do you think that book's events affected her actions here?

8. Troy describes how Jessamyn changed once she started dating Tobin: "Falling for him meant giving up a big chunk of herself." Troy values her own independence, but sometimes she wishes she weren't so logical about love. What were some of the significant sacrifices she and others made for their loved ones? Did you think they were worth it?

9. Did your feelings about Tobin change, and how? How did his parents' actions affect him and his choices? How do you think his life would have turned out had he not died?

10. Which characters did you trust more than others, and why? Were you surprised by the resolution of the mysteries? What do you think about Troy and Win's decision not to tell Jessamyn or the Winslows about Cadey?

11. How does the title illustrate the themes of the book, besides the Adirondacks sometimes being a "cold and lonely place"?

12. What do you think might be next for Troy Chance? And for the other characters?